C000197728

Pendle

By

Paul Southern

Copyright © 2018 Paul Southern

The right of Paul Southern to be identified as the Author of the Work has been asserted by him in accordance Copyright, Designs and Patents Act 1988.

First published in 2018 by Bloodhound Books

Apart from any use permitted under UK copyright law, this publication may only be reproduced, stored, or transmitted, in any form, or by any means, with prior permission in writing of the publisher or, in the case of reprographic production, in accordance with the terms of licences issued by the Copyright Licensing Agency.

All characters in this publication are fictitious and any resemblance to real persons, living or dead, is purely coincidental.

www.bloodhoundbooks.com

Print ISBN 978-1-912604-09-8

Pyari Sophia

Aap ki mustaqbil ke liyay baba ki pyari si dua 'Allah tumhe
hamesha shaad aur abaad rakhe' insha'Allah.

Pendle Hill, 1612

The last of the evening sunlight flickered through the trees, painting the forest floor in fiery shades of red and gold. Quicksilver shadows flitted in and out, over bluebell and ramson, round aspen and alder, and the air rang with the shouts and screams of children chasing each other around. 'Jack be nimble, Jack be quick, Jack jump over the candlestick!'

Two of them, dressed in ragged linen, ran along the edge of a small, babbling stream. The first, a girl of nine or ten, had unkempt, golden hair that flowed behind her like sunlight. She was lithe and strong and jumped higher than the boy who followed her. He was a year or two younger, pale and thin, with long limbs and torn clothes and curly, brown hair that hid his blackened face. 'Thou'll not catcheth me, pauper John. Neither thou nor thy horse,' she said, baiting him.

He was carrying a wooden hobby horse, really a stick with a sinister horse's head on, carved unevenly and with flax for a mane. He rode it as if it were real, jumping over briar and fern in his effort to catch her. He neighed loudly when he got near, but she was always one step ahead. She laughed and shrieked and led him down strange paths, far from the ones he knew, but he didn't care. He loved her like a boy does when he first loves a girl, with all his heart, wanting just to be near her.

Eventually, she came to a stream and vaulted it like a deer. She stayed on the far bank to taunt him again. 'Thou'll not catcheth me, pauper John. Thy horse is lame.'

He rushed in, neighing wildly, and nearly lost his footing. Coughing and spluttering, his foot struck a rock and he cried out in pain, but the girl didn't stop. 'Run faster, pauper John. John be nimble, John be quick.'

She disappeared into the forest delves in the shadow of the hill. The sun had gone down behind it and the shouts and screams of the other children had faded.

'Don't leave me, Lizzie!' he called out. 'Don't leave me hereabout!'

'I will if I want,' she said, appearing suddenly from behind a rowan tree. 'I'll do just as I want.'

A tear sprang to his eye and he wiped it with his dirty, linen sleeve. He didn't want her to see him cry. He put the hobby horse down on the bank and hauled himself up by some old tree roots. His linen breeches and shirt were wet through. He heard her voice up the hill, trailing down towards him – 'John be nimble, John be quick' – but he didn't know the woods as well as she and worried he was going to get lost. He looked across the stream and thought he should go home, but her voice came again, goading him. He got hold of the hobby horse and dragged it up the hill, panting with the effort. The shadows had lengthened, making it impossible to work out any landmarks or what direction she'd gone. Soon her voice was lost and so was he.

He sat on a moss-covered tree stump and looked at the hobby horse. Its red eyes stared back at him. In the gloom they appeared real. His father had painted them like that. It was a war horse and needed to look frightening. Maybe it would protect him from the things in the wood? Before she got sick, his mother had told him to keep out. There was something in there, she said, something much worse than the wild animals. He knew who she meant. The villagers had seen him up by Barley Farm a few moons back, a tall figure in black, carrying a stick. Some of the other children said he'd come over Pendle Hill from Chatburn and Grindleton. Witch country, that was. Everyone knew that. It's why everyone was getting sick, why the cows were dying in the fields. It's why Lizzie's mother, Goody Chattox, had died.

He shivered and tried to ride the hobby horse down the slope, making his way over the knotted ground as best he could.

'Lizzie!' he shouted. 'Lizzie, where art thou?'

But the woods were silent. She *must* have gone back.

Twilight now spread across the sky like a thin, blue gauze and the birds of the night began calling to each other. He felt things flit through the branches above his head – bats, maybe, or nightjars, or tawny owls looking for field mice. There were wild creatures in the wood, evil foxes and wolves. And there were stoats and weasels, out hunting for rabbits. Some in the village also spoke about witches – Ginny Greenteeth, for one – who had come from over the hill. They could turn a boy into a toad or a rabbit with a twitch of their nose. What could be worse than that?

As if merely thinking about them had been enough to summon one from the wood, there was a sudden rustling to his right from behind an old hawthorn tree. 'Lizzie? Is that thee?' he asked. 'Don't thou be scaring me if 'tis.'

The rustling stopped.

'Prithee, Lizzie. I want to go home,' he said.

There was a crunch of dry leaves and the snap of a branch, then something broke cover. He wanted to run but his feet were frozen to the ground, his limbs as dead as the earth. A shape emerged from behind the hawthorn. It grew taller as it came towards him. For a moment, he felt like a rabbit, hypnotised by a stoat. Was it a witch? He managed to prise his legs apart, inch-by-inch, forcing them wider. Then, at the very last second, he broke free and found himself running away. But the figure leapt after him and grabbed him by the hand.

He turned and stared into the eyes of Thomas Whittle, the apprentice blacksmith. His heart thundered in his chest. He was relieved he recognised him, but also terrified in case he'd done something wrong.

'Master John,' Tom said coldly. His long, flaxen hair stuck to his face, partially covering the pocked and pitted skin. In the daytime, his face was a bag of leaking sores that the children shied away from. 'What art thou hither for? 'Tis evening anon and thy father will want to know whither thou art.'

John stared at him, petrified as the rabbit. He felt the giant smith's hands round his wrists, fettering him like he was in the stocks.

Paul Southern

'I'm looking for someone, sir.'

'Who, pray?'

'Lizzie Chattox, sir.'

Tom went quiet. 'Lizzie? I think she's fallen, John. Happen thou can bring her mint and nightshade and we can help her?'

'I know them, sir.'

'Then, quick, come with me.'

Tom led him hurriedly round the hawthorn tree, down a slope towards a colonnade of silver aspen trees. The wood got darker.

A shadow of fear grew in John's heart. There, on the ground, her skirts raised to her chest and naked underneath was Lizzie. She was quiet and still. Something terrible had happened to her and he didn't know what. He wanted to put her skirts back over her. He'd once seen his mother like that, with his father on top of her, and knew that it was bad – they'd both cried out and their bodies shook like the Devil had got hold of them.

Tom began touching Lizzie with his long, tumescent fingers. Lizzie seemed to shudder, then turned quiet again.

'What hath happened to her?' John asked. 'What hast thou done?'

Tom's face was red with choler and riven with sweat.

'Mine own duty, Master John.'

Lizzie's golden hair hung loosely and unkempt from her head. Her eyes, which an hour ago were bright with mischief, were now closed.

'Is she dead?' John asked hopelessly.

Tom shook his head as if trying to shake something from his mind.

'No,' he said. ''Tis not her time yet.'

'Her time?'

'Aye. Everyone hath one, Master John. 'Tis why we all have to be prepared.'

He picked up some iron tools and a long, leather scabbard from the forest floor.

'Me, as well?' John asked quietly.

A nightjar flew into the branches above them and the leaves trembled.

'Especially thee, lad. Thou hast been chosen.'

'Chosen for what?' John asked desperately.

Tom raised his arm to silence him. 'I don't like it any more than thee, but the village is sick and we need to stop it.'

At that moment, Lizzie coughed and spluttered.

'Be careful,' Tom warned. 'Thou art going to wake her and that's going to make your suffering all the worse. We don't want her to see, do we?'

Tears swelled in John's eyes and this time he couldn't stanch them.

'Thou mean to kill me?'

'I hast to, lad. I was chosen to. We hast to put an end to things, to the animals dying and the sickness in the village. Even thine own mother. Thou want to save her anon, don't thou?'

John thought of his mother shivering in her bed. The fever had not left her the past month. Her friend, Goody Chattox, had died of it. She said she would be next. He nodded slowly.

'She said 'twas the Hobbledy Man.'

Tom looked at him strangely, as if seeing a light in the darkness. 'Thou hast also seen him, lad?'

John shook his head.

'Then you're lucky. He's in these parts. I saw him two nights past, near the village. He was looking to take someone. A child, haply.'

'What didst thou do?'

'I ran like the wind away from him, master. I told the village elders. That's when they made their decision.'

John's eyes were wild with fright and fear.

'To do what?'

'To stop him, Master John, or bring ruin on the world. God spare us from the servants of the Devil. For that's what they say he is. They drew lots to choose and mine came up shortest. Kill John Malkin, they said, and make peace with him.'

John looked down. He thought of everything he could to save himself, but the talk of the Devil and his mother and the Hobbledy Man had sent a shadow across his little soul and he doubted he could do anything.

Tom drew a knife from the long, leather scabbard. It was from the smithy, ten inches of cruel iron smelt for ruin. 'Thou want the Hobbledy Man to go away? Thou want thy mother to be better?'

'Isn't there any other way?' John cried.

Tom shook his head.

'I wish there was, Master John. But 'tis gone too far. If I don't carryeth out his wishes, the Hobbledy Man will take something of mine. So 'tis written. Look away anon and close thine ears. The night will cover thy tears.'

John looked at Lizzie for the last time and felt his bladder empty and the urine run down his leg. It gathered in a pool by his feet. He turned and stared at the silver boughs of the aspen trees.

Behind him, Tom lifted the knife.

'I have no choice, lad, thou understand that? Be brave anon.'

The iron sliced through the night air.

A dark, wet line appeared on John's neck where it cut through his throat. Blood oozed out onto the ground, collected in a little pool by a stone. His hobby horse fell beside him, its red eyes flaring in anger at the betrayal, but powerless to stop it.

Tom stood over the stricken body and his cheeks burned with shame. Maybe the Hobbledy Man would see the body and go away now?

The last flicker of light had fled the sky and a strange rumination gripped the valley. Children slept easier in their beds and the cows were safe in their fields again. The land returned to plenty and the sickness passed. There would be no more sightings of the Hobbledy Man, not for many a long year.

1

The call came in at 2 a.m. Johnny Malkin rolled off the couch, grabbed his phone and swiped the unlock button. The number was withheld, a sure sign of bad news. Sky Sports was still on, regurgitating last night's Champions League results. He grabbed the remote, turned the volume down, and answered. 'Hello.'

'Johnny?' It was Kat. 'You need to get down to the cells now. It's one of yours.'

'Yeah? Who is it?'

'Nathan Walsh.'

'For fuck's sake. What's he done now?'

'Breaking and entering…resisting arrest…the custody sergeant will go through it all.'

'Tell them I'll be there as soon as I can. Is he okay?'

'They say he's acting funny. Actually, they said he's off his head. Taken something but he won't say what.'

Johnny kicked a Domino's pizza box towards the TV and searched for his trainers. 'He probably doesn't know himself. The boy's a walking pharmacy.' He found the trainers and laced them up. 'You're on late tonight.'

'Cath's on maternity leave.'

'Is she? When did that happen?'

'About nine months ago, I reckon.'

'Nine months?' It slowly sank in. 'Ah, yeah. Very good.'

He wrestled with his coat, ran his hand through what was left of his hair, and grabbed his keys from atop a large pile of unopened case reports.

'Hey, Kat. You still there?'

'Till four.'

'You want to catch up later? Lunch?'

'Are you free?'

'Barring emergencies.'

There was a pause, then a laugh. 'We'll see.'

She hung up. He shook his head, pulled a face at the phone. 'Like you've got any better offers.'

He picked the pizza box up, tried another bite of Margherita, and spat it out. He opened the front door. The cold hit him full on. It was amazing how much colder it was on this side of the hill. Someone had once told him the reason for it but, like a lot of things recently, it had been forgotten. He threw the pizza box in the wheelie bin at the end of the drive and climbed into his black Ford Focus.

Nathan Walsh: if ever there was a kid with problems, it was him. His care plan was longer than the Bible, with as many twists and turns as a bad soap opera. Then again, how many ways were there to escape a life like his? His dad was locked up, his mother an alcoholic who hired her mouth out, and whose lovers regularly beat him black and blue to remind him that neglect wasn't the worst fate you could inflict on a child. The hospital had no record of what she was taking when she was pregnant, just the stuff she declared, but he was suffering withdrawal symptoms the moment he came into the world. You could spend every day with Nathan and you wouldn't sort him out – even if you hadn't another twenty-one Nathans on your files. You were a sticking plaster at best.

He sped down the A682 towards Nelson. On his right, the dark, rolling landscape was wreathed in silver, spectral moonlight. Pendle Water, flush from the recent rain, trailed him towards the village of Barrowford. In the darkness, the beige Yorkshire stone embankment looked like the ramparts of some mediaeval castle and the terraced houses looked like one building with a hundred front doors. The river eventually meandered away towards the M65 before crossing again underneath Scotland Road. Then the greenery ended and the bleak outline of Nelson came into view. This was Nathan's patch: a town with nothing to do and nowhere to go, long forgotten by time. Johnny drove past Bingo Playland Amusements and the old 70's bus station, where kids gathered to smoke late night weed, and parked round the corner from the police station.

The desk sergeant nodded when he came in. He was, perhaps, forty, but looked older, with short, grey hair at the temples and a bald patch on top like a monk.

'You the cavalry?' he said.

Johnny nodded. 'How is he?'

The sergeant looked down at the charge sheet. 'Been keeping us busy. Drug possession, criminal damage, assault and making a right mess of his cell. You any idea what he's on?'

'Ketamine. Crystal meth sometimes.'

'Lovely. I'll tell the FME. You want to see him?'

Johnny looked at the clock on the wall. It was 2.21. 'Someone has to.'

The desk sergeant called the custody sergeant who was reading a copy of the *Metro* in the corner of the waiting area. He came over, took out a bunch of keys, and led Johnny down a long, white corridor. At the end was a large white door with a grille at the top. He slid back a panel and had a look inside. 'Fuck!' he exclaimed. 'Fuck, fuck, fuck!'

'What is it?' said Johnny, suddenly alarmed.

The custody sergeant shouted down the corridor, 'Dan, get the FME now! Hurry!'

The desk sergeant appeared from round the corner, then ran through a pair of double doors to the other end of the corridor.

The custody sergeant fumbled with his keys, made several attempts before he got the right one in the lock, then pushed open the door.

Johnny was right behind him. Over his shoulder, he could see Nathan. He was in the middle of the cell, lying on his side. A stream of vomit had spewed across his t-shirt and onto the floor. It wasn't the only thing that stank. There were some brown smears along one wall. What the hell had he done? Stencilled it in shit?

The custody sergeant looked panicked. 'He's fucking overdosed, hasn't he?' He bent down beside the body and checked the pulse. 'He's barely breathing. Fuck. I only checked him ten minutes ago.'

Johnny pushed past him. 'Where's the FME?'

'He could be anywhere. Out on call.'

Johnny knelt down. Nathan's face was paler than he'd ever seen it. He'd lost consciousness. 'Nathan, can you hear me, son?' More vomit slewed out of his throat, with what looked like bile. He'd been mixing it again. His breath smelt of booze. 'He's going to choke to death, if we don't do something. His stomach needs pumping.'

'So how do we do that?' asked the custody sergeant.

'We don't. We need the FME fast and we need an ambulance. I'm going to try and keep his airwaves free.' He opened Nathan's mouth to make sure he hadn't swallowed his tongue.

The custody sergeant ran out, shouting. Whether he'd really looked in on Nathan ten minutes ago was of no importance now. It was all about keeping the kid alive. The term on the streets was falling into a K-hole, but it may as well have been a black hole. You left the real world behind, out of body, out of mind, locked in tranquiliser heaven, just you and the fucking wild hallucinations. When you got out, *if* you got out, you'd remember nothing.

'Nathan, listen to me, we're gonna get you out of this,' Johnny urged. 'You're going to be okay. The ambulance is going to be here in a few minutes and they're going to pump your stomach and you're going to be okay.' But in Johnny's head, he was thinking the worst already and wondering if he'd done everything he could.

Have I missed something?

It was written above his desk in the office. It was written on his desk at home. It was imprinted in his mind, the mantra of the social worker. Could he have predicted it? He saw Nathan yesterday; he'd checked the room he was staying in, he'd checked he'd eaten, he'd checked he wasn't on anything and needed urgent medical attention. He'd spoken to him, and though Nathan had hardly been on the best form, he wasn't on the worst either and had responded. He could fill a progress report in and say things had been okay. But now things weren't okay and Nathan had inhaled more of this fucking horse tranquiliser. He was overdosing and this was far out of the reach of his training.

Have I missed something?

Of course, he'd missed something. That was why Nathan was like this.

More bile came out of Nathan's mouth, covering his hand. Where the hell was the ambulance? He kept Nathan on his side with his head pointed slightly down. He felt his pulse. It was feeble.

Don't die, you bastard.

He looked at the shit on the wall and suddenly realised the smears weren't random but made into badly drawn letters. He'd written something there.

C O H M

What the fuck was that?

It was then he heard the footsteps running down the corridor and the clang of metal. There were two paramedics, one male and one female, in the doorway. One had a wheelchair.

'Ketamine?' the male paramedic said.

Johnny nodded.

'Any idea when he took it?'

'None.' He was covering his back. Should he have known?

The male paramedic put an oxygen mask over Nathan's mouth. 'Give him point five mill of atropine,' he said to the female paramedic.

She prepared the needle.

They managed to get Nathan onto the wheelchair. The man held his head while the woman stuck the needle in his arm. Nathan's eyes remained closed. They wheeled him out the door, down the corridor, and past the desk sergeant's counter.

The desk sergeant eyed them stoically as if he encountered this kind of thing every day, but he nodded at Johnny with something approaching understanding and not his usual cynicism.

'You coming with us?' the male paramedic asked him.

'I'm all he's got.' Johnny said.

'More than some, then,' the paramedic said.

As they left, Johnny caught the time on the station clock. It was 3.11.

A light drizzle was coming down. Johnny followed the ambulance to Burnley General.

It ran through his head all the way there.

Have I missed something?

2

'You look terrible,' Kat said.

'I feel it.'

'Have you slept?'

'No. I'm back at the hospital later.'

'How is he?'

'Not good.'

Kat looked at him sadly. She hadn't touched her food, just kind of messed with it the way women did when there was something on their mind, or they weren't happy, or both.

'I suppose you'll be tired tonight, then?'

'Yeah, I guess so.'

She stared at him as if she was about to say something, then changed her mind.

'You must be tired, too,' he said.

'I am. We're really busy at the moment.'

He looked down at the pie he'd ordered.

'The boss thinks something's going down,' she said.

'Yeah? Like what?' he said.

'Those grooming gangs…'

Johnny rolled his eyes. 'Them again?'

'Some girls have come forward.'

'They say that all the time, but they won't.'

'They may this time.'

'No, what will happen is what always happens. Front office will get the call, it will be referred up top, and it will come straight back down again. The department doesn't want to offend anyone. Meanwhile, some fourteen-year-old white girl, who shouldn't be on the streets anyway, will be passed around and poked by a gang of Asian men who are laughing at us because we aren't doing anything about it.'

She let the rant end. 'They need evidence, Johnny.'

'They don't need evidence. They need a backbone. No one in the community is going to talk to us, are they? They pretend they don't speak English. Close ranks.'

'Well, isn't that what all families do?'

'Yeah, but we still go after them, don't we? We'd go after Seamus for fiddling with his sister but we won't investigate Saleem for doing the same thing because the council don't want the bad press. Isn't that right?'

She shook her head sadly.

'You know what would happen if a white gang were abusing young Asian girls on the streets?' he continued. 'There'd be a fucking war. They'd take the law into their own hands and shoot the bastards. And, you know what? They'd be right to do so.'

Kat sighed. 'Weren't we coming for something to eat, Johnny? You know, relaxing?'

It was true.

'You're right,' he said. 'I'm sorry.'

She stared at him in that way again. 'I don't think this is working out, John.'

So there it was, what she'd been meaning to say all along. He could tell it was serious when she shortened his name. All the familiarity was gone.

He looked round the room at the other diners in the Bay Horse Inn. He heard the clink of cutlery and the chime of polite conversation and the laughter of children pretending to be grown up, and then he thought of a hospital bed in Burnley General and a sixteen-year-old boy with a tube down his throat, undergoing gastric lavage. He couldn't eat, either.

He looked at Kat. Her bleached blonde hair was cut into a bob and clung to her newly bronzed skin. The Barrowford tanning parlour had done a grand job. She was twenty-nine and could do a lot better than him, there was no denying it.

'Yeah, I know,' he said.

'I've been thinking…'

He knew those words only ever prefaced something bad.

'I think we should have kids.'

An elderly lady with silver-rimmed spectacles, pretending to read her menu on the table to his right, raised her eyebrows and gave him a saucy look.

'What?'

'You know. Kids. I think we should settle down.'

She'd blindsided him, taken him unawares. That wasn't in the rulebook.

'Right…'

'Well, what do you think?'

The elderly lady regarded him mirthfully. 'I hope you don't mind me intruding,' she said, craning her neck confidentially. 'Of course it's none of my business, but my advice would be to say yes.'

Kat smiled. Her teeth were white as snow.

'She's a very beautiful girl,' the elderly lady went on, 'and very beautiful girls don't come along every day. Children are a great blessing.'

Johnny nodded and wondered if the whole thing had been planned. They'd been coming here long enough to get to know the regulars. 'You know that for a fact?' he challenged her.

'I most certainly do,' she said. 'Now, I'm going to get back to my menu and you're going to be a gentleman.'

Kat had a huge smile on her face. For a moment, the tiredness was forgotten, and a shot of life came coursing through her. 'Well?' she said.

'Well,' he said. 'Looks like we're going to be a family.'

Her face glowed in pregnant expectation. He didn't think he'd seen her so beautiful or so happy. Maybe Cath having a baby had done it to her, set her biological clock ticking? Now she was overdosed on the realisation.

'Things are going be different, though,' she said.

'Different?' he said.

'Yeah. You're going to get your priorities right. You're going to find time for us.'

'Time?'

'For me and baby. And you're going to stop drinking.'

She had a long list of things she wanted changing. He listened carefully, then less carefully, until it became a background noise, like the babbling of a stream far away.

'So?' she said finally.

'So?' he repeated.

'Are you going to be tired tonight?'

It suddenly all made sense.

He smiled. 'No sleeping on the job, eh?'

As they left, the elderly lady caught his eye and gestured to him to come over. 'She's just getting the nest ready, as we used to say. Well done. And good luck.'

For a moment, the years fell off her and he glimpsed what she would have looked like when she was younger. She had beautiful eyes and a petite face, slightly foreign looking. He guessed she would have been quite a catch in her heyday. Even now her history and her manner gave a kind of foxiness bordering on sex appeal.

'Thank you,' he said. 'Really.'

They drove back down Pasture Lane to Barrowford. Pendle Valley stretched out on either side, bathed in warm afternoon sunlight. On a day like this, the place was as inviting as the holiday brochures in the local tourist information centre made out: a rambler's paradise. He didn't say much, and Kat seemed happy enough to stay in the moment, thinking of babies and the future. When he dropped her off she had a smile on her face, and when he kissed her goodbye it meant something, the way it often didn't. It didn't feel like he was saying goodbye to anything. It felt like a new beginning.

He saw her in the rear-view mirror and wished he could take a picture of her, to remind him. Then he turned a corner and she vanished. Time? How was he going to find time when there was no time even to sleep? A kind of haze descended on him as he headed back to the hospital. He was taking Nathan back to the police station, back to answer questions, so his life could be reset and the same old crap happen again. There'd never be a new beginning for Nathan, just a million false dawns. If he left his job, sure there would be someone to take his place, but the continuity he promised, that he promised all of them, would be gone. He would have passed the buck, moved on, forgotten them all, like every social worker before him.

Nathan was in a bed at the far end of the ward. He didn't look at him when he sat down next to him, he just kept staring straight ahead.

'How you doin', son? They looking after you?'

There was no reply.

'You don't have to talk if you don't want to. I'll do it for both of us.'

No reply again.

'We have to go to the station when you're better, have a talk with the police.'

Nathan shook his head.

'You'll have to, son. We have to sort you out.'

'Leave me alone or I'll call the nurse.'

'I'll call her for you, if you like. I need to speak to her, anyway.'

'Fuck you.'

An amiable ward sister in a light blue dress approached them. 'You are?'

'John Malkin. I'm Nathan's social worker.'

'He's not,' said Nathan. 'He's a cunt and I want him to go.'

'We don't use language like that, Mr Walsh,' the nurse said to him. 'It upsets the other patients.'

Johnny looked round the ward and thought most of them wouldn't bat an eyelid. It was that kind of place. 'How is he?' he asked.

The sister took the notes from the side of his bed. 'Blood pressure is still high, but he's stable otherwise.'

'So, he's free to go?'

'He's free but the doctor would like to keep him another night.'

'What for?'

'Just a precaution.' She took him to one side. 'He was assessed by a ward psychologist last night. He was showing signs of severe psychosis. They think he may try to harm himself again.'

Nathan looked up, as if guessing what they were saying. 'I'm not staying in this shithole,' he said. 'And you can't make me.'

The sister rapped his bed sheets. 'You'll do as you're told, Mr Walsh.'

He recoiled from the blow as if he'd been punched.

When the sister had gone, Johnny sat down next to him.

'You fucking told them, didn't you?' Nathan said.

'Told who, son?'

'The police. You told them what I was taking.'

'I had to.'

'That was our secret. You said you'd never tell anyone.'

'You could have died.'

'I wanted to die.'

Johnny looked at his fragile, fucked up sixteen-year-old features – the narrow-boned, shaven head, the wasted pock-marked skin, the grimace of pain that passed for a smile – and realised it was true. The world was already too much for him. 'You can't.'

'Why not?'

'Because I won't let you.'

'Cos you're a cunt?'

'Because I care for you, son.'

For a moment, nothing registered. There was that same bone-hard stare from dead eyes. Then, slowly, they began to water, like an underground spring coming to an arid land that had never known love or emotion. It broke the dam he had constructed around himself and tears poured down his face. He sobbed and lay on his side on the bed.

The sister reappeared and took it in. She bit her lip and looked at Johnny. 'I called the doctor. He'll talk to you as soon as he can. Do you need anything?'

Johnny shook his head. 'No.'

He looked at Nathan's defeated body and his defeated soul crumpled on the hospital bed and thought of children who hadn't been born yet. Would his own be spared the agony Nathan was going through? Could he guarantee them that?

He sat on the hospital bed and stretched his arm out. He rubbed Nathan's shoulder gently. Nathan didn't respond. He was holed up somewhere, in his own world.

C O H M

3

It was 9.30 p.m. and the rain came down in grey, unending waves. Jenna waited under the trolley shelter in Morrisons' car park, watching the last of the shoppers pack their cars up and go home. The silver saloon was late. *He* was late. She checked her phone, smoothed her coat down over her legs. For a moment she thought of her mum and the thought made her feel uncomfortable. She lit a cigarette and inhaled sharply. Her cheekbones stood out like cut glass.

After a couple of minutes, the silver saloon turned up and the passenger door opened from inside. She got in quickly. 'You're late,' she said.

'You got wet?'

'What do you think?'

'Where's your friend?'

'She couldn't make it.'

The driver was wearing sunglasses, but she knew the hard, dead eyes behind them would be cross. When he was cross, he got really cross. She'd seen him like that with other girls and it frightened her. But he'd been nice to her so far.

'Why not?'

Jenna shrugged. 'I think she's seeing her boyfriend.'

'She has a boyfriend?'

'Yeah.' She said it as casually as she could, but she worried he'd see through the lie.

'I told you to bring her. Mo likes her. He thinks she's pretty.'

She felt a twang of jealousy. 'She is.'

He pulled out of the car park. The rain came down heavier. You couldn't see more than twenty metres ahead, even with the windscreen wipers working overtime. The headlights on the oncoming cars blurred and squinted like dying suns.

'Where are we goin'?' she asked.

'It's a secret today. You like secrets?'

She looked down at her phone. 'Ya know I do.'

She felt his hand on her knee. He pinched it twice, reassuringly.

They drove out of Nelson and up towards Barrowford. It was where the posh girls from her school lived.

'We've never been this way before.'

'I told you, it's a secret.'

She glanced at her phone again and read a message.

U with him now?

She texted back quickly.

Yeah

She didn't know where they were. It was dark and cold and the rain was unrelenting. It made her think of the book she was reading in English class: 'Wuthering Heights'. The streetlights vanished from the side of the road and soon they were out in the country. He seemed a little on edge, like he was thinking about other things, things other than her. She played him a song on her phone and he smiled. It made her feel better.

Soon, she could make out the black outline of Pendle Hill. When she was young, she went walking up there on a school trip. She remembered the teacher talking about how people used to believe in witches and how people round there used to think the Devil was real and those who followed him played in the woods and worshipped him.

Where r u goin?

I dunno.

The headlights lit up hedges and gates and road signs, but they were too quick for her to take in. There was a bridge over a river and that was about it.

He pulled into a car park and drove to the far end, near some trees and furthest from the road.

'Is this the secret?' she said. 'A car park in the country?'

He took a packet of fine white powder from his pocket. 'Here,' he said. 'Have a line. It will do you good.'

'We're just going to sit 'ere?'

He shook his head. 'No.'

She looked at the powder sceptically. 'What is it?'

'Something special. Go on. Try it.'

A faint chemical smell wound like a snake into her nostrils. She inhaled the powder. He touched her knee again and she felt awkward. He touched her hair and then asked her to unbutton her coat. The buckle on her coat took two goes to undo. Then he kissed her slowly on the mouth. She felt the stubble on her chin and his nose on her cheek. It excited her to see his reaction. It reassured her, made her feel like she was something, made her feel grown up.

But things didn't go quite as planned. After kissing her, he began to talk. He mentioned his wife. Then he laid his cards on the table. 'Jenna, I need you to help me.'

She could see her face reflected in his sunglasses and wondered what he was thinking of. 'How?' she said.

'I need you to get some money for me. I want us to get a little place together, so we don't have to keep doing things like this. It will be safer.'

'Like a house?'

'Yeah.'

'Where?'

'Wherever you like. We can see each other. And, after your exams, we can live there.'

'On our own?'

'Of course. I'm going to move out.'

He'd said things like that in the past but it had never happened. He said the moment wasn't right. But tonight, something was different about him.

'So, what can I do?' she said.

He looked at his watch. As if on cue, there was a flash of headlights behind them. Another car drew up alongside.

'You know 'em?' she asked.

'Don't worry. It's just some friends.' He didn't sound altogether convincing.

Instinctively, she clutched her phone tighter.

'Wait in the car,' he said.

A cold wind blew in. She watched him walk round the front. She wondered if it was a business deal he was making. She'd seen some of his 'friends' before. Older men, normally. They'd been nice enough to her, but occasionally some had perved at her and she was scared of them.

The driver's window on the other car wound down. She could hear him talking to the driver but she couldn't see them properly. Then the passenger door opened and she felt the rain on her legs.

'What do they want?' she said.

'You,' he said.

The word nailed her to her seat. 'What d'ya mean?' It slowly sunk in and a terrible, inescapable fear took hold of her.

He leant over her and took her phone from her trembling fingers. 'You won't need that,' he said.

She let him take it and hated herself for being so weak. 'I don't understand. I thought ya loved me?' she said.

It sounded so pathetic.

He kissed her cheek softly. 'I need you to do this for me, Jenna. Please.'

She got out slowly. The rear door of the other car opened and she got in. She was too terrified to run away. She was too terrified to do anything other than what they said.

An hour later, she got back in the silver saloon. He said nothing and she said nothing. He took his sunglasses off to look at her. His eyes were full of something like remorse.

'I wanna go home,' she said simply.

He pulled out of the car park and the headlights lit up the hedges and gates and road signs once more.

'Can I have my phone back?' she said.

He reached into his coat pocket and gave it to her.

She guessed he must have looked at her messages but she didn't check. She didn't want him to ask what she was doing.

When they got back to Nelson, she felt a strange relief sweep over her. She hadn't died, had she? No one had hit her. No one had beaten her. They had just used her. Or, maybe, she had used herself.

He drove into Morrisons' car park and began to talk again. Half of it sounded like he was talking to himself, trying to justify himself, but half of it was addressed to her, talking about the house they were going to get together.

'Did ya get ya money, then?' she asked.

'Yes,' he said.

'I hope it was worth it.'

He paused. The rain drummed against the roof of the car. 'They want to see you again,' he said. 'Somewhere different.'

'Well, you can tell 'em to fuck off.'

'We can't, Jen. They took some pictures while you were in the car.'

'What do you mean?'

He took out his phone and let her look.

She froze. The girl in the photos, could that really be her? 'What are they gonna do with them?'

'Nothing, so long as you do what they say.'

She could hardly think. She imagined the images being passed around school, appearing on her Facebook page, on her Twitter feed, and then her mum finding out. It would destroy her. 'You can't let them do that. I need you to get them back.'

'I'll try,' he said.

'You have to,' she said imploringly.

'I can't promise you, Jen.'

'If you don't, I'm gonna kill myself.'

She said it earnestly and it stopped him dead.

'Don't be stupid,' he said.

Tears sprang to her eyes. 'D'ya know what you've fuckin' done to me?'

He put his hand on her knee and stroked it. 'Of course. And it's killing me, too.'

She shook her head bitterly. The rain drummed on the roof. 'No, you don't.'

After a minute, he spoke again. 'Maybe, there is a way out.'

'How?' she said.

'Your friend.'

'Alisha? What about her?'

'Can you bring her next time?'

'Why would I do that?'

'Because they're interested in her, that's why.'

'Well, I can't.'

'I can get the photos back. I can get them deleted. You want them deleted, don't you?'

'What if she won't come?'

He put his sunglasses back on. 'Then you'll have to make her.' He reached across her lap to the glove compartment and took a clear, plastic bag out. There was something inside. 'Here,' he said. 'There's something for you.'

'What is it?' she asked.

'Something you've been asking for.'

She put her hand inside and drew out a white box. She read the familiar type on the side.

iPhone7

'You won't need your old one,' he said.

A feeling of childish consolation crept through her. That was something she could show off to her friends, not those horrible pictures.

Before she got out of the car, he squeezed her knee again. She knew he was trying to buy her forgiveness but couldn't bring herself to tell him. Truth be told, she didn't really know how she felt about anything any more. Her body didn't feel like it was her own. Nor her mind. She ran across the car park with her coat wrapped tightly about her. The rain had stopped but the cold was bitter. Her mum would be furious. She should have been back an hour ago.

She ran past the mosque on Pendle Street. Its green dome looked like a giant football. Before she made her way down Every Street, she turned to her left. In the distance, she could see the silhouette of Pendle Hill again, but that wasn't what drew her attention. In the middle of the road was a tall, gangly figure in black. He had a stick in his hand. He stared at her for a moment, then began hobbling down the road like an insect on crutches. She'd never seen him round there before, nor anyone like him, in fact. He would have fitted the pages of wild 'Wuthering Heights' more than the streets of Nelson.

For a moment, she almost forgot the dark, tempestuous events of the night, and felt the shadow of some other evil had come to the town.

4

Eight weeks later

The police Range Rover ploughed through the huge pool that had formed on Barley Lane, sending sheets of spray into the hedgerows. The wipers did their best to clear the water from the windscreen, but the rain kept on falling. PC Shaf Khan felt the wheels lock up as he rounded the final bend and killed his speed. He looked out into the forbidding scene. The local saying, '*if you can see Pendle Hill, it's about to rain, if you can't, it's already started*', came to mind. The five days a year you could actually see anything brought the hillwalkers and tourists out, but for the seasoned walker, treks up the hill and across the valley were a test of endurance and a battle against the elements.

Shaf pulled his high visibility, yellow jacket tightly around him and got out of the car. An unearthly blast of wind forced him back and made him squint. Ahead of him was a small farmstead. As he struggled down the footpath towards it, he heard the sound of dogs barking in an outhouse. He cursed quietly. If there was one thing he hated, it was dogs.

There was a light on downstairs in the main building: an old, stone cottage. He rapped on the large wooden door and then on the window. The wind lashed against it and he drew his collar up further, burrowing his neck inside.

'C'mon on, answer,' he whispered.

After a few seconds, he heard a bolt shoot back and the front door opened. In the doorway was a giant of a man. He was six feet two, in his fifties, with a grey beard and a rugged, weathered face. His left eye squinted to the left, but the right was straight and true and stared at him like a rook, beady with concentration.

'Mr Carver?' Shaf said.

'Aye.'

'You called us?'

'That's right. An hour ago.'

'I'm sorry. We got here as quick as we could. May I come in?'

'Aye, best you do. The night is bitter.'

Shaf felt another cold blast at his back. Mr Carver led him inside, down a narrow hallway into a large, stone kitchen. Shaf guessed the features must have been original; it had that olde worlde feel. There were low, heavy, wooden beams on the ceiling and cold, white, stone walls. The floor was stone too and the furniture was made of wood: sturdy oak chairs and a large, old oak table. There was a roaring fire on a large range at one side, which threw out great heat and, in front of it, was a big black dog chewing on a huge bone. Shaf imagined it chewing his leg and hoped it wouldn't get up.

'He'll not eat ya,' Mr Carver said, as if sensing his anxiety.

Shaf looked at it, unconvinced. 'You reported intruders, Mr Carver?'

'Aye, the last three nights,' he said.

As he said it, there was a light footfall behind him.

Shaf turned and saw a girl of nineteen or twenty, with a long white dress on, standing in the doorway. Her left eye was squinted, too, and spoiled what was a very pretty face. Or, perhaps, spoiled was the wrong word. Rather, it seemed to enhance the beauty of the rest of it. She had long, brown hair which covered her shoulders and breasts, and rustic brown skin with tiny freckles round her nose.

Shaf turned back to Mr Carver. 'Has anything been taken?'

'Milk from the cowsheds has been spilt. And they've tried the front door.'

'Have they come at the same time each night?'

'Aye. The wee hours o' the morn. Two, maybe. The dogs have all been woken. They wud'na wake without cause.'

Shaf took out a pen and a small pad and began writing. 'Have you actually seen them? How many there were?'

The fire crackled and the dog lacerated the bone but Mr Carver was quiet. He was looking past him towards the girl.

'I have na, no.'

The girl came into the room and stood beside him. She stood framed in the firelight, a willowy girl with shadows dancing up and down her body. She took his hands. 'Why don't you tell him, Dad? That's why you called them, isn't it? So they can investigate properly.'

'I rang because ya asked me, Beth. Nothing else.'

She turned to Shaf and her green eyes flickered in the glow of the fire. Her freckles twitched as she spoke. 'My father won't talk because he's scared, that's all,' she said. 'He's scared you won't believe him.'

Shaf looked at Mr Carver. 'We treat every report of a crime the same. It will all be investigated.'

'Aye, and there's the fault. Sometimes, it does'na need to be,' he replied.

'I'm sorry,' the girl said. 'Please, take a seat, officer.' She took a large iron kettle off the range. 'Can I get you some tea?'

'No, I'm fine,' Shaf said.

She looked at her father, put the kettle down and then spoke, warily at first, as if trying to get his approval, then more confidently as her belief got stronger. 'It started three nights ago. It was the dogs that alerted us. We lock them up in the outhouse, apart from Fang here.' She pointed to the dog. 'He'd rip the others apart if he was with them too long.'

Shaf gave it another wary look.

'I looked out from my bedroom window but I couldn't see anything,' she went on, 'and after about half an hour, the barking stopped, and we didn't hear anything till morning. When we got up, we found the cowshed had been opened and some pails knocked over. We thought it must have been a fox at first, although the pails are very heavy. Anyway, two nights ago the same thing happened, only this time some marks appeared on our front door.' She gave her father another guarded look. 'We didn't hear anything, though. Just the dogs barking.'

'Marks?' Shaf asked.

Her eyes never left her father's. 'Yes. Four lines, cut into the wood. We thought it may have been an animal but it's too high up.'

The fire crackled.

'Did they go into the cowshed again?'

'Yes, just like the day before. There was a pail on the floor, too. Then, last night, my dad slept downstairs.' She nodded to the right, through the doorway she'd just come from. 'I couldn't sleep so I waited upstairs. Right on cue, the dogs started barking and, this time, Fang joined in. He was at the kitchen window here, barking like a fury.'

Shaf looked at Mr Carver for some kind of verification but he was staring out of the window as if reliving everything. The wind lashed against the frame and sucked the fire up the chimney as it passed over the cottage, and strange demon shadows played on the table. Shaf stopped writing.

'My father owns a gun,' she said. 'He has a license for it. He brought it out the back room where he keeps it locked up. I was looking out from the upstairs window to see if I could see anything, but I couldn't. Then I heard the front door open and Fang barking and the light from the cottage flooded out as far as the garden wall.'

Shaf sat entranced, wrapped in the story.

'It was then I saw it,' she said.

'*It?*' he said.

She nodded. 'I told you, you wouldn't believe us.'

Mr Carver got up as if he could take no more of it. 'That's enough, Beth. I said it was just your imagination playing tricks on ye.' He glowered into the fire. 'Someone's been prowling, that's all, officer. That's why we called ye. Show him to the door, Beth. We've gone and reported it now, done what ye wanted. Let them do what they have to now.'

She nodded obediently but her eyes were wild and bright. She led Shaf back into the hallway and opened the front door.

'What did you mean by *it*?' he said. 'What did you see?'

She ignored him. The wind blew in and her voice was nearly drowned out in its roar. 'We heard more screams tonight, officer. They were coming from over by Black Moss.'

'The reservoirs?' he said.

'They're only five minutes away. The lane you're on runs right by them.'

'Is that why you called?'

'They weren't normal screams, officer. We thought it may have something to do with the intruders. Who else would be out on a night like this?'

As if in answer, another gust of wind blew right down the hallway, sending in a shower of rain. Her hair blew wildly behind her and her white dress clung to her body. Shaf tried not to notice the nipples pointing through the material. 'If the intruders come back, call us,' he said.

'I will,' she said.

He braced himself against the wind and rain and plunged into the darkness. The door shut behind him with a bang. He got out his torch and turned it on the door. He saw four lines in the wood, just the way she had described them. There were three vertical lines going down and one going off to the right, with what looked like a dot above it, as if someone had tried to scour an i into the wood. He examined the rest of the yard and made his way down the footpath to the end of the garden. The dogs were mercifully quiet in their outhouse.

As he took one last look at the cottage, he noticed a light come on upstairs. The curtains weren't drawn and he could see inside. The girl, Beth, was standing there, looking down at him. She had a candle in her hand. That wasn't what grabbed his attention, though. It was that she was no longer wearing her dress. Or anything. He turned quickly and hurried back to the Range Rover, aware of her looking at him. When he got in, he radioed base and requested background checks on the residents of the farm. They all came back spotlessly clean, not even a parking offence.

He turned the key in the ignition and flicked the headlights on. As he did, he caught movement in the corner of his eye, something scurrying behind the gate. An animal, maybe, but he thought of what the girl had said and began to feel uneasy. He turned the car round and drove down Barley Lane towards the reservoirs.

The headlights lit up the narrow, stone walls on either side. Any mistake and he'd end up crashing into one. He wanted to file a report and head back down to Nelson, but he didn't want screams hanging over his career, no matter how flimsy the evidence. He realised when he joined the Lancashire Constabulary that he had to be twice the officer everyone else was. No short cuts, no deviating, just taking the line between the narrow, stone walls of prejudice.

The road was like a slender grey thread that wound into the darkness. After a couple of minutes, he came to the lip of Lower Black Moss Reservoir. He parked the Range Rover alongside and got out, holding aloft his torch, then looked over the dank, stone wall. The wind blew right across the water, down from Pendle Hill, and sent icy blasts towards him. Waves lapped and chopped against the banks. He felt the cold spreading to his bones, even through his jacket and gloves.

On the other side of the valley, a nursery of trees had been planted in plastic cases to protect them from the biting wind. They looked like tiny gravestones. Higher up, the dark, brooding coniferous plantation of Aitken Wood covered the hill's crown. There was nothing there, no sign of anyone. He could tick that box now and go back to the warmth. He'd have nothing bad to say about Nelson now, either.

Then, just as he was about to get back in the car, a sound wound down from the top of the hill, one he couldn't ignore. It was a high-pitched scream. What the hell was going on tonight? He flashed his torch across the wide expanse of cottongrass and gravestones, up towards Aitken Wood. He couldn't see anything, but on a night like this, he'd need a lighthouse to do so. The torch was like a candle in a tempest.

'Hey!' he shouted up. 'Anyone there?'

There was a muddy path that wound up the slope. His boots squelched as he climbed. He reached a line of spruce trees and took shelter there. The rain stopped and the wind ceased its battery. He looked round, his heart thundering in his chest. The running, the cold, the fear, the weird encounter with the Carvers, had put him on supernatural edge. He thought again of what Beth had seen at the farmhouse. *It?* What the hell was that? A big cat? They had reports of them round here, from farmers as far away as Clitheroe and Chatburn way. But a big cat surely couldn't make marks on your front door like that, even on its hind legs.

'Hello!' he shouted again. 'Is anyone there?'

The screaming had stopped. There was nothing but the wind in the eaves and the rain falling on the trees. He continued for a hundred metres along a narrow path. They'd made a Sculpture Trail here a few years ago, celebrating the Pendle Witches. In the darkness, the statues seemed to take on lives of their own. It needed only a little magic of the imagination.

There was a snapping sound to his left and he turned quickly. The torchlight revealed nothing. Then he caught something hanging on the branch of a tree about ten metres away, twitching in the air. He shuddered. It was a bird of some kind, black as night. Was it trapped? He approached it slowly. Why hadn't it flown off? It was about the size of a man's head, with a long, black beak. Then he realised it wasn't a bird. It was a mask, hung on the branch. He'd never seen anything like it. It smelt faintly of perfume or spruce and had two giant, red glass eyepieces that stared back at him. As he was about to touch it, the snapping sound came again, this time from his right. He jumped back, expecting something to bolt from the undergrowth. 'Police!' he shouted. 'Who's there?'

The words sounded empty and hollow. Or was that just his voice? There was no law in the woods, at least no manmade one.

She appeared out of the corner of his eye like an apparition and it took him several moments to realise she wasn't one. She was fourteen or fifteen, with long, unkempt, blonde hair and a dirty, white coat. As soon as she saw his face, she stopped.

'Are ya one of 'em?' she said, frightened.

'One of who?'

She looked at the bird mask on the branch.

'I'm a police officer,' he said.

She said nothing.

'Did you scream just now?' he said. 'I was on patrol by the reservoir.' He indicated back through the woods even though he had no idea which direction he was pointing. 'I heard screams. They were coming from up here.'

The girl paused. 'It's my friend.'

The way she said it didn't sound great. 'What's happened?'

'You're too late,' she said.

'Too late for what?'

'To help her. I think she's dead. I think they killed her.'

Shaf felt tendrils of fear spreading to the rest of his body, reaching down into his stomach, making his arms shake and his legs feel unsteady. It was all he could do to keep his voice steady. 'Listen,' he said. 'I'm here to help you. Where is she?'

She looked at him, as silent as one of the statues.

He edged closer to her. 'If you want to help her, you'll have to tell me.'

He took his radio out, tried to call base, but it only crackled with static. They were on their own. 'Just tell me where she is, then we can help her.' He extended his hand slowly, the way he had been trained.

She must have guessed what he was about to do because, at the last moment, she ran.

'Hey!' he shouted. 'Stop!'

She was light on her feet and, even though her coat was white, she blended into the woods seamlessly. He crashed through the undergrowth after her. The way he ran would have alerted every bird and animal within a five-mile radius, but speed was of the essence, not the finer points of tracking. Several times he nearly tripped on tree roots as he careered downhill. Then, suddenly, he came to a small stream. He could have vaulted it with a single stride, but he shied at it like a jump horse on race day.

The stream flowed down to a shallow pool about ten metres away that lay in the shadow of an old rowan tree. Standing beside it was the girl, and next to her was a prone figure on the bank.

'Hey!' he said. 'Please wait.'

He approached them slowly. And this time, she didn't run away. There was a faint plop from the centre of the pool and his eyes were quickly drawn there. For a brief second, he thought he saw something, a figure or a shadow, disappearing into it, but when he got there, the pool was still and silent. There were no ripples on the surface to indicate anything had been there and certainly no figure in the middle. What there was, was a lingering smell in the air, mephitic and unpleasant. He bent down. The figure on the ground was a girl, about the same age as the girl in the white coat. She had dark brown hair and olive skin, Mediterranean or Asian. Her hair was wet and had some kind of weed entangled in it.

Had she drowned? He felt for her pulse but his hands were cold and he detected nothing.

'Is this your friend?' he said to the girl in the white coat.

She nodded, hypnotised.

He put his hands on the prone girl's chest and began to push. One. Two. Three.

'How long was she in the water?' he said.

The girl in the white coat said nothing, her eyes fixed on her friend.

'C'mon,' he said. 'Breathe. You've got to breathe.'

Four, Five, Six.

A jet of water came out of the girl's mouth. It was black and covered his yellow jacket.

'Shit,' he said.

Seven, Eight, Nine.

His hands pumped the chest rhythmically. More black water came out.

Then nothing.

He was pumping in vain. She was dying on him.

Then, with a violent convulsion, her chest heaved and she coughed and spluttered.

'Breathe,' he said again. 'Breathe!'

He turned her on her side, let gravity drain the rest of the water from her lungs. The noisome smell came with it.

He tried his radio again, prayed for a signal. After a few seconds, a voice cut through.

'Bravo Delta Echo Sierra seven eight six. Urgent,' he said quickly.

There was static on the other end, drowning out the voice.

He repeated the request, then pressed the orange button at the top of the set. It was only used if an officer was in imminent danger, but he felt he'd reached that point. The girl in his arms needed medical attention and the potential assailants could still be in the area. That justified his choice.

He got his own phone out, tried to find a signal, but the network was down. So much for Airwave, so much for 4G. Losing your signal was common on the top of Pendle Hill, but not down here. It must have been the storm.

The girl in the white coat stared at him. Anger turned to sympathy. He recognised the signs of trauma. She wasn't thinking clearly, if she was thinking at all.

She shuffled slowly towards him. 'Will she be okay?' she said.

'I hope so,' he said. 'But she needs a doctor.'

She came a bit nearer still. 'Her name's Alisha.'

He looked at her. 'And what's yours?'

'Jenna. Jenna Dunham.'

He nodded. 'Well, backup will be here in no time, Jenna. I don't want you running off. We'll get your friend to hospital and we'll get you sorted. You understand?'

She pushed her hair out of her eyes. 'You really a policeman?'

'Yes.' He showed her his collar number.

'Am I in trouble?'

'No.'

She sat on the bank. A light spray came down from the branches above them. The rain on the tree canopy intensified. It sounded like the distant roar of the sea. He readjusted his hold on Alisha, kept her as still as he could, and tried to shield her from the spray. 'What were you doing out here?' he said.

'We was runnin',' she said.

'Running?'

'Runnin' away.'

'From what?'

She picked up a stick and drew some lines in the mud. There was something that looked like a bird's beak. He thought of the strange bird mask he'd seen on the tree and wondered if it was the same. Then he saw something else beside it: three vertical lines and one that veered to the right. He felt the fear creep up on him again. It was the mark made on the door of Carver's farmhouse.

'What's that?' he said.

'You don't know?' she said.

He shook his head.

'You will do soon,' she said. 'Everyone will know.'

The way she said it chilled him. He hoped backup wouldn't take long. He was beginning to feel something was dreadfully wrong round here, with the girls and with the whole wood.

5

The silver Skoda Rapid shot past Farmfoods where Chav Central, The Hour Glass pub, used to stand, and sped up Walton Lane towards Marsden Park. It was 9.32 p.m. and the roads were deserted. It continued up to the cemetery as if the police chopper were on top of it, then the driver hit the brakes and got out. He had a shaved head and his face was scarred and pitted with acne. A few seconds later, a black car came down the hill the other way and pulled up behind him. A man got out and they shook hands briefly. The driver opened the Skoda's glove compartment and put a clear plastic bag inside it. He then got out his mobile phone and made a call.

'You okay?' There was some agitated chatter on the other end. 'No, I'm not with someone else. I'll be back in a bit. Fuckin' calm down, will ya?' He held the phone away from his ear. 'Yeah, of course.'

He put the phone in the dashboard holder and accelerated up the hill, turned the music up full blast till the car began to rap with it. He had one more fare to go. Thursdays were normally dead but tonight was the deadest ever. It's like the whole town had fallen asleep.

He got to Marsden Park and slowed down by the play area. It was an odd fucking point to pick anyone up. The kid looked about sixteen, with a shaved head and the narrow-slit features of all the local chavs. You couldn't judge a book by its cover, but in this case you could. He turned the music down and opened the window. 'Nathan?' he said.

The kid nodded, then pointed to a large holdall by his feet. 'Can I put this in ya boot?'

The driver smelt a rat. 'What is it?'

'Football gear.'

More likely swag, the driver thought. 'You got your fare?' he asked.

The kid grinned, took out a twenty note from his pocket. 'You's can 'av it all upfront, pal.'

The driver swung the Skoda round on to the park side of the road and got out. The moment he did, three lads came running out from behind the green hut in the play area. Nathan opened the holdall and handed something to the nearest one. The driver caught the glint of silver. Before he could get back to the car, a knuckleduster was smashed flush in his face. His nose burst and his skull shuddered. He thought he'd seen the lad somewhere before but, with his head reeling and his eyes full of blood, he couldn't think where. He sank to his knees.

'Nice wheels, bro,' Knuckleduster said. 'Can we take it for a spin?' Before he could answer, the knuckleduster was smashed into his face again.

The blow made him cry out. His nose ran like a river. They stood round him like rats. He felt something cold and metallic on his neck and winced at its sharpness.

'Don't worry,' Knuckleduster said. 'I'm not gonna cut your head off like your mate Jihadi John does. We're not animals here. I just want ya to take a message back to ya paedo pals.'

The driver felt the blade sink its teeth into him.

'We know what you're up to. We know who's doin' it and we're gonna do summat, y'understand? One of ya sisters, or ya wife, we'll video it for ya.' The blade drew blood. 'Now, cos we're not cunts, we're gonna give ya car back, but we're gonna skin it first, and then we're gonna take a picture of ya like this and post it all over and if you so much as look at one of our girls again, you's a dead man. Geddit, John?'

Another punch took the air from his lungs. He heard them open the doors of the Skoda and saw their shitty white hands all over his seats. They'd find the ketamine, of course, and his phone. He cursed them and a wave of anger came coursing through him.

It seemed to come out of the very ground he was kneeling on. For a moment, the sky got darker and he was sure there was someone else by his car. He counted the figures and they came to five, then blood seeped into his eyes and they were all gone. All that was left was the blinding pain and the humiliation.

When they'd gone, a door opened in one of the houses on the opposite side of the road and a woman came out. 'You all right?' she shouted.

He nodded, but she came over anyway – a real Good Samaritan. She was thirty, maybe forty, maybe even fifty. With his eyes puffed up and blood everywhere, it was hard to make anything out.

'You want me to ring an ambulance?' she said.

He shook his head again. 'No. Thanks.'

'I don't like to see that stuff anywhere, especially on my doorstep,' she said. 'It's not right.'

'You know who they were?' he asked, revenge already on his mind.

'Aye,' she said. 'But if the police come knocking, I don't. Those lads wouldn't a' done that for no reason. Whatever you did, you better stop. You understand?'

He looked at her grimly.

'Look, let me get you a towel,' she went on. 'There's blood everywhere.'

He could feel it on his neck and his t-shirt. It would be all over the car, too. He'd need to get that cleaned up. He'd need to get everything cleaned up.

'I'm okay,' he said. 'Really.'

But she wasn't for dissuading. As she disappeared back inside her house, he hit the accelerator and sped off up the hill, taking Hallam Road back into town. His phone was locked but there was a lot of shit on there, things that shouldn't be there. He had Find My iPhone on and could erase it remotely but he needed to get to a computer fast. He needed to wipe it before those shits found anything.

If they didn't kill him, Tariq would.

6

Johnny picked up his phone and looked at the time again. It was 2.16 a.m. and he couldn't sleep. This last year, he couldn't sleep. What began as a one-off, and something the alcohol could sort out, had become a long, waking nightmare. The doctor said he was thinking too much about it and put him on a course of CBT, but that didn't fix it either. Expecting you weren't going to sleep meant you wouldn't. It was as simple as that. There were tablets for relaxing and tablets for anxiety and tablets for depression but none of them worked. And none of them really mixed well with alcohol. The latest one, mirtazapine, was given to him off-label by a locum as a last resort. It gave him dreams bordering on hallucinations and made him wake up wanting to punch a wall, but any kind of sleep was better than none. What he really wanted was to get to back to normal, but with work the way it was, the long hours and the pressure he was under, it wasn't going to happen.

He turned on to his side and looked at Kat. Her back was to him and she was sleeping soundly. Her Barrowford brown skin glowed in the soft light of the table lamps. She'd fallen asleep reading. He tried that, along with bananas, sex, valerian, meditation and some diazepam he'd got from a dispenser at Burnley General when the doctor refused to give him any more, but none of it was a long-term cure. You had to listen to your body and let it do what it wanted, not fill it with drugs. He dealt with enough headcases every day to know that drugs were never the way forward. The irony was that so many other social workers took them too, prescription or not.

He put his hand on Kat's back and felt the warmth of her skin. She stirred slightly. He thought about what she'd said, about finding time, about changing his job and about the baby. They'd been having baby sex for two months, or at least on the days leading up to and during ovulation. She'd read books about it – the ones that sent her to sleep – and pencilled days in her Pregnancy Diary. It meant the absolute world to her. And it meant the same to him – almost. The problem was, with all the forms and timings and thinking about babies, it had robbed him of any excitement. When they'd had an argument, or when they were out in the country somewhere and the mood took them, the sex was great – unpredictable and great. All this other stuff had killed his libido, just as the lack of sleep had.

He looked again at his phone. 2.31 a.m. now. Where the hell had those fifteen minutes just gone? Had he dozed off and not realised? He had a meeting with Daphne Cooper, the vacuous, air-brushed team leader, later to review his cases. He could see her now, with her laptop open in front of her, ready to dissect his latest failings. There was a standing joke amongst the other social workers that the laptop actually housed her brain, because she didn't seem to be able to think without switching it on. It gave her direct access to the recommendations of Professor Eileen Munro, the latest expert on social care in the UK. Have a word without her laptop on and she was lost for words, which in most cases was a good thing.

Johnny's brain was in overdrive. There was no way he was going to sleep, even with the mirtazapine. He lifted the duvet carefully and slid out of bed. He covered Kat's back, left the room, and went into the lounge. He turned the TV on, lay on the couch, and went through his cases in his head. He wondered if he had made a 'defensible decision' – the department's new mantra – for each of them. Was a care plan clear? Was the pathway plan the right one? Christ, he may as well have been taking smack, he was so wired. Kat was right: the job had taken over his life. He'd have to bring that up with Daphne, too. He wanted to reduce his caseload. He'd have to, otherwise he'd go mad.

'Shut up,' he told himself. 'Shut up and go to sleep.'

He looked at his phone again. 2.54 a.m. He flicked through the channels. Plenty of shopping ones, a couple of UFO documentaries, a plastic blonde on Babestation asking him if he was hard – he wasn't, some religious programmes asking him to think about God, and Sky Sports.

He closed his eyes, turned the sound down low, and tried to shut out the chatter. The CBT woman had told him to think about somewhere peaceful, somewhere remote, somewhere no one could disturb him. He'd tried somewhere exotic like a desert island before, but it didn't feel real, so he concentrated on places he knew well, like Pendle Hill. He'd walked up there from Barley village with Kat in their very early days. It was a clear summer's day, the sky an unbroken blue from horizon to horizon. He'd asked her to commit the scene to memory at the time because he knew it probably wouldn't ever be like that again. She'd laughed and leant on his shoulder, the way girlfriends do, with her face up close to his cheek, about to kiss him. They hadn't been going out more than a week. He didn't remember if they'd slept together that day, but he remembered wanting to. They took in the view down to Clitheroe Castle and across the Ribble Valley even as far as Blackpool and then down the east side to the Black Moss Reservoirs and Ogden Clough and then up to Colne. Yes, she'd laughed at him, but not since. They *hadn't* had a day like it.

He was on top of the hill now and the wind was blowing through the green bracken and the thick cottongrass and the purple heather. He could see the lights of Barrowford twinkling in the distance and the lights of the M65 running south-west. It was evening hurrying towards night and there was a chill in the air. He wanted there to be sunshine, to be like the day he went there with Kat, but he'd been told to let his imagination go. If you fought it, your conscious thoughts would take over and you'd never sleep. The reservoirs glinted in the dull light, the black eyes of a land that didn't sleep, either. There were no shutters to pull over them, no lids to close off the night, just the empty spaces of the sky to look into. Johnny saw it all like he was watching a film.

He let himself go, hoped that reality wouldn't come looking for him. The wind got stronger and he felt cold. Then, suddenly, he heard a cry down the hill. It came echoing up the sides of the valley and broke upon the crown where he lay. At first, it didn't register what it was – maybe the cry of an animal or bird. Then it came again, louder than before, and he knew it was human. His body was rigid with sleep paralysis. He couldn't move a muscle, couldn't even take a breath. It was crushing him.

'Breathe, you bastard, breathe,' he told himself.

He took in great gulps of air but it felt like something was blocking his throat.

'For fuck's sake.'

He felt movement on his face, then a sharp, stinging pain on his cheek.

The straitjacket paralysis was suddenly gone. Air burst into his lungs.

'What the…'

He opened his eyes and looked straight into Kat's.

She was sitting on the couch beside him.

'Where am I? What…' It took a few seconds to register. 'What time is it?'

'Six.'

'Really? I slept that long?'

She nodded.

He noticed the huge grin on her face. 'You're kidding?'

She shook her head. She was excited about something, like a little girl about to explode on her birthday.

'What's up?'

'I'm happy.'

'Great.'

'I'm unbelievably happy.'

'You want to tell me why?'

She held a blue and white plastic strip in front of his face. He looked along it and saw the clear, unmistakeable plus sign in the little window.

'You're pregnant?' he asked, shocked.

She nodded.

'I can't believe it,' he said. 'I thought it'd take months. Years.'

'Planning,' she said.

'So I'm going to be a dad?'

She kissed him on the lips. 'The best dad ever.'

The weight on his chest from the sleep paralysis was replaced with a different kind of weight: the gravity of expectations and responsibility. He was fast-forwarding already to changing his son's nappy, taking him to school, watching a football match with him. Excitement mixed with trepidation. He didn't know how to react. There were too many conflicting thoughts and emotions. One thing was consistent, though – Kat was out of this world with happiness.

She made breakfast. The meeting with Daphne Copper slipped to the back of his mind. Between taking bites from her toast and talking about what she was going to do now she was pregnant, there was no time to do anything but nod.

Finally, after finishing her breakfast, she looked at his plate. 'You've not eaten.'

'I'm not hungry,' he said.

She tucked her blonde hair behind her ears and stared at him. 'I love you, Johnny. I know you're going through shit at work. We all are.'

'Thanks,' he said.

'When the baby's born, I want us both to get out. I can't hack it in Duty and Assessment any more.'

'I don't blame you,' he said.

'You're going to get out, aren't you? You're going to look for something else?'

The three hours' sleep was weighing heavy on him. 'Yeah, of course.'

'You have a meeting with Daphne later. You can mention it to her.'

'How did you know?'

She stood up and cleared the table. 'She mentioned it to me yesterday. She asked how you were.'

He didn't know what shocked him more: that Daphne had actually expressed concern for one of her staff, or that she'd potentially broken protocol by asking another member of staff about them. 'Did you have to fill out a risk assessment form?'

'No. I said she should ask you herself.'

'Quite right,' he said.

He got up from the table and went upstairs to the bathroom. She'd left the pregnancy test packet by the sink. Clear Blue, it said, just like the sky over Pendle Hill that day. He looked in the bathroom mirror. His eyes were bleary but not totally awash with tiredness. He shaved and washed and hoped that it would bring some colour to his cheeks.

Kat saw him to the front door and waved as he left. 'Baby says goodbye, too,' she said and pointed to her stomach.

'Goodbye, baby,' he said, smiling, but the words had an ominous feel and he regretted saying them.

Daphne Cooper's office was bright and cheery, with several cast-signed posters of the musicals she'd been to on the walls. *Les Mis* took pride of place, the iconic picture of Cosette a reminder of why they were all there and what they were working towards: the elimination of child cruelty and exploitation. Unfortunately, this wholly laudable aim – religiously championed by other managers – was left ultimately unrealised, bound by fifty shades of departmental grey. Daphne was in her late forties, unmarried, a lover of horses, and an insufferable egotist.

She invited Johnny to sit next to her. The open laptop was between them so he could see the screen. 'I've designed a new care plan template,' she said excitedly. 'I want you all to follow it. I'm asking everyone to fill it in by next week. Do you think you could manage that?'

'Is that on top of my forty-two other cases or will someone be taking over those?' Johnny said.

'It will help streamline your workload and allow me to see which areas need prioritising and which areas you need help with. That way, we can focus our attention in a more focussed way.'

'I'm just thinking of the time it'll take up,' he said.

'Well, that's just what I'm saying. In the long run, this is going to *reduce* your time and workload.'

'I fail to see how.'

She humphed. 'Well, I'd like you to start straightaway, John.'

'Of course,' he said.

She smiled. 'Now, about your cases. I was looking through your notes and was a little bit worried you were being a little hasty…'

'If I think a child's at risk, I'll say so.'

'It can be very damaging to the child, not to speak of the family, if we rush in and take them into care.'

'I quite agree.'

'So we must make sure that what we are doing is the right thing to do.'

'You know, I've never really thought of it like that.'

She paused. 'You're being sarcastic?'

'I am. Take the case you're looking at there. Nathan Walsh. I had a look at his file the other day. You know, just checking I hadn't missed something. It's quite extensive and I thought I'd double check the background before I did anything, or put in a request to have a meeting to discuss the possibility of doing something. That kid has been on our radar since he was born and, if you'll forgive me for saying, I don't think we've served him too well. In fact, I think we've fucked up his life good and proper because we didn't intervene sooner. He's addicted to ketamine and crystal meth and shit knows what else. He has no education to speak of, and currently he appears to be hanging round with a group of neo-Nazi, EDL types who are taking exception to a bunch of Asian taxi drivers who are passing round young white girls like a shisha pipe. All of which leads me to conclude that we're still not doing our job and that the kids we should be protecting are being fucked over. Is that right or, again, have I missed something?'

Daphne looked at him impotently. There was nothing about dealing with rebarbative staff currently on the laptop. 'That's quite a tirade, John. I hadn't realised you felt quite that badly about the job.'

'It's not about the job. Or about me. It's about protecting children. That's what we're in this for, isn't it?'

She pulled a slightly matronly look, trying to get back on top. 'Do you need some time off, John?'

He thought about what Kat had said. Should he just tell her he wanted out now, go home, get another job, leave the children behind?

'I could do with less cases,' he said.

'I know. And I wish I could help you there.'

'But you can't, because the council has slashed our budget.'

'Yes,' she said.

'So we're stuck.'

'We're both stuck,' she said, and closed her laptop with as much authority as she could muster. 'And it's not going to change.'

She stood up, looked smart and officious in her high heels and pleated skirt, but he could tell he'd rocked her. She'd have to fill in her own forms about this meeting and put in recommendations about what to do.

'We're finished, then?' he said.

'Almost,' she said, and paused as if wondering how to say something. 'As you know, Front Office have been inundated recently with stories about grooming gangs.'

'You don't say.'

'We don't know how much is true, obviously. It's all unverifiable.'

'It always is.'

'Because no one will come forward,' she said.

'Because no one will listen.'

'Well, they might this time.'

'How's that?'

'Two girls were found in Aitken Wood a few nights ago. They were picked up by the police. One's in hospital, the other's currently in our care. They say they were taken there by a group of…men…and assaulted. You can imagine the details.'

He could. 'Are they going to talk?'

'Who knows. We'll see.'

'So why tell me?'

'We're short-staffed, John. Chronically so. We need someone who can look after them and find out.'

'And you want me to?'

'I was asked to ask you.'

'Someone with a backbone, then. Doesn't sound like the council.'

'I can temporarily relieve you of some of your cases.'

'Fuck, it must be serious. What about your new care plan template?'

'You can put that on hold, too.' She opened the door to her office. 'This could be very big, John. And very damaging. You've seen what's happened in Rochdale and Rotherham. The fallout could be enormous. It could set race relations back generations.'

'If they're not already.'

'You were chosen, John, because of your robust approach,' she warned. 'Don't let it go to your head. The Asian community is an integral part of our town. They are overwhelmingly decent, law-abiding people. We want to keep them like that.'

7

Dan, the desk sergeant, looked at Shaf in a seen-it-all-before kind of way. 'You're here to see the Super?'

'Yes. Ten o'clock.'

'Not often we get him in here. You been a bad boy?'

Shaf looked at the shabby interior of the Nelson HQ. It wasn't like the Burnley station, a proper building built in a time when there was such a thing as civic pride. 'Hardly. I think he wanted to be near the action.'

'Well, that makes a change. I'll let him know you're here.'

Shaf adjusted his uniform, straightened his back, held his hat squarely under his arm.

After a couple of minutes, Dan returned. His pate glistened under the artificial strip lights. 'Good luck.'

Shaf nodded, walked down to the end of the corridor, and knocked on a bare, brown door.

'Come in.'

The superintendent was sitting at a long, brown desk. He was a large man in his fifties, with a ruddy face and once granite chin that had now become podgy. He was flanked on either side by two DCIs, one Asian and one white. 'PC Khan,' he said. 'I don't think we've met in person.'

'Actually, we did, sir. Last year. At the Lancashire Neighbourhood Policing Awards ceremony.'

The superintendent nodded. 'Ah, of course. I should have remembered. Please, take a seat. I hope you don't mind DCI Evans and DCI Ali sitting in. I thought it important we all get together before this gets out.'

Gets out? Shaf swallowed and sat down.

'Now, I can't begin to stress how delicate this situation is and how we need to be very careful in how we react to it. Is that clear?'

'Yes, sir.'

'DCI Ali here has been investigating grooming gangs in the area for the past six months. We're well aware of the chronic failures in other forces to deal with this and we don't want to add ourselves to that number. Is that understood?'

'Yes, sir.'

The superintendent opened a file on the table and pulled out a two-page statement.

Shaf recognised it instantly. It was the one he'd submitted after finding the girls in Aitken Wood.

'It's still your contention that the girls' story checks out? That there is some credibility to it?'

'I just reported what they said, sir.'

'They were in a very bad way, weren't they?'

'Yes, sir.'

'What made you go out to the reservoirs? Your report says you were investigating a possible intruder at Blackthorn Farm.'

'It's all in the report, sir. I was told by Mr Carver's daughter that they'd heard screams.'

The superintendent fixed him with a strange look. 'You mean Beth?'

Shaf nodded. There was something oddly familiar about the way he said her name.

DCI Evans passed a sheet of paper across the table and the superintendent picked it up. 'Well, that *is* curious. I went over to the farm yesterday, checking you hadn't missed anything. I asked Beth about the screams and this is the statement she gave. In it, she denies saying anything of the sort to you.'

Shaf had a flashback of her looking out of the room with the candle in her hand. 'Well, that's not true, sir.'

The superintendent stared at him as if waiting for the lie to come out, but Shaf kept on the straight and narrow. A good officer always kept that line.

'Very well, PC Khan. So, let's say she *did* hear screams. You radioed base to get a check on them and then made your way to the reservoirs, where you yourself heard a scream in the woods?'

'That's right, sir.'

'And then your radio stopped working?'

'Yes, sir, it's all in the report.'

The superintendent smiled. 'Of course it is.' He paused, then glanced at DCI Ali. 'It's not a great distance to the wood from the farm, is it?'

'No, sir. About half a mile.'

'So, it would be unlikely the radio would have developed a fault in that time, or that the signal would have deteriorated so much in such a short distance.'

'I'm not an expert, sir.'

A slow, sinuous doubt began to creep into his mind. This wasn't fact checking or making sure they'd got the story right. He was on trial.

'No, but we have people who are. DCI Ali here has a team in Manchester dedicated to electronic surveillance. They kindly had a look at your unit. As you know, each radio keeps a log of calls made on it.'

Shaf glanced at the DCI. For a moment, there was a flicker in his eye, something like sympathy. They were both up against it in this job. If today, Shaf was facing the firing squad, tomorrow it could be him.

'Between the call you made at the farm and you pressing the emergency button in the woods, there was nothing. No call out. No call in.'

The doubt spread to Shaf's throat. He felt it tightening. 'Then there must be something wrong with the unit, sir. I made two calls. On both occasions, I couldn't get through.'

The superintendent sat back and looked at the ceiling as if for guidance, then resumed in a more conciliatory tone. 'You have an exemplary record of service, PC Khan. Your colleagues speak very highly of you. It's essential that we hold on to officers like you.

We need more of you, frankly. The community talks to you more readily than they would to me or DCI Evans.'

'That's more the fault of the community than the police service, sir.'

'That may be, but the problem is there, whether we like it or not. As I said, we have to tread very carefully. Losing an officer like you would look very bad. It discourages others from joining, as well as making out there is still institutionalised racism in the force.'

'I'm not sure I follow, sir. Am I losing my job because the Carvers changed their story? Or that my radio wasn't working?' There was a long silence. 'With respect, sir, I still don't know what this is all about. I thought I was here to talk about the girls.'

The superintendent looked again at DCI Ali, who nodded back. 'The girls have made some serious accusations against you, PC Khan. We thought we'd give you the chance to talk off the record first.'

Off the record? So, there it was. They weren't checking the girls' story out. They were checking his – the non-existent screams, the radio that stopped working.

'I saved their lives, sir.'

'The blonde girl, Jenna Dunham, claims you sexually assaulted her friend and then assaulted her.'

'That's a lie, sir. I saved their lives.'

DCI Ali shuffled in his seat.

The superintendent stared at him. 'They're not very grateful, are they, PC Khan? Not after what you did. That's why I asked you about their credibility. Girls like that just can't be trusted. Just look at their backgrounds. Jenna Dunham, arrested twice before for shoplifting. Alisha Ali, father's doing time for fraud and tax evasion, mother on the permanent sick. Hardly credible sources.'

'There's a lot from broken homes round here, sir. A lot of good kids, too.'

'Yes, quite. But the minority always ruin it for the majority.'

Instinctively, Shaf glanced at DCI Ali and wondered if there was anything implied in that, or if it had even registered with him. But DCI Ali showed no emotion. He had a pugilist's face and an iron stare. It was his turn now.

He spoke in a broad Lancashire accent, a mix of Darwen and Blackburn. 'As the Super said, I've been investigating these grooming gangs for the past six months. We checked the girl's story out as far as we could. There is CCTV on the A682 but we couldn't trace the silver car they referred to. Neither of them had the registration, either. Just a description of the perpetrators.' He read from a sheet. 'Five males. Aged between 19 and 40. Pakistani origin. Nothing else. We searched the wood and The Cabin car park. We made routine inquiries in Barley, door to door and The Pendle Inn. Nothing. If their story is true, it seems they were assaulted elsewhere and dumped in the wood. They'd both taken ketamine. There's a lot of that going round at the moment. It's used in a lot of date rapes. You're not going to remember much of anything after snorting that shit.'

'What about forensics, though?' said Shaf. 'The Asian girl wasn't breathing. Something *had* happened to her.'

'We surmise she'd taken too much ketamine and fallen in the pool,' the DCI said. 'Lucky the paramedics got there on time and lucky you performed CPR on her. You *did* save her life.'

'So their accusations against me?'

The DCI looked at the superintendent.

'We're putting it down to the drugs and their state of mind, PC Khan,' the superintendent said. 'Hallucinations are common on ketamine. Either that or they're just lying, like a lot of these girls do.'

Shaf thought of the screams and the hallucinations in the wood and the figure in the pool. They weren't lies. He thought of the rain coming down and the look of fear on the girl Jenna's face. That wasn't imagined. 'You don't think there's anything to the grooming story?'

The superintendent said nothing.

'We have nothing to go on,' DCI Ali said. 'Just rumours and unsubstantiated reports. This isn't a big city like Manchester. The community wraps itself up. If there was something, we'd be the last to hear about it.'

Shaf looked from one to the other. They were closing ranks, too.

'We'll have to suspend you for a week or two,' the superintendent said finally.

'We have to be seen to be investigating everything at the moment, especially ourselves. Public scrutiny has never been greater. In a week or two, you'll be back on the beat and, I assure you, nothing will go on your record.'

The words weren't said cruelly, but Shaf felt betrayed by them. He'd never got in trouble before.

'The incident will go to press, of course. We can't keep it out. But we'll keep names and identities and race out of the picture.'

Shaf could see it right now: 'Muggers in Marsden Park'; 'Assault on pregnant girl in Leeds Road'; 'Police on the lookout for six men with no physical description'. The local white community had cottoned on to it, as had the BNP, but somehow the *Nelson Leader* and *Lancashire Telegraph* kept churning it out, trying to diffuse racial tensions.

'What do I do in the meantime, sir?

'Take a break, Shaf. Look after your mum.'

'My mum?' Someone had been asking questions.

'You live with her, don't you?'

'Yes, sir.'

He picked up his hat and left the room. He felt like he'd been suspended from school. Dan, the desk sergeant, nodded at him as he passed. He didn't want *him* thinking anything. He had to keep up appearances. He'd been doing that from the day he joined the force and would continue to do so. *His mum?* He thought of what he'd tell her. She'd ask, of course. She asked about everything. Since dad died and his sisters got married and left home, he was all she had.

He turned left out of the police station, got into his car, and drove down Leeds Road, past the Pendle Community Hospital. This was an Asian area, full of people like him, second and third generation, descended from men like his grandfather who'd come to work in the mills. Now, instead of wearing suits, they wore trackie bottoms and Air Max trainers, listened to Tupac and Ice Cube, and wanted to be gangstas or join IS. He passed the takeaways and halal meat shops and came to Santa's Pizza parlour. He drove around and wondered how anyone was going to change things. The people treated him with as much suspicion as the white officers, and more so in white areas like Marsden Park.

He took a left on to the A6068 and headed towards the motorway. Pendle Hill could be seen in the distance, a black line on the horizon, darker and more forbidding than the mass of grey clouds above it. As he sped away from it back home, it began to rain, and the wipers swept the raindrops off the windscreen. He realised a film of water was collecting somewhere else. There were tears in his eyes. He doubled back on to Scotland Road and headed along the A682 towards Barrowford. He was officially off duty and could do what he wanted. He

hadn't been told to stay away from anyone. He'd been told to take a break.

The rain came down harder. He'd missed something, they'd missed something, in the woods. He passed through the village of Roughlee and headed back towards Barley.

8

It was a small, white terraced house in the Marsden Park area of town, ex-council and probably BNP. No matter how often Johnny had heard the 'same old story', he had to pretend otherwise. Responses at the door varied considerably; you had those who were crushed by a visit from social services, as if it reflected badly on their parenting; there were those who welcomed it, some kind of support after all the years putting up with ungrateful kids on their own; and then there were those who greeted you at the door with fists raised and teeth gnashing, yelling 'fuck off'. You could make assumptions from where people lived but it wasn't always an accurate barometer.

The small garden nestled behind a tidy, well-tended privet hedge. That was a good sign. Normally, social workers went out in twos, or with the police in tow, but this was deemed low risk. He rang the doorbell and, after a few moments, a woman in her thirties opened the door. She was quiet and pensive and thin. Her hair was thin, too, and as jaded as her expression. She could have been pretty when she was younger, but worry lines and the tell-tale signs of alcohol had dimmed the cynosure of youth.

'Mrs Dunham?' Johnny said.

'It's Ms.'

'I'm sorry. We spoke on the phone. My name's John Malkin. From social services.'

'Yes, I know.'

She let him in, showed him to a small living room. On a beige settee was a teenage girl with sharp cheekbones and long, blonde hair. It covered her face like a pair of curtains.

'Please, sit down,' said Ms Dunham, pointing to a chair opposite the settee. 'Jenna, luv, this is the social worker.'

Jenna didn't say anything.

Johnny sat down and took a form out of his case. On it were the barrage of questions he always had to ask himself.

1. Did you see the child?

2. Did you see the child alone?

3. Did you see the child's bedroom?

There were always boxes to tick. At the back of his mind, the paranoia had already set in.

Have I missed something?

Jenna's fists opened and clenched.

'This has all come as a bit of shock, Mr Malkin,' said Ms Dunham.

'I can imagine,' said Johnny sympathetically.

'Jenna's a good girl. She was doin' really well at school. I had no idea this was goin' on. Still, it's parents that are responsible, ain't it? It's our job to know.'

'It can be very difficult,' said Johnny.

'It's her friends that put her up to it.'

Johnny looked at Jenna. If he had a pound for every time he'd heard that, he could retire. 'Do you think I could talk to her alone, Ms Dunham?'

She looked more grateful than offended. 'You can try.' She pulled the door to behind her.

Separating the child from the parent didn't always work, but it was a good way of gauging the relationship.

Jenna still hadn't moved, except her fists.

'I'm from child protection, Jenna,' he began. 'We were called by the police. To make sure you're okay.'

'Go away,' she said after a moment. Her voice wasn't aggressive, more sullen and resentful like a young child's.

'I will do, but I need to ask you some questions first.'

'I answered all the questions at the police station.'

'These are different questions.'

She shook her head, tucked her long, blonde hair behind her ears. She wore mascara and lip gloss and looked a lot older than her fifteen years.

'*I* want to ask a question. Do you think I'm pretty?' she said.

A sudden, cold chill penetrated his heart.

'Well?' She waited for a response. 'You can't say, can you?'

She was right.

'Do you think someone's a pervert if they think it but don't say it?'

'Not a pervert, no.'

'What's the difference?'

It was rare he got to the heart of the matter so quickly. 'A pervert's behaviour is abnormal. There's nothing abnormal about thinking someone is pretty, but saying it may not always be appropriate.'

'That's a cop out.'

'I agree.'

'You want to know if I'm okay?'

'Yes,' he said.

'I'm not. Let's talk about something else, instead.'

'Like what?'

'If you think I'm pretty.'

He drummed his pen on his leg. 'How are things with your mum?'

'Go and ask her.'

'I wanted to hear it from you.'

'So you can tick one of the boxes on your form?'

'Yes.'

'Here,' she said. 'I can help ya.' She reached over and took it from him, then began reading it. 'It's a bit boring, ain't it?'

'Yes,' he said. 'They tend to be.'

'I'll make some changes for ya.'

'Go ahead,' he said, handing her the pen.

He watched her write. She had an odd grip and the writing was a bit of a scrawl, but her concentration never wavered. That was a good sign. She wrote for perhaps two minutes and didn't stop till she put her signature at the bottom. 'There,' she said, and handed the form back to him. 'I hope you find it helpful.'

He looked down.

To whom it may concern

My name is Jenna Dunham and I've just been raped, at least I think I was. I was given a drug and don't remember much of what happened. The man I love didn't rape me but he gave me to his mates to rape. I don't feel great down there and I feel pretty sick with myself and my life. I wish I'd lisened to my mum and not gone out. She is not to blame, tho. I am. There's a pervert from socal services with me now called John who thinks I'm pretty but wont say it because hes scared hell be like the rapists. He thinks he can help but he cant. No one can. It wont matter anyway soon because something is going to happen. Something really bad and no one can stop that either. This town wont be around much longer.

Jenna Dunham

He got to the end of the paragraph and then looked at her. 'You put "something is going to happen", Jenna. What do you mean by that?'

'Just what I said.'

'You mean to you?'

'No. To all of us.'

'Like what?'

She shook her head.

'You're not thinking of harming yourself, are you, Jenna?' The clenching and unclenching started again.

'I'm not feeling too good, John. Did you read what I wrote?'

'Yes, I did.'

'Filling boxes in isn't going to help me. You sitting there isn't going to help me. Nothing can help me. Or us.'

Paranoia, guilt, delusions, despair, anger, mistrust: he could tick all the boxes now. And she was right, it wasn't going to make her feel any better. The damage had already been done. Social work was always about playing catch up, always putting sticking plasters on wounds that required surgery.

'Do you want me to go?' he asked.

'Yes.'

'What will you do?'

'My mum wants me to go back to school.'

'Do you think you're up for it?'

'I wanna see Alisha.'

'That's your friend?'

'She was in hospital. My mum doesn't want me going near her any more. She said it's her fault what happened.'

'And was it?'

She shook her head. 'No.'

'It was the men's fault?'

'Yeah, but not Tariq.'

He jotted the name down. 'That's your boyfriend?'

'Yeah.'

'How long have you known him?'

'Does it matter? A few months, maybe.'

'Why don't you think it's his fault?'

'Cos he loves me. He got me a new iPhone.' She took it out of her sweatshirt pocket. 'It's a seven.'

'Nice,' he said.

'He looks after me. He said he wants to get us a little place soon, so we can live together…' Her voice trailed off.

'Did you tell the police all this, Jenna?'

'I don't remember what I told them.'

'You know it's against the law for Tariq to have sex with you, even if he does love you?'

She started playing with her phone. 'Do you have someone who loves you, John?'

'I guess.'

'How long have you known them?'

'Several years.'

'Do you live with them?'

'No.'

'Then I don't think you're in love.'

She was clued up, that was for sure. He scanned what she'd written again. *This town wont be around much longer.* The phrase struck him as odd, and odder now that he'd spoken to her. Town wasn't a mistake.

There was a knock on the door and Ms Dunham came back in. 'Is everything okay?' she asked.

Jenna said nothing. She retreated into her shell and Johnny noted it down. There was a box for that, too.

He asked to see Jenna's bedroom and Ms Dunham showed him upstairs. It wasn't much more than a box and was full of the usual teenage clutter: clothes and posters of One Direction and Rihanna and some GHD hair straighteners. There was nothing different here from a thousand other girls' bedrooms across the country, yet something plainly was. Like the girls who'd been groomed in Rochdale and Rotherham, or girls who'd killed themselves over cyberbullying, or girls who'd communicated with jihadis in Syria and gone to join IS, something had gone wrong. A cancer had spread undetected through their rooms, metastasised through their belongings, entered their heads, until no amount of social chemotherapy could save them.

'Well?' Ms Dunham said. 'What are you going to tell them?'

'Who?'

'Whoever you tell things to.'

'I'm going to tell them she's well looked after here, Ms Dunham. She has everything she needs.'

'You're not going to take her away?'

'No.'

She looked relieved and led him back down the stairs. The living room door was open. Jenna hadn't moved from the settee.

'The bastards who did this to her,' said Ms Dunham. 'You need to kill them.'

Johnny nodded. 'I'm going to speak to my boss. Hopefully get a care plan in place. Some counselling, maybe.' If it sounded awfully hollow and useless, it's because it was.

'You've dealt with cases like this before?' Ms Dunham asked.

'Loads, I'm afraid.' He paused before he left, ran through the mental inventory of questions he was supposed to ask. The note

Jenna wrote niggled at him. 'Has Jenna ever self-harmed before?' he asked.

Ms Dunham shook her head. 'No, why?'

'She's never spoken to you about leaving home?'

'No. Never.'

'Good. Keep a close eye on her for the next few days. I'm going to talk to her school and the police. I'll be back in touch as soon as I can.'

Ms Dunham did her best to hold herself together but he could see she was torn apart.

He got into the Ford Focus and put Jenna's file down on the passenger seat. At the moment, it was slim, but he knew it would soon be bursting with referrals and reports. Counselling was what she needed, but the wait time was long. That was the problem with the whole set-up. Even when you could get help, it was never now. All he could do was keep them talking.

He put a call into her school, Marsden Heights, and asked to speak to her pastoral manager. He was told she was busy, too busy to talk. He was told the same thing yesterday. No one wanted to talk, even those who should.

He got another file out of his case, one so large it was held together with string. No need to guess whose it was. *Nathan Walsh. 11 a.m. Nelson Youth Centre.* That's if he was there. More often than not, he'd not turn up and Johnny would end up having to chase him halfway across town.

They called it The Zone, a state-of-the art facility for the kids in the area. The Department of Education had pumped loads of money into it and it definitely had an effect. The good kids had somewhere to go and something to do and, in a town like Nelson, that was no bad thing. But for those who'd fallen off the map, it was like sticking a library in a desert. All very well if you could read, but what you really needed was water. Meanwhile, the social services' budget was frozen.

For once, Nathan *was* there. He'd shaved his head again and there were some cuts on his skull. Not the greatest way to impress his new landlord.

'You ever going to let that grow, son?' Johnny asked.

'I like it.'

'You ever heard of fashion?'

'You seen yerself, ya cunt?'

There was a spark in Nathan's eyes today. That could either be a good thing or a bad thing. Good that they'd be able to communicate for a while; bad that he'd taken something and would get withdrawal symptoms later.

'We're running out of places to put you, Nathan.'

'I don't need a place,' he said.

'Where are you going to stay, then?'

'At me mates.'

'And who are they? Good lads?'

'Sound.'

'Where do they live?'

'Up on Leeds Road.'

Johnny knew who they were. Everyone knew who they were. 'You've got enough problems, son. You don't want to be hanging round EDL nutcases.'

Nathan screwed his eyes up, maybe remembering how Johnny took care of him in the police station and at the hospital. 'They're not nutcases.'

Johnny shrugged. 'You want to get in the car?'

It was the one thing Nathan did like.

He ran a hand across his skull and grinned. For a brief moment, Johnny saw another Nathan, the one who hadn't made up that file in his case, who wasn't even on the radar of social services. He was a racing driver or a fighter pilot. He was a games designer for GTA, designing one for the streets of Nelson or Burnley.

He put his case on the back seat and Nathan got in the passenger side.

The wheels screeched as they drove off.

'Nice,' said Nathan. He'd taught him that one.

Johnny grinned, too. Today might not be as bad as he thought. He might get back before eight. He might have a chance to get a takeaway with Kat. He might have a chance to talk to the baby.

'*I don't think you're in love.*'

Bang. It hit him like a stone, one of those innocuous statements that seemed to work like poison, gradually entering the bloodstream and then paralysing you.

He glanced at Nathan. His narrow-slit eyes were focussed on the road, turning every corner, accelerating on every straight.

'What have your mates told you about the EDL?' he said.

'That they'll look after us.'

'And how will they do that?'

'They'll give us jobs.'

'You could get a job now.'

'I couldn't. They're all gone. The Pakis have taken them.'

'Only the ones you couldn't be arsed doing.'

Nathan's grin had gone, the spark in his eyes had dimmed, and a strange, sombre expression appeared on his face. 'It won't matter soon, any road.'

The way he said it, determined, resigned, made Johnny turn. There was a flicker of recognition at what he said. 'Why?'

'Cos summat's gonna happen.'

They were on Halifax Road. In the distance, the grey bulwark of Pendle Hill rose above the houses. He hit the brakes hard, pulled up onto the pavement. 'What the hell are you talking about?' he said.

Nathan's eyes squinted. 'You can't stop it now. No one can, Johnny. This town ain't gonna be here much longer. Pendle's gonna go up in flames.'

9

Shaf looked in his rear-view mirror for the hundredth time before turning into The Cabin car park. He couldn't shake the feeling he was being followed. Maybe the superintendent had put a tail on him? Maybe they were watching him now? But there was no one around except some hill walkers. He had half a mind to go back to Blackthorn Farm and have a word with the Carvers about why they'd changed their statement, but that would be his career over if the superintendent found out.

He got out of the car, walked up the hill behind The Cabin and headed for Aitken Wood. The trees looked more benign in the daylight. He heard a tractor in a nearby field and, far away, the sound of an electric saw. He stepped into the shadows on the edge of the wood and made his way up to the Sculpture Trail. There was a gateway made of two mammoth tusks and a life-size witchfinder to guide the way. After a few minutes, he came to the part of the wood he'd been that night. He would have recognised it even without the ribbons of police tape that still clung there. Officially, it was no longer a crime scene, so he was free to cross it. There was the stream leading to the shallow pool. The old rowan tree spread its branches across it as if guarding a secret, but there were no figures in the water, no ripples, and no bodies on the bank this time. The noxious smell had also gone. Everything seemed different.

He was tempted to use his radio to see if he could get a signal, then remembered they'd taken it off him. He remembered the voices on the other end so clearly. How could it not have appeared on the logs? And he'd used his phone, too. *His phone.* Of course. He nearly dropped it getting it out. He'd rung 999, hadn't he? That would have shown up. He scrolled through the recent calls list but it wasn't there. Had he inadvertently wiped it?

He looked round, retraced his steps up the hill, to the place where he'd first seen Jenna. She'd come out of the undergrowth near here. He looked for the tree with the bird mask on but couldn't find it. Had he got the place wrong, or had someone taken it? He extended his hand and touched the bough of a Scots pine. Maybe it was this one? The bark was smooth and wet. As he did so, there was a rustle behind him. He looked round and shivered. He hurried along the trail and out of the woods, till he came to the stretch of exposed bracken and cottongrass that reached down to the reservoirs. On the other side of the valley, Pendle Hill rose up, wreathed in low-hanging mist, as if someone was reciting secret incantations up there.

He descended the hill and came to the green iron railing overlooking Lower Black Moss Reservoir. As he stood there, his eyes were drawn to something floating in it, maybe ten metres from shore and some twenty metres to his left. It looked like the bird mask. Its long beak stuck out of the water like a trunk. It floated by like an old Viking funeral ship but, buoyed by the gentle currents and blown by the soft wind, it came to ground about twenty metres to his right. He vaulted over the railing and went down to the water's edge, found a stick and guided it to a shallow spot on the lip of the shore. He lifted it out and examined it. Its red, glass eyes were lifeless now but there was an unpleasant, musky smell coming from it.

As he held it up, he was suddenly aware of barking in the distance. He clambered up the railing and saw a big, black dog running up Barley Lane towards him, with two men in pursuit. He measured the distance back to Aitken Wood in his head, wondered if he could outrun it. He didn't fancy getting tied up in the long grass and having it chase him. He doubted it would do wonders for the reputation of the Lancashire Constabulary, either. There was no option – he'd have to face it.

As it approached, the dog began to look more familiar. It was the one he'd seen in Carver's kitchen, or one like it. It would be on him in seconds.

'Heel, Grip!' one of the men shouted. 'Heel!'

It leapt straight across the road towards him. He raised his arms to protect himself, his yellow jacket unfurled. But the dog didn't seem to want to take a chunk out of him. It was after the bird mask in his hand. When he raised them, it leapt up, its tongue lolling out of its mouth, its jaws wide, snarling.

'Throw it away!' one of the men cried. 'Throw it in the water!'

Shaf backed away and hurled the mask over the railings into the reservoir. If the dog wanted it that badly, it could get it. He thought it would turn on him, but it sniffed the sides of the railing and then the wall. It was going mad, looking for a way over. It succeeded in getting half its body over the top, then squirmed and wriggled and barked, its lower legs kicking the air in a frantic effort to do so. For a brutal moment, he considered giving it a helping hand. Then, one of its hind legs reached the cross bar and it got over. It tested the side of the bank and skidded down to the reservoir's edge before jumping in. There was a loud splash.

The two men reached him moments too late. They wore fleece jackets and boots and were covered in mud. They were probably in their twenties but looked older. The harsh Pennine climate had eroded their features, placed crags on their faces and curled their hair. They were burly lads, though, and strong.

'Ferry him out, Tib. Quick,' said the nearest.

'Nah, leave 'im, y'understand. He's gone, Thomas.'

'I canna. I 'as to save 'im,' Thomas said.

Tib held him back. 'Ya canna, y'understand.'

There was barking in the water. The mask had floated out to the centre of the reservoir and the dog was swimming after it, a black shadow in the icy grey.

Thomas turned to Shaf. 'I canna leave 'im to die. I canna.' He rushed for the railing.

Instinctively, Shaf put an arm out to stop him. 'It's deep water there, sir. You can't jump in.'

'Fancy I know more about this place than you, officer. Now leave me be,' Thomas said.

He shrugged Shaf off but not fast enough. Tib quickly wrapped both his arms about him and wrestled him to the ground. 'Listen, Thomas!' he shouted. 'The dog's gone. It's not ya dog any more. It's not 'im!'

They all looked into the water and saw the dog struggling to stay afloat. Shaf remembered a handler telling him once that the big ones have no endurance. A couple of minutes and they're sucking through their teeth. This one yelped pathetically. The cold water was freezing its limbs, making it difficult to swim. The bird mask was just out of its reach, a jawline away. The dog's head bobbed underwater, then came back up. It gave another yelp. The mask was further away. It sank under the water again and this time did not come back up. There were some ripples and bubbles on the surface and the struggle for life was over. There was still serenity and the soft wind blew the mask into the centre of the reservoir and the gentle currents took it out of sight.

Thomas hung his head and Tib put his arm round him. 'It's over now, Thomas,' he said. 'He's gone.'

Shaf looked out into the centre of the water, too stunned to react. He thought of the night at Carver's farm and what had happened in the woods. 'You're from Blackthorn Farm?' he asked.

'Aye,' said Tib.

'The dog was yours?'

'Thomas's, sir, as you can guess.'

In normal circumstances, he would have arrested them for failing to control a dangerous dog, for letting it attack a police officer, but things weren't normal. And he wasn't even meant to be on duty. 'You've worked round here long?'

'All our lives, sir. We was born in Newchurch,' said Tib.

'You want me to get a boat sent out?'

'To get 'im? He's forty feet under, sir. You're nivver going to find 'im.' He paused. 'You're not goin' to send other officers out, are you, sir? Mr Carver would be mad with us for losin' 'is dog.'

Shaf shook his head. 'Not if you don't want.' He looked at them and remembered why he'd come. 'I suspect you've had your fill of the police at the moment anyway, haven't you?'

Tib paused. 'Sir?'

'I heard you had an intruder at the farm a few nights ago.'

At the words, Tib seemed to flinch. He couldn't disguise his discomfort. Nor could Thomas, who turned round and gave him a queer look.

'Did either of you see anything?'

'We haven't, officer. Neither of us have,' Thomas said. There was an abruptness and surliness about him, no doubt magnified by the loss of his dog.

'We thought it may have been connected to the attack on those two girls.'

They went still as Easter Island statues, caught in the wind and rain.

'The wood's a dangerous place at night,' said Tib.

'Animals,' Thomas said. 'Wild animals. It's not a place to get lost.'

Shaf looked into the reservoir. 'I'm sorry about your dog,' he said. 'That was a horrible thing to happen.'

'You canna go against what is written,' Thomas said.

'Written?'

'Aye, sir.'

'Here,' Shaf said. 'Here's my number. If you see anything or hear anything, let me know.' He held a card out but Thomas's hands stayed resolutely at his side.

Eventually, Tib reached in and took it.

'Before you go,' Shaf said, 'I wonder if you could help me with something?'

They regarded him cautiously.

'I was in the woods before and I saw a mark carved into a tree. I wondered if it was a farming sign.' He picked up the stick he'd used to steer the bird mask and drew some lines in the ground where the soil was loose and sandy. He made three vertical lines going down and then one that veered off to the right, before putting a dot on it.

Tib and Thomas exchanged a quick look, then something like panic seemed to take hold of them.

'Where have you seen that?' asked Thomas.

Shaf pointed in the direction of Aitken Wood.

'I told ya, didn' I?' said Tib. 'The time is comin'.'

Thomas shook his head. 'It's not what was said. It canna be.'

Tib pointed at Shaf. 'Even the officer has seen it.'

'He's mistaken. He's lyin'. It's not time.'

Tib stared at the marks in the ground. 'Sir, you cover them up now and you forget you ever saw them, y'understand.' There was a wildness in his eyes and such an expression on his face that Shaf felt it, too.

'What is it?' he asked. 'What do they mean?'

But Thomas was pulling Tib away back down the road. The sane part of him thought it was all an elaborate ruse, but the look in their faces was too real, too convincing to manufacture. These weren't seasoned and sophisticated criminals from Nelson and Burnley. They were barely literate farm workers.

Tib finally broke free of Thomas's grip. 'Run!' he shouted to Shaf.

'Why?' Shaf shouted back. But Tib's voice was lost.

The sense of the supernatural that he'd felt in the woods that night was now all around him. He fought it back, trying to apply cold police rationalism to what he'd seen. How stupid to have let them get to him. They were probably laughing all the way back to the farm. But he kept coming back to the dog and how it was now dead at the bottom of the reservoir. That was a fact that could not be explained away.

Thomas and Tib were now little more than dots in the distance.

He made his way back up to Aitken Wood. The wind whispered in the leaves and the mist made its way through the thick cottongrass behind him.

10

9.25 p.m. Nelson. The taxi base was only a stone's throw from the police station, nestled on Manchester Road among a strip of kebab houses, sweet centres, money exchanges and hi-fi shops. Two private hires were parked outside, their drivers sheltering from the rain. It was the usual northern kind of high street. A couple of barking women in short skirts, armed with curry and chips and tanked up on booze, bartered with the operator over how much it would cost to take them home. He was polite and insistent and they were increasingly aggressive. They aimed a bag of chips and curry at him and the windows of the taxi base took a direct hit. He swore at them and they told him to fuck off, emboldened by the drink and each other.

Some Asian lads in the next-door takeaway came out to have a look at what was going on. They wore Nike Air Max trainers with the tongues out, Nike black trackie bottoms and Nike hoodies – the uniform of the street. Their heads were shaved, regulation number one, and their faces swarthy.

'Hey, Shoaib!' one of them shouted. 'Look over 'ere!' He approached the women. 'Come on, girls, how about we calm down?'

The girls told him to fuck off but he was undeterred. He knew drink did funny things to girls and that he could charm them if given the time. 'I can give yers a lift home, if you like? No need to pay.'

The girls started to laugh and asked him who he thought he was and what did he think they were, but now his mates joined in and they started to have a bit of banter and the girls laughed at the jokes and forgot about the curry and chips and the radio operator.

'Seriously, you twos are dynamite,' the smooth guy said. 'Why don't you come in our cars and we can smoke a bit. It's pissin' down.'

It really was.

The operator had gone inside and the two private hire drivers outside wound their windows up and read their copies of the *Lancashire Telegraph* waiting for a fare, or something else.

The two girls followed the lads till they got to a black car. It was a fast car and a pussy magnet. Immortal Technique was on the system, the Boss speakers were boss and the bass was heavy. They were all making banter now. Then Shoaib got carried away and touched one of the girls' bottoms. At first, she didn't really notice, it was a bit of playful fun, but then he smacked it a bit and she turned round and asked him what the hell he was doing. He backed off and his friend had to intervene.

'Whoa, sorry, girls! Shoaib was just excited. He thinks you're dynamite. He just got carried away. If you weren't so attractive, he wouldn't have done it.'

The music nearly drowned him out and they were dizzy and wet and really did want to go home. One got in the car and nearly threw up, but the other sat in the back seat and took a drag on a reefer and was soon snogging Shoaib.

It would probably have gone further – a lot further – but the music suddenly cut out and they were no longer listening to Immortal Technique, but to people shouting. The girls were dragged out of the car and told to run. The rain soaked their skirts and their flimsy coats and their bare legs but there was no option. There were ten, twelve, maybe fifteen men in masks with sticks in their hands. Some wore Union Jacks, and some wore the St George's Cross.

Shoaib was on the ground. Something terrible had happened. His head had split open and blood oozed out of the top of his skull. The car windows were smashed and glass flew everywhere. The men in the masks ran down the road to the taxi base and smashed its windows. Alarms went off. The operator was dragged out and kicked to the ground. He tried to fend off the blows, but soon he was like a rag doll being punched and pummelled regardless.

The two private hire drivers had only just woken to the violence and tried to drive off, but a shower of metal came out of the night sky, landing on their bonnets and smashing their windscreens. They were dragged out on to Manchester Road and beaten to the ground. Bone shattered on the concrete and blood stained the tarmac. Rags were lit and stuffed into petrol tanks, then there were two huge bangs like gunfire as the petrol tanks exploded, engulfing the cars in fiery flames that leapt twenty feet into the air. As they did, the sound of sirens could be heard. Blue lights flashed in the distance. The emergency services didn't have far to come. They were on the scene in minutes – police officers, fire crews, paramedics – attending the wounded and putting out the fires. The side streets began to fill with people, some woken, some curious, some ghoulish, some asking questions, some frightened.

Then police began taping off the area. Other units were drafted in from Burnley and Colne. The chatter on the police radios was electric. Rumours began circulating almost immediately. The EDL were involved.

It was just the start of it.

Johnny lay looking up at the bedroom ceiling, trying to calm his breathing. His thoughts were racing and would not switch off. Whenever he closed his eyes and tried to think of Pendle Hill, he would see Nathan and Jenna running along it, shouting at him. Something's going to happen, they said. They'd *both* said it.

He turned onto his side, looked at Kat. She'd spent every night at his house since finding out she was pregnant. She'd unofficially moved in. It was different having her round all the time. Things started moving of their own accord: razors from the bathroom, socks from his wardrobe, crisps from the kitchen. Then things started appearing: an army of shampoos and hairsprays, a skip full of clothes and a mountain of chocolate wrappers. She had a craving for chocolate, she said. Or baby had. If she didn't eat, she felt sick.

He felt sick. He got up, went into the lounge, put the TV on. He lay on the couch, tried to calm down.

The next thing he knew, she was beside him.

'You're not going to get to sleep if you keep walking round.'

'I'm not trying to fall asleep,' he said. 'I'm practising something called stimulus control.'

'What's that? Not touching your dick?'

He opened one eye. 'I'm sorry. Did I wake you?'

'No. Baby did.' She sat down beside him, pulled her legs under her to keep warm. 'Can you get me some crisps?'

'Haven't you just been up?'

'Yes, but I'm tired now.'

He shook his head, got up, and went into the kitchen. He opened a cupboard door and reached down a six pack of Walkers Salt & Vinegar. He stuck the kettle on. When he went back into the lounge, she'd got herself cosy on the settee, and was lying on her side.

He threw the crisps at her.

'Thanks,' she said.

She'd changed channel, was watching the BBC News. 'Have you seen this?' she said.

'What?'

'They're reporting overnight disturbances in Nelson and Burnley.'

'What? Earthquakes?'

'No. Rioting. Attacks on shops.'

He sat down beside her, saw the breaking news headline at the bottom of the screen.

'What the hell?'

The news ticker kept repeating the same line. It was just reports so far. They hadn't got any reporters on the scene, but just the mention of it on national news meant it was serious.

'You okay?' she said.

'Yeah,' he said. 'Just a bit weird seeing it.'

'I don't think it'll get as far as Barrowford,' she said.

'Maybe not.' He paused. 'You haven't had any weird stuff coming into Front Office recently?'

'We get weird stuff all the time.'

'I mean like really weird, like something bad was going to happen.'

'To what?'

'Oh, I dunno. The town. Two of my kids told me today.'

'You think they were talking about this?' She pointed to the TV.

'I don't know. They don't know each other so I don't see what else.'

'It's probably all over Facebook or Twitter. The police will be on to them soon enough.' She picked up her tea and the six pack of crisps. 'I'm going back to bed. You coming?'

'In a bit,' he said. 'I don't think I'm going to sleep tonight.'

She looked at him sadly. 'Johnny, why don't you go back to the doctor? Talk to him again.'

'He can't do anything.'

'He might.'

'He can't. He doesn't understand.'

She rubbed her stomach. 'Are you going to say goodnight to baby?'

He looked at her stomach. It wasn't showing any sign of growing yet but it soon would. It would protrude from her waist like Pendle Hill. There would be two landmarks on the horizon. He got up and touched her stomach. 'Goodnight, Mummy,' he said. 'Goodnight, Baby.'

She kissed him gently on the lips.

He went to the sideboard, picked up the laptop, and sat back down on the couch. He googled disturbances in Nelson and Burnley. There were some reports trickling through. Some said there had been trouble in Colne, too. A lot of tweets were coming in, mainly from kids, judging by the language: crazy shit goin down, pigs out in force, gangs of youths throwing stones, EDL idiots causing trouble again. He was drawn to one by someone called @plaguedoctor. His or her Twitter page had a picture of some plague victims being shepherded into a house by a sinister figure in a giant bird mask. The mask had a great downward pointing beak and two large red eyepieces above it. The figure carried a wooden cane and wore a wide-brimmed black hat, a long black overcoat and long leather boots.

@plaguedoctor The end of the world is nigh.

@plaguedoctor No one can stop Him now. The beacons are lit.

@plaguedoctor I saw Him again today. In a field by Newchurch.

@plaguedoctor Fires in Nelson and Colne, Ring the bells and call Him home.

The guy, if it was a guy, had a few hundred followers, all tweeting the same kind of thing. They were either Medievalists or crackpots or maybe both, but the last of his tweets made the hairs on Johnny's neck stand up.

@plaguedoctor RIP John Malkin. No one shall forget the price you paid. #COBM

It took a few moments to sink in. Yes, it *was* his name. Talk about coincidence. He searched the hashtag but there wasn't much there. Maybe it was an acronym? The results were pretty obscure: the Church of Body Modification or the Cost of Being Muslim.

He turned back to the television. The News had switched from the studio to a reporter. They'd got as far as Burnley. It read 'Live' at the bottom of the screen.

He turned the sound up.

The female reporter was on a street somewhere and there was a large crowd of people behind her. Blue lights flashed intermittently and police in yellow jackets filed past.

'The first disturbance was reported in Nelson about nine thirty this evening and quickly spread to other towns, in what appears to have been a series of choreographed attacks on taxi bases and local shops. Police say there has been no looting of the premises in question. There have, however, been serious attacks on individuals. To date, seven people have been admitted to hospital, two in a critical condition. We're joined now by a local councillor, Rabnawaz Ahmed, who witnessed one of the attacks in Burnley first hand.'

The camera panned to the councillor, a man in his fifties with a face like a leather parchment. He was clearly distressed.

'Councillor, could you tell us what you saw, please?'

'Yes, of course. I was driving through the area after one of my surgeries when I saw a gang of about twenty men gathering outside the taxi base over there.' He pointed off camera. 'There were drivers being dragged out of their cars and then all hell broke loose. Stones were thrown and the next thing I know, there was a huge bang and the taxi base was on fire. It was horrible.'

'Did you get to see the faces of the gang, Councillor? People we've spoken to have said they were all white and members of the EDL. Could you confirm that?'

'I can't, but if they were, it is very unfortunate,' said the councillor. 'We've had excellent race relations in this town and have built many bridges since the dreadful riots in 2001. There is no excuse for criminal behaviour in any part of our community, from whatever quarter.'

Johnny shook his head at the screen. More politically correct posturing. It was going on beneath their very noses and they were choosing to ignore it. He could join the dots together from here. Taxi cab bases, that's where all the grooming rumours had started. If the authorities didn't want to deal with the shit, some other idiots would. Idiots like Nathan. It would be just like him to get involved in crap like this and, if he was, he'd be doing time. He couldn't keep him out indefinitely.

He turned the TV down, lay on his back, and picked up the laptop.

RIP John Malkin.

He took some deep breaths, tried to think of nothing.

Into his mind came Jenna, Nathan, Kat, the baby.

He lay the laptop on his stomach.

It was then that Pendle Hill came into focus. Only it wasn't Pendle Hill. It was Kat's belly. She was screaming in agony, her thighs apart. Something was coming out of the forest between them. He was doubled up in fear. First came a beak and then a hat. A fully formed plague doctor emerged from her womb. It looked round for a moment, then stared at him through its large red eyepieces. He backed away down the hill and it came running after him. He made for the Black Moss Reservoirs and, all the time, he heard it chasing him. When he reached the bottom, he had no more energy left and he turned to face it. It walked straight towards him. Then it slowly took its mask off.

He was staring straight at Nathan.

He was locked in his body again, struggling to get out, struggling to breathe. After what felt like minutes, he felt the blow on his face, and he was staring up at Kat.

Her look said it all.

'Okay,' he said. 'I'll make another appointment. I promise.'

The fucking mirtazapine.

11

The house was a modest three-bed semi on the outskirts of Burnley. His dad had left it to them, part of the last will and testament before lung cancer took him. Mum didn't want to move; she had too many memories locked up here. There were pictures of him in every room, some at the factory, some back in Rawalpindi, one riding a horse at the front of a phalanx of other riders. That sepia tinted image had never faded from view – it was the tough, no nonsense, manly man. Shaf could have chosen other careers – he had three A levels from Clitheroe Grammar school – but that picture of his father on the horse had settled his fate. He had to follow in his footsteps.

He sat at the breakfast table. Mum had made eggs the way she did every day and, even though he wasn't the least bit hungry, he finished them. Not to eat them would mean something was wrong at work, or he was ill.

He was ready to leave at nine when the doorbell rang. He put his jacket on, peered through the glass panel at a silhouetted figure.

'*Asalamu alaykum, Auntie. PC Khan unda hai?*'

He recognised the voice immediately and felt his stomach churn. Something had happened. They'd found out where he was yesterday; they found out about the dog.

He went into the hall, saw him framed in the doorway. 'It's okay, Mum. It's the DCI. I was expecting him.'

Shaf showed him into the lounge, tried to keep calm. Mum beamed at him proudly as they passed. She was on her best form when visitors came round. She liked to keep up appearances. '*Naashta lena hai? Chai?*' she said.

DCI Ali smiled at her. '*Nahin, Auntie.* I've already eaten. Thank you.'

She closed the door behind them, still beaming.

The DCI looked at him. 'You were expecting me, then?'

'I didn't tell her I was suspended, sir. I didn't want her to worry.'

'Not the easiest thing to explain away, I suppose.' He made himself comfortable on the sofa, like he'd lived there for the last thirty years.

Shaf looked at the clock on the mantelpiece, watched the second hand turn. Anxiety accompanied every tick. 'You didn't come for breakfast, sir?'

'No, it was about the riots last night, actually.'

'I saw the news. Absolutely shocking.'

'You had no inkling?'

'None, sir. I would have told the Super if I had.'

DCI Ali rubbed his chin as if he'd been in a fight. 'I was one of the first on the scene. The taxi base on Manchester Road was completely gutted.'

'It's lucky no one was killed.'

'You don't think it could have been coincidence, do you? The places that were targeted, they were all connected, weren't they?'

'I don't know, sir.'

'Oh, come on, Shaf. This is your patch. You know what's going on. We've had most of them under observation. These grooming gangs—'

'I thought you said you had nothing concrete, sir.'

'That was yesterday. We've not been able to divulge what we've known before. The operation was so covert, we weren't even able to tell other officers. We think we have a mole in the department.'

Shaf kept quiet. Was this another test, like the interview?

'Every place that was attacked last night was on our surveillance list. Could be coincidence but it looks to me like someone's been tipped off and taken matters into their own hands.'

Shaf tapped his fingers on the table. 'Should you be telling me this, sir? I mean, it's meant to be classified, isn't it?'

The DCI snorted derisorily. 'Do you always play by the book, Shaf?'

'I try to, sir.'

'Then I think the secret's safe with you.'

Shaf wondered if it was meant as a compliment or a dig.

'You could be of real assistance to my team, Shaf. How about you come and help us?'

Shaf stopped tapping. Was he offering him a job? 'I can't help at the moment, sir, if you remember.'

DCI Ali nodded. 'Of course not. Your suspension. But I think we could work round that. You could help us in an *unofficial* capacity.'

'You mean as an informant?'

'It would get you out the house. No more having to think of excuses for Mum.'

Shaf paused. 'How legit is it?'

'It's a bit under the radar. But it's in a good cause. If people really knew how close they were to mad men, paedos, terrorists, psychos and serial killers out there, they wouldn't step out of their houses. You can't fight a fire with water guns, can you?'

Tick. Tock. The second hand moved round inexorably. It was his move to make. 'Have I a choice, sir?'

'Of course. You can sit here for the next two weeks, wondering if you've got a job to go back to and then find you haven't, or you can come and work with me.'

'I didn't touch those girls,' Shaf said adamantly.

'I don't doubt it. But things have a funny way of staying on people's records.'

There was a knock at the lounge door and his mum popped her head round. She'd brought a tray of *chai* and biscuits with her.

The DCI smiled. 'You didn't have to, *Auntie*.'

'*Chup ka*. You need to eat,' she said, and looked rosy in his attention.

Shaf watched her pour the *chai* and again saw the flicker in the DCI's eye. It wasn't quite sympathy this time, more of recognition.

'They're all the same, aren't they?' the DCI said as she left.

'Mothers?'

'*Asian* mothers.'

'I guess.'

'You know, there's not many of us in the force, Shaf. We need to stick together. Look after each other.'

Shaf watched him drink his tea and remembered what Dad said, that Pakis were all out for themselves and you couldn't trust any of them. It was part of the DNA.

'So, what do you say, then?' the DCI asked.

Shaf thought for a moment. He thought of the drowned dog in Lower Black Moss Reservoir and the figure he'd seen in the pool. He thought of Thomas and Tib and how they'd reacted to the strange marks in the ground, and Beth Carver, naked at the window. He thought of Jenna Dunham and Alisha Ali changing their story and accusing him of sexual assault. He could use his new role to find out what was going on. 'Okay,' he said. 'I'll do it. On one condition.'

'What's that?' said the DCI.

'We do things by the book.'

DCI Ali drank his *chai*. 'There is no book, Shaf. There never was. It's just about us and them and being on the right side of things.' He reached into his jacket pocket and brought out a small, red notepad and a pen. 'You can't trust technology nowadays, you know. One of the problems working with those guys in surveillance is learning how vulnerable we all are. Everything you consider private – emails, texts, phone calls – can be intercepted. It really is quite frightening. Which is why I didn't ring you beforehand.' He began to write. When he'd finished, he tore the top page out, folded it up, and held it out. 'Here's a list of names. You may know some of them. I want to know what you know and anything you can find out about them.'

'In relation to what?'

'In relation to everything.'

Shaf took the note and read it. Some of the names he *did* recognise, but most he didn't. Then, at the bottom, he stopped. He thought maybe his eyes had read it wrong, or that it was actually a name on the watermark. But no, it was in the same shaky calligraphy as the others.

'John Whittle?' he asked incredulously. 'The superintendent?'

The DCI said nothing.

Shaf shook his head. 'I'm not sure I'm going to be able to help, sir. I mean, he knows me. Why not get the IPCC involved?'

'We launch an internal investigation, he's going to hear about it. You're clean and you're currently off duty.'

'But what if I get caught?'

DCI Ali put his *chai* down. 'Doing this is your only chance of getting your job back, Shaf. Keep thinking of that.' He got up from the sofa. 'I'll be in touch.' He showed himself to the door and didn't look back.

Shaf watched him drive off from the hall. His mum joined him, smiling at him proudly.

'Did he like the *chai*?' she said.

'Yes, Mum. He did.'

'What did he want?'

'To offer me a new job.'

Her whole face lit up. 'Oh, *Mash'Allah*.'

He thought better of telling her what it was. At least he had one to go to.

12

Everywhere Johnny drove, there were police cars. They must have called every available unit in Lancashire to deal with the rioting. For a day, at least, Nelson and Burnley felt like Manchester or London, with things on the go and news cameras on the doorstep. He came out of his GP's surgery late, having failed to convince the receptionist that their policy of 'ring at eight for a same day appointment' was bullshit. They were very busy, she said. *Busy?* Everyone was busy.

He drove out to Brierfield. Marsden Heights had finally got back. Their pastoral care manager, Ms Houghton, was willing to speak to him now. The school was tucked away off Halifax Road, a modern blue and white building with a central turret that made it look like the centre of government, and some nice, well-tended playing fields. Ms Houghton greeted him at the school office. She was probably late twenties, but with glasses and a hairstyle that made her look late forties. She shook his hand lightly and apologised for not getting back sooner. 'We've been very, very busy,' she said. 'It's exam time.' He felt like putting in a call to the doctor's receptionist to tell her.

'I remember it well,' he said.

She took him into a small office with a nice aspect over the playing fields, looking towards Pendle Hill. 'Please, have a seat,' she said. 'You're here to talk about Jenna Dunham and Alisha Ali?'

'Yes. I thought you could give us some good background information. Alisha's family have been reluctant to speak to us.'

'You'll forgive me for asking why social services appointed a male social worker in a case like this?'

'We work on a case-by-case basis. I do what I'm told,' he said.

'Quite,' she said. 'The Headteacher can't be with us but he wanted me to tell you the school will do anything to support the girls at this terrible time. We are all in great shock.'

Johnny pulled out a form with a long list of questions and tick boxes on it, took a cursory look down it, then scrunched it up and threw it back in his case. 'Thanks. I'll try not to take too much of your time.' He took out a pen and paper. 'Jenna's mum said she's doing really well at school. Is that the case?'

Ms Houghton considered the question. 'She's not the most academically gifted child we have but she gets her work done. That's better than a lot.'

'She's not been in trouble before? Any suspensions? Cases of inappropriate behaviour?'

More careful consideration. 'Jenna's normally a quiet girl but she can get herself involved in stuff she shouldn't.'

'What about Alisha?' he said.

'Alisha is different.'

'In what way?'

She looked out of the window. 'She can be quite a coarse girl. A lot of staff have commented on it. I wouldn't say she was out of control but if I was her mum, which I'm not, of course, I'd be worried.'

'What about?'

'The way she acts.'

'Which is?'

'Frankly, like a tart.'

'I see.'

'It's not that she dresses like one. You can't do that in school. But a few male teachers have expressed concern and reported incidents.'

'Verbal ones or physical ones?'

'Verbal.'

'Can you give me an example?'

'I can't remember, off the top of my head. Not all the incidents have been logged.'

He stopped. 'Is that normal practice?'

'Not normal, but not unusual. A teacher has to be very sure something was said and preferably have proof from another member of staff. You can't go accusing pupils without good reason.'

'So, you're not able to give me an example? If she's at risk, you'll be doing her a favour.'

'I believe she offered to give her French teacher a blowjob, Mr Malkin. If he gave her a good mark in her oral exam.'

Johnny stopped the smile just in time, wondered if she got it, too. 'Jenna's said nothing like that to the teachers?'

'Not that I'm aware.'

'Would you say Alisha's behaviour affects Jenna?'

'It affects most people.'

'You think it more likely Jenna would follow what Alisha was doing than the other way round?'

'I'm sure of it.'

'What about boyfriends? Did either of them have one?'

'It's impossible to say. A lot of the boys hung around Alisha, but then she encouraged them. Jenna was more…distant.' She rubbed her hands together as if trying to keep warm. 'There's something I didn't mention to the police before, Mr Malkin, but I've thought about it since and wondered whether I should have. A few weeks ago, it may have been longer, Jenna spoke to me after an English lesson. That's the subject I teach when I'm not doing pastoral care. I was filling in for one of the teachers on maternity leave. Anyway, we'd been reading "Wuthering Heights". I loved it when I was their age and I got them all to read it. Jenna was really taken with the lead character in it, Cathy, and her meeting with Heathcliff on the moor. You can tell when a child is interested in something. It's the way they read the text, the way they identify with the character when they're talking about them. That lesson, Jenna identified. It's like she was Cathy, if only for a little while.'

'That must have been gratifying for you.'

'It was. Although I'd probably have forgotten all about it if I hadn't heard what happened to them. It was only then that it struck me how relevant it may be.'

Johnny's pen nestled on the paper.

'It was the Monday after the lesson on "Wuthering Heights", so there had been a weekend between. Alisha was with her. They said they were arguing about who should be called Cath as it was a cool name. They said they'd been up on Pendle Hill, looking out for Heathcliff. I thought they were joking, really. The hill is high, as you know, and the weather's never great. Anyway, we were talking for a few minutes and Alisha said they'd been in a wood, following the Sculpture Trail. She said they'd got lost in there and needed a farmer walking some dogs to lead them out.'

'Aitken Wood?' Johnny said.

'That's the one,' said Ms Houghton.

Johnny's pen twitched in his hand. He'd come looking for information about Jenna's background, not about what may have happened to her.

'Do you think I should tell the police?' she said.

'Definitely,' he said. 'The more they have to go on, the better.' He put his pen down. 'Had Jenna ever mentioned running away to you before?'

'Never.'

'Or that she was worried about something?'

'Not that I recall.'

He thought of Jenna's note and what Nathan had said. 'Have any children ever mentioned to you that something really bad was going to happen round here?'

'What a strange question. Like what?'

'Oh, I dunno. Like the riots last night? Something in the town.'

'I can assure you that if we'd heard anything like that, we would have told the police. I'm sure Jenna and Alisha wouldn't have known, either. We pride ourselves on our excellent race relations in school. Any hint of racism is dealt with straightaway.'

'The girls were aware of grooming gangs?'

'Of course. And online paedophiles. And drugs. And everything else. It's all covered in PSHE and I cover it in my pastoral care. We leave nothing to chance.'

She took her glasses off and lost about ten years. Give her a fashionable bob and she'd be quids in, Johnny thought.

He put the paper and pen in his pocket and rubbed his eyes.

'You look tired, Mr Malkin,' she said.

'I am,' he said. 'These cases mount up.' He put his jacket on. 'You've been very helpful, Ms Houghton. Thank you.'

She showed him to the door. 'My pleasure. Your name, you know, has a lot of local significance.'

'Yeah, so I've been told. Malkin Tower.'

'Indeed. It was the home of one of the Pendle Witches, although probably more a cottage than a real tower. It's where the coven was said to meet.'

'I've never been there,' he said.

'Some say it's by Lower Black Moss Reservoir. A cottage was found there with a mummified cat sealed into its walls.'

'Lovely. You seem to know a lot about it?'

'I've got the children to do a local history project on it enough times. And I've always taken an interest in the hill.' She looked out of the window towards it. 'It draws you to it, don't you think? We're very lucky to live here.'

'I wouldn't go that far. What do the children make of it all?'

'The witches? They're fascinated, naturally.'

It made sense. Children were instinctively attracted to the dark side, like they were attracted to everything taboo and illegal. 'What about Jenna or Alisha? Did they ever mention them?'

'They didn't,' she said, and a barrier seemed to come down.

He looked out. She was right about the hill. It did draw you to it. He had a flashback of last night's dream, the plague doctor emerging out of Kat's womb, chasing him. 'You know, there's a line from a song I read last night. Some kind of pagan thing, or nursery rhyme. I think it's from round here. I wonder if you've heard of it?'

'I'm not much for modern music, I'm afraid.'

He closed his eyes, saw it imprinted in his mind. *'Fires in Nelson and Colne, Ring the bells and call Him home.* Something like that,' he recited.

'Well, isn't that curious,' she said, shocked. 'Where on earth did you see that?'

'It was on a website.'

'It's a very old rhyme, although I think you may have got the words wrong.' She went to a waist-high bookcase by the window and ran her finger along it. 'I've seen something about it not too long ago.' She took out some books and laid them on the table. 'Here,' she said, bringing out one called 'The True History of the Pendle Witches'. 'There was something on it in here.' She scanned a few pages in the middle, turned a few more, then stopped at a page with a drawing of a strange-looking man.

'You have a great memory,' Johnny said.

'For certain things,' she said.

She handed him the book, pointed to an extensive footnote at the bottom of the page.

Johnny looked at the picture and had a horrible feeling of déjà vu. Had he been here before, staring at this? The man in it, if indeed it was a man, was tall but bent at the waist, and carried a long, slender cane in his right hand. He had a face like a hobgoblin, with a prominent jaw and a long nose. Behind him was a picture of a wild wood with the inscription 'The Forest of Pendle' written underneath it.

He narrowed his eyes to read the footnote.

[23] *One of the strangest legends of the Pendle area concerns that of the Hobbledy Man. Although it hard to place an exact point when he first surfaced in local folklore, mention of him goes as far back as the famous 17th century witch trials. Indeed, there seems to have been some confusion between the Hobbledy Man and the famous witchfinder, Matthew Hopkins, although Hopkins was not known to have travelled to the Pendle Valley area. It may be that the Hobbledy Man was confused with other witchfinders. Certainly, it was a time of great local uncertainty and fear. The witchfinders had the power of life and death over the villagers. There are reports of sightings of the Hobbledy Man throughout the Royal Forest of Pendle, to the south*

and east of the famous hill, most particularly in Padiham, Greenhead,
Barley and Roughlee.

Around the time of the Pendle Witch Trials, a cult grew up around
the Hobbledy Man. Known as the Cult of the Hobbledy Man (COHM),
its followers believed that the sighting of him signalled the imminent
ending of the world and that a sacrifice was needed to appease him.
There have been recurrent sightings of the Hobbledy Man in subsequent
centuries although it is not known if there are still any adherents. The
Cult of the Hobbledy Man is sometimes known as the Cult of Black
Moss (COBM), a reference to the reservoir at the base of the eastern
slope of Pendle Hill. How and why this alternative name originated
is open to some speculation as the reservoirs were only built in 1894.

He stared at the letters. *COHM.* He was sure he'd seen them before
but couldn't think where.

On the opposite page were a few lines from a children's song
of the time, an untitled ballad called *Beacon Fire.*

Who'll light the fire on the beacon pyre?
Who'll lay the holly on his bed?
Who'll plant the seeds of next year's crop?
Who'll keep the cattle well fed?
Fire on the hill and fire in the woods,
Lay them on a wheel of stone,
Out comes the knife to take his life,
Now ring the bells and call Him home.

They weren't the exact words but they were close enough. He
looked at Ms Houghton and, for a brief second, imagined it wasn't
memory that had spurred her to bring that book out, but part of
some conspiracy that she was a part of. Had something other than
fate brought him here?

He shook his head in an effort to rid himself of the déjà vu
and handed the book back to her. 'Thanks,' he said. 'Now I know
where they were from.'

She smiled helpfully and lost another couple of years.

They had another light handshake and then he was gone.

In the car, on the way back to the office, he thought of the tweets he'd seen – *The end of the world is nigh, No one can stop Him now, The beacons are lit* – and a cold fear crept up on him. They knew something. Maybe Nathan did, too. And Jenna. He had to get a grip, calm down, put them to the back of his mind. It was the sleep, or lack of it. That's what was making him feel this way.

Reality wound its way slowly back in. It was a legend, a coincidence. There was no Hobbledy Man. He made mental notes as to what he would say to Daphne Cooper. He could hardly classify Jenna as at risk. She had the support of her mum and the school. Alisha, on the other hand, was a different case. But there wasn't much they could do if the family wouldn't talk and there was a police case ongoing.

He looked at his phone. He had other appointments to go to. Two, in fact. He'd already cancelled them twice before. They weren't urgent but they needed to be done.

The offices were more than usually busy when he got in. Last night's violence had brought in an avalanche of calls. Paperwork had to be completed, then everyone had to be out.

Kat was in the corridor, clutching a bundle of pink and yellow forms. She looked worried. 'Daphne wants to see you.'

'Great.'

'Now,' she said. She hurried off, then turned, suddenly remembering something. 'What did the doctor say?'

'The usual. I'm not ill enough to see him.'

'But you are ill, John.'

She didn't mean it badly, he knew that. But hearing it out of her mouth, so clinical and matter-of-fact, was as shocking as if it had come from a real doctor.

'I'm sorry,' she said.

'You're right,' he said. 'I'll go back to him. I'll tell him it's an emergency.'

By the time he got to the top of the stairs on the second floor, it nearly was. He rubbed his chest to settle himself, then knocked on Daphne's door.

The reply was instantaneous, as if she'd been spying on him through it.

'Come in.'

She was behind her desk, looking at her laptop. 'We're absolutely inundated, John. We can't breathe for calls.'

'Kat said you wanted to see me.'

'Yes. I need you to go to Nelson police station. Nathan Walsh is in custody.'

'What's he done now?'

'It would be quicker if I told you what he hasn't. He was out last night during the riot.'

Johnny cursed. He knew he should have checked on him.

'He's not in a good way. The desk sergeant said he was delirious last night, kept saying that he needed to see you.'

'That's not like him.'

'That's what I thought,' she said.

'Did he say why?'

She paused. 'He said he had a message for you.'

A message?

His heart skipped a beat. He imagined Nathan on his own in the police interrogation room. Then it came back. Of course – that's where he'd seen the letters. **C O H M.** Nathan had written them on the wall.

This town ain't gonna be here much longer. Pendle's gonna go up in flames.

He wasn't imagining things.

13

He could hear the chanting well before he got to the station. There was a phalanx of police officers guarding the main entrance and, facing them, a hundred, maybe two hundred, EDL supporters, their voices raised to fever pitch, all shouting in unison. It was like being at a football ground in the bad old days.

'EDL! EDL! EDL!' they shouted, followed by a chorus of 'Scum! Scum! Scum!' when they saw an Asian being led into the building. The violence in their expressions was palpable. Johnny had never seen a crowd so worked up. It heaved, bulged, threatened to break the thin blue line that protected the building. A couple of police motorcyclists pulled up on Manchester Road and proceeded no further. Johnny did the same. There was no way he was driving through that lot.

'EDL! EDL! EDL!'

Then, from down the road, came rival voices – equally hostile, equally strident.

'Racists go home! Racists go home!'

There were women in headscarves in the group, but the bulk of them were young, Asian men, the kind he'd seen in trouble.

The groups got closer and closer and the thin blue line, or thin yellow line as they all wore yellow jackets, separated them as best it could.

Hands went up from the EDL when they saw the rival mob. 'Islamic State Fuck Off! This is England!' Then isolated cries of 'Justice for our Troops!' Gnarled fists and contorted faces, necks with veins like ropes, and skulls with iron intent, faced down the enemy.

The Asian group was about twice as large and quickly overwhelmed the police lines. Sirens could be heard in the distance, but already, there were clashes.

'Racists go home! Racists go home!'

Johnny tried to get to the station on foot but an officer with a riot shield shoved an angry baton in his face.

'I need to see my client,' Johnny said.

'You want to get yourself killed?" the officer shouted. 'Stand back!'

It was then Johnny saw the handheld TV cameras and crews spilling out of vans coming towards him. The BBC were there, so were Sky and ITV, all trying to get their story.

'I need to see my client,' he repeated, holding up his ID card. 'Not going to look good if you knock me out on TV, is it?'

The officer mouthed 'Fuck you' but let him through. The riot shield fell back into place.

There were clashes breaking out all over now. A group of Asians had pulled an EDL supporter out of the main group and was stamping on his head. A new cry of 'Pigs! Pigs!' went up.

'EDL! EDL!'

'Racists go home!'

Then screams and punches and the thin yellow line was finally breached.

A flotilla of police carrier vans arrived, the first sign that things were getting out of hand. Someone had fucked up royally. Police in blue stormtrooper uniforms, Tactical Aid Units and PSU from the big cities spilled out onto the streets. Shields came up. Horses and dogs were deployed. Batons were raised.

Johnny shook his head. Fear, curiosity, adrenaline all coursed through him. As much as he wanted to get away, there was another part of him that wanted to see it, to witness the violence at first hand, to see the shambolic madness of Friday and Saturday nights ratcheted up by a cocktail of hatred, bigotry and misunderstanding.

He managed to sneak into the station, only to find the madness of the crowd outside was matched by the detainees inside. There were five Asian men with bloodied faces and black eyes being protected by an armed guard of Tactical Aid officers. On the other side of the waiting area twenty handcuffed members of the EDL were being kept back by an equal number of police.

The cry went up. 'Scum! Scum! Scum!' It rocked the very foundations of the station, threatened to take the roof off.

The Asian men were silent. It was impossible to gauge their reaction as their faces were so beaten up.

Then the EDL broke out in unison. 'Paedos! Paedos! Paki Paedos!'

It came from outside, too.

The police officers were edgy, like horses near a fire.

As he was about to file through the lines, he felt a hand on his shoulder. It was Dan, the desk sergeant.

'You're brave,' he said.

'What the hell's happening?' Johnny said.

'We're trying to get them out of harm's way,' he said, indicating the Asian men. 'But we can't move them till those cretins calm down.' He nodded at the EDL supporters. 'This station wasn't built for so many people.' He led Johnny behind his counter, then through a door behind it. 'You'll be safe here for a bit. At least until we've moved them.'

'Are they all under arrest?'

'Aye, and about a hundred more in Burnley. The world's gone mad.'

'You know what started it?'

The desk sergeant rolled his eyes at his naivety. 'I think we all know what started it.'

There were more shouts in the waiting area and the Asian men were finally moved out.

The cry of 'Paki paedos' was taken up again outside.

The desk sergeant was right. The world *had* gone mad.

'Where's Nathan?' he asked.

'In the holding cell.'

'Is he okay?'

The desk sergeant gave him another funny look. 'You're giving me a bit of a grilling today, aren't you?'

'I was told he was delirious.'

'He was. Proper off his head, hallucinating, the lot.'

'He'd taken something?'

'The FME said so. He'll give you the report.'

'When can I see him?'

'When I get the all clear.' He looked out the door. 'Look, bud, this is probably none of my business, but I must ask you. That kid, should he even be walking the streets?'

'How do you mean?'

'We see all sorts of shit in here. Joyriders, drunks, smackheads. All this stuff outside, that's a big step up for us. But your kid... Christ, he needs help. I've been in the force twenty years and never seen anything like the stunts he was pulling last night. Even the knobs out there, who were arrested with him, were taken aback. We had to put him in isolation.'

'To protect him?'

'No. To protect *them*. It took five of us to get him down and sedate him. He was like a bloody animal.'

Johnny listened in despair. He'd left it too late. Nathan was going to get himself committed.

The desk sergeant opened the door a fraction. 'Looks like we're okay. I'll take you over to him.'

The waiting area looked like a battlefield, with equipment strewn across the floor and the injured being tended to. The sound of chanting outside had reduced in volume and the police line had forced the mob away from the building. The occasional siren cut through: police, fire, ambulance.

'Bloody madness,' the desk sergeant said.

At the words, a shadow fell across the room, and Johnny again remembered the tweets: *The end of the world is nigh.* For a brief second, tiredness and the light transformed the police in riot shields, some with gas masks on their faces, to plague doctors, walking over the corpses of the plague-stricken fallen.

Scum! Scum!

The chants faded.

The desk sergeant unlocked a door opposite the room Nathan had previously been locked up in. There was nothing in it apart from a mattress squared up to the far wall and a pisspot beside it.

'Just the bare essentials,' the desk sergeant said.

Nathan was sitting huddled on the floor, his head bowed, his hands holding the back of it, rocking back and forth, mumbling to himself. He hadn't heard the door open.

'Nathan?' Johnny said.

He kept rocking as if he was in a trance.

'He's been like that a while now,' the desk sergeant said.

There was a strong smell of ammonia. Johnny got on the floor and sat next to him.

'Son, can you hear me?'

More rocking, more mumbling.

'How long's he been like this?'

The desk sergeant shrugged. 'Since the FME left him. Maybe two, three hours.'

Johnny put a hand on Nathan's shaved head. The nicks and cuts had hardened into black scabs like plague sores. 'Nathan, can you hear me?'

Nathan stopped rocking, stopped mumbling. Slowly, he removed his head from its protective shell and let the strip light pierce the narrow apertures of his eyes.

'Who is it?'

'It's Johnny.'

Nathan turned his head towards him. It's like he was blind, mole-like, following his voice rather than seeing him.

'Johnny, is it you?'

'Yes, son.'

Nathan nodded nervously. ''Av' they gone now?'

'Who?'

'The others.'

Johnny looked round. 'Everyone's gone.'

Nathan's eyes opened slightly. His pupils were dilated. He blinked to keep the light at bay, then used his hands to ward it off.

'What happened last night, son? How come you got involved?'

'I was told to, Johnny.'

'By who?'

Nathan went quiet. 'By *Him*.'

'The sergeant?'

'No. *Him*. That's why I needed to see ya. To tell ya. No one else would believe me. No one.' He buried his head again, began to shake.

'He was like this last night?' Johnny asked.

'He was off his trolley before,' the desk sergeant said. 'Totally gone.'

Johnny put his hand on Nathan's shoulder. 'Nathan, you have to tell me what happened. It's the only way I can help you. You're okay now. You're safe.'

Nathan looked up but his eyes were wide and black. Johnny had the feeling he was looking into an animal's eyes, feral and wild.

'You don't understand,' Nathan whispered. 'No one's safe. That's what I'm tryin' to tell yous.'

Johnny felt his fear. It was dripping off him.

'I was out with 'em last night, Johnny. I know ya told me not to but I was bored. We was only havin' a laugh at first, then it got serious. I didn't do nothin'. Really I didn't. Then it started goin' crazy.' His eyes were not focussed on him but on an invisible point on the wall where the past was. 'Someone lit a fire and then there was fightin'. That didn't bother me. I could take those Paki cunts any road. I threw a brick at 'em. I admit that. It hit a car maybe. But I never hurt no one.' He was sweating now and feverish. 'It was then I saw *Him*.'

He hit his head with his hands, banging it to get rid of the memory. Johnny tried to stop him.

'I thought it couldn't be, there's no one there. But he was. He was standin' in the shadows, lookin' at me.'

Johnny managed to pin his arms to his sides. 'Who was it, Nathan?'

Nathan was in a trance. 'He was tall and bent, like a spider. He came round the fire to see me. He had a stick in his hand, one you use for walkin'. I told him to fuck off. He gave me the creeps. Then he said he had a message to give. I said I wasn't taking no messages but he bent down and I couldn't get away.' Nathan's hands were now like talons, clawing the air. His eyes were wide like black, pewter dishes. He tried to get up but Johnny held him back.

'What did he say, Nathan? You must tell me.' Nathan's anxiety transfused into him as readily as if they were on the same drip.

Nathan struggled for a few more seconds, then sank in a saggy heap on the floor, sobbing. When he'd stopped, a look of near normality returned to his face. He looked at Johnny and didn't blink. 'He said he had a message for you and that I had to take it.'

'For me?'

'Yeah.'

'What the hell are you talking about?'

'*Tell John Malkin the beacon fires are lit and that he's been chosen*, he said.'

The shock nearly killed him. He held his chest to stop the palpitations, gulped instead of breathing.

Nathan saw his chance and ran for the door.

The desk sergeant stood in his way, took the impact head on. Two other officers came in, grabbed hold of him and peeled him off.

But Nathan wasn't looking at them. His eyes were trained solely on Johnny. He was sobbing and crying. 'You don't understand, Johnny. But you must. You must go. It's gonna be too late.'

The officers had him on the floor, pinned underneath their boots.

Johnny felt tears spring to his eyes. Nathan was helpless. 'Don't hurt him. Please don't hurt him.' But he was thinking about himself, too. His head spun at the madness of what he'd just heard.

They handcuffed Nathan and made him sit on the floor. Johnny had never seen him so lost or so desolate. He felt the same way himself.

'I'll call the FME again to check him out,' the desk sergeant said. 'Don't want anyone making any accusations, do we?'

Johnny looked at the officers. They'd just been outside controlling a riot, stopping the town from ripping itself apart. Little wonder if the adrenaline was still flowing.

The desk sergeant turned before he left the room. 'You're all the same, aren't you? You think we're animals.'

Everyone was an animal today.

14

The west side of Pendle Hill, where the Ribble Valley softly undulates and rolls down towards Longridge and Ribchester, was bathed in hazy afternoon sunlight. This was the affluent side of the hill where solicitors, bank managers and television producers lived. It had so far been unaffected by the outbreaks of violence in Nelson and Burnley, but there was still pensiveness in the air and people looked up at the hill and wondered if it would be their protector or allow the violence to cross and be visited upon them.

Shaf had been trailing the silver Jag since midday after it had come out of Burnley Police HQ. There was no surprise it had been there, maybe more that it hadn't been there longer; after all, the town was in flames, the area a powder keg of uncertainty and fear. He followed it along the A59 till it came to Clitheroe, an arty town neatly stacked with tea rooms and little boutiques. He watched the driver get out at a Sainsbury's car park and made a note of the time. He thought he was going to get a day or two to think about what he'd signed up for, not a couple of hours, but DCI Ali wasn't hanging around. There must have been a hundred other candidates, more skilled in surveillance, and less likely to get caught, than he was. Why the hell choose him?

John Whittle came out of Sainsbury's a quarter of an hour later with two bags of shopping – one loaded with food, the other with drink. He fielded a call on his way to his Jag. There were a few 'fucks' and then a prompt 'goodbye'. Shaf wondered what people would say if they knew their superintendent was dealing with the riots by loading up his car with booze. Then again, judging by everybody else in the department, this was exactly the way they dealt with a crisis.

Whittle pulled out of the car park and turned north along Chatburn Road. He passed the grammar school Shaf used to go to. Shaf remembered the day his father found out he had a place. 'My son, the grammar school boy, the *Royal* Grammar School boy, has made me proud,' he said. Mum was in the background, as ever. He had to say hello to relations in Pakistan he'd never even heard of and hold court with neighbours he barely knew. It was the day his life changed, if only mum and dad knew how much.

He looked at Pendle Hill, now looming on his right. That was something that had never changed. After a couple of miles winding north through the countryside, Whittle turned right down a narrow lane towards a large, stone house. Shaf drove on about a hundred metres and pulled up. He looked in the rear-view mirror. He turned the car round and drove back down the road, parked in a garden centre car park about fifty metres from the house on the left. He could see the silver Jag on the driveway but there was no sign of anyone inside.

He waited about five minutes and then noticed another car winding down the lane. It was a battered Land Rover with a muddied body and muddier windows. He guessed there must be a farm near, but no, the Land Rover parked outside the stone house and two men got out. He recognised them instantly. It was Tib and Thomas, Carver's farm workers.

He wound his window down, tried to pick out their voices. Judging by their manner, and their constant gesticulating, there was some kind of argument going on. Then the front door of the house opened and the superintendent came out. The three of them began talking. Thomas gesticulated some more and had to be restrained by Tib. Finally, after several minutes, they got back in their Land Rover and reversed back down the lane at speed.

Shaf remembered the superintendent's words, that the Carvers had changed their story about hearing the screams. Did they all know each other? He hit the steering wheel hard and turned the car. The superintendent would have to wait.

The Land Rover shot south down Chatburn Road. It was doing about sixty which, on the narrow road, was twice as fast as it should. Whatever Tib and Thomas needed to do, they weren't bothered about running themselves into a tree or an oncoming car. They took a quick left at a desolate looking roundabout on to the A671, where the trees looked as though they'd been blighted by a spell, and then sped on. They were doing over seventy now. If he'd have been on duty, he'd have to have pulled them over. But, of course, he wasn't on duty. He wasn't even meant to be following them.

There were sparse hedgerows and sprinkled withered and brown woodland on either side of the road, hiding barren fields and offering shelter from the elements. Tib and Thomas turned right on to the A59. Shaf guessed where there were going: Blackthorn Farm. Doubts began to surface about what he was doing. What did he hope to achieve by it? His mind was whirring as fast as the car.

Then, as he approached the big roundabout at the end of the dual carriageway, the rain came down suddenly and hard. One moment the road was dry, the next there was water everywhere. Shaf felt the brakes lock up and the car begin to aquaplane. He managed to get some kind of traction on it but the Land Rover was less fortunate. It ploughed straight across the roundabout, hitting an Esso petrol tanker and then ricocheted into the crop circle centre of the reservation. It flipped on its side and rolled over a few times before landing on its roof. The Esso tanker continued at speed for about ten metres, then spun in a circle, colliding with a red Ford Fiesta before hitting a lamppost and a sign that pointed the way to Burnley and Padiham.

There was a horrible silence in which time stopped and the rain lashed down. The tanker driver opened the cab just in time. There was an explosion underneath the tanker, then a dull roar and the whole thing set alight. It was met with a greater roar as the tank ignited. Orange flames shot up into the sky, sixty feet high.

Shaf felt the heat even in his car.

The tanker driver lay on the grass, shielding his face from the flames and the burning debris. Shaf got out and ran over to him.

The rain lashed down, beating back the flames on the tanker, but was unable to quell them. This was a petrol fire, unaffected by water. It couldn't cool the raging temperature or prevent the plumes of thick, black smoke from billowing into the sky. Indeed, the rain seemed to aggravate the beast, spreading the fire and heating the raindrops. Shaf put his arms up to protect his face. A blast of wind sent the flames dangerously in his direction.

He reached the driver just in time. 'You okay?' he said.

The man nodded fearfully.

Shaf helped him up, shielded him from the fire as best he could, then led him away. There was another mini-explosion in the tank and another billowing cloud of smoke, blacker than the night sky, mushrooming out from the writhing tentacles of flames.

He looked back at the red Fiesta, stuck on the roundabout, its engine concertinaed. The driver, a young woman, had managed to get out and was running into the trees on the grass verge for shelter.

The Land Rover which Tib and Thomas had driven was like a stranded turtle on its back in the centre of the crop circle roundabout. But there was no sign of them. He ran over to it. If the flames got to it, or if petrol was leaking, that would explode, too. He knelt on the grass and looked inside.

Tib was struggling to get his brother out, but was hampered by his seatbelt and the shattered glass. There was a fierce cut on his cheek where a piece had embedded itself. Shaf tried to open the driver's door but it was stuck fast. He went round to the passenger side, managed to get it open. It took two heaves to get it over the thick grass and wide enough for him to reach in.

In the panic of the moment, Tib didn't recognise him.

'Can you get out?' Shaf shouted at him. 'You need to get out *now.*'

'I canna. I canna leave 'im. He's gonna die.'

Shaf reached around and felt the buckle of Thomas's seatbelt. He was slumped and unconscious. He pressed the red release button but it refused to budge. 'Just get yourself out!' he shouted to Tib. 'You aren't going to help him where you are.'

Tib shook his head and then a slow light of recognition spread across his face.

'Get me something sharp,' said Shaf. 'Quickly.'

He put his fingers on Thomas's neck, found the pulse. He was alive. Just. He guessed he must have some kind of internal injury.

Tib slid out of his seat and crawled out of the passenger side. Shaf yanked at Thomas's belt, tried to rip it out by force, but it wouldn't move. He tried to extend it so he could pull it over Thomas's head, but the fact he was face downwards, and the weight of his body, had shortened the give. He would have to lift him and pull the belt at the same time.

''Ere,' said Tib, behind him. 'Try this.' He was holding out a shard of glass, about six inches long.

Shaf took it, placed it against an exposed part of the belt, and was surprised how easily it cut through the black polyester. He nicked himself in the process and winced. Thomas's body and gravity did the rest. He slid out on top of him. Tib helped pull him out and they managed to drag him away from the Land Rover. The rain spattered his face.

'Is he alive?' asked Tib.

Shaf checked the pulse again. 'Yes, but he needs medical attention quickly.'

He looked at the flaming oil tanker, wondered if anyone had called the emergency services yet. There was a line of cars building up on the A59, unable to get round the Fiesta and the fire. Cars were coming up from Whalley and Blackburn, wanting to take the Burnley and Padiham exit.

He got out his phone and dialled 999.

A woman answered straightaway.

'I need an ambulance,' Shaf said. 'Two injured, one serious and currently unconscious.' He was on autopilot.

Some drivers got out of their cars and took pictures of the stricken tanker. He didn't blame them. There *was* something eerie about the sight.

Tib shielded Thomas's face from the rain but every few seconds he would look over at it pensively. 'Guess that's it, then,' he said.

'That's what?' said Shaf.

'The start of the end.'

'What are you talking about?'

'It's written down, ain't it? When the beacon fires are lit. You seen the marks yerself in the woods, sir. The ones you drew in the ground.'

There was the sound of sirens in the air. Shaf wondered what he'd say to the police when they arrived. The last thing he needed to do was draw attention to himself, especially as he was meant to be five miles away, watching the superintendent's house. The correct thing to do would be wait and make a statement, but he had a gnawing feeling in his stomach telling him to get out of there. Checking Thomas's pulse one last time, he left him with Tib and ran to the verge where he'd left his car. He slewed it across the wet grass, past the burning tanker, and took the A671 to Burnley. There was a chance he'd run into the emergency services this way, but more than likely they'd be coming down from Clitheroe. For the first time in his professional life, he was doing the wrong thing. There was a crime scene to contain and evidence to give and statements to take, but this was not the time. As the rain lashed down and the car sped past the lines of hawthorn and blackthorn bushes, he felt the cold clockwork of some other destiny propelling him forward, its hands and face his own, but to what end he didn't know.

'*The time is comin'.*'

15

The River Calder ran silently past the old Cistercian abbey, barely disturbing the steep, mossy shore. Oak and ash trees leant over the side, casting dark, ruminative shadows on the north bank, and the air murmured strange incantations. It rose above the path that ran through the trees, then blew over the old, cloistral walls like a mother blowing on her sleeping child, hoping to watch them stir. But nothing moved. There were lights on in the adjacent retreat, the only part of the abbey that was still used, but they cast a meagre light outside and there was no sound from within.

The breeze continued over the old seventh century parish church of St Mary and All Saints, around the clock tower that tolled eleven and then between the granite gravestones. It turned and twisted down Church Lane and then turned on to The Sands, past the old, stone wall of the abbey grounds. It blew westward for a few hundred metres until it came to an old stone gatehouse, the north-western entrance to the abbey grounds, and passed under its cold, stone arch. In times past, when the abbey was used, before the dissolution of the monasteries, the gatekeeper would have kept an eye on visitors, turned away those who were not welcome, and dispensed alms, food and drink to the poor and maimed. Now, any traveller could walk down Ridding Lane from Whalley Arches, the great Victorian viaduct that spanned the river.

The breeze followed this ancient path, through the gnarled and twisted oaks that hung like gibbets over its walls. Between the fingers of their branches, and in the shadow of the viaduct, was a field. The moon rose over it, casting a sickly glow. Along the lane, which now glowed moonlit white, six figures walked in single file. They stopped in the shadow of the gatehouse, three men and three women, all wearing monastic gowns. The breeze blew their gowns and the cowls of their hoods.

The tallest of the men turned to the others. 'Are we all agreed, then? It has to be done?'

One by one, they nodded their assent, until he came to the last, one of the women.

'Beth?' he said.

'It has to be done,' she said. 'It's written. We can't forget the price that was paid.'

He handed her a small plastic packet and she put it in her gown.

The only thing left of the church were its foundations, imprinted in the ground like a date stamp and running north-west to south-east, but the cloistral walls of the rest of the abbey were still there, crenellated and imposing. On the west side, there was a large wall with two square cut windows and four arches. Through one of these entrances, the six figures made their way. They moved silently to a stone annexe on the south side of the ruins. The walls were higher here and the windows criss-crossed with stone sills and pieces of wood. There were three rooms inside: the monk's day room, the parlour and, lastly, the vestry, where ceremonial vestments and liturgical objects had once been stored. The six figures disappeared inside the latter.

'Are you sure about this?' the tall man said. His voice was broken with doubt.

'We must do what is right,' said Beth. 'We have to give back what was taken.'

'You took what I gave you?'

She removed her hood. She had long, brown hair, green eyes, tiny freckles, and her left eye was squinted to the left.

'You have about ten minutes till it kicks in.'

'I'm okay,' she said. 'It has to be done, Tom.'

The other girls took off their hoods. They had long, rich, straw coloured, country hair and wore braids of flowers. They began to lay a path of holly from the vestry to one of the windows in the annexe.

Tom and Beth followed them in.

The other two men were standing guard at either side of the window. Through it, the breeze blew in the scent of the river.

'You sure you saw him?' Tom asked.

'Last night,' said the man on the left. 'He came along the path by the river.'

'What if it doesn't work?' one of the straw-haired girls said. 'I mean, there's no guarantee, is there?'

Tom looked admonishingly at her. 'You're doubting the words, Claire?'

She shook her head, aware that the others were looking at her.

'One was chosen from amongst you,' Tom said. 'There is *no* other way.'

'There is,' said the man on the right of the window.

They all turned to him.

'And which of us is going to take *that* path?' Tom challenged him. 'Are you really going to kill someone? We may have no choice, Adam.'

As he said it, a shadow passed the annexe window, blocking the meagre light the night brought in.

'Christ,' the man on the left said. 'I think he's coming, Tom.'

Claire and the other straw-haired girl disappeared into the vestry, hoping the shadows would hide them.

Beth stood in the centre of the annexe, frozen with fear. She wore sandals on her feet and the cold air rode up her gown and gave her goose pimples. She could hear Tom breathing heavily at her side. There was nothing he could do now to save her. There was nothing any of them could do.

Slowly, a long shadow appeared in the entrance of the annexe, creeping across the grass. It was unrecognisable at first, all elongated by the moonlight, but gradually a form took shape. It was a tall man with a bird's head. He wore a long, black, leather coat and brandished a long stick in his right hand.

Tom's fingers struggled with the fittings on Beth's gown. He had to pull some of the buttons off before she was free of it. She felt it slide down her and land at her feet. Her body felt the extra cold immediately. But for her sandals, she was naked.

The Bird Man beat his stick on the stone wall and Tom was gone, too, leaving her to her fate. The Bird Man looked taller in the dark and more powerfully built, edging towards her like a patient, old spider testing its web to see what it had caught. As he got nearer, she realised the bird's head was in fact a giant bird mask with a pointed beak and two red glass eyepieces, the kind of apparel mediaeval plague doctors used to wear. She felt disorientated and knew it wasn't just the ketamine causing it. He walked round her three times, and each time the circuit got closer till his leather coat brushed her skin. On the final occasion, she felt a gloved hand on her right breast. The shock of it, and the roughness of his touch, made her shudder, but she had nowhere to turn. Then he began to feel her all over. The abruptness of his fingers, the coldness of the night air, and the emotionless stare of the red eyes kept her rooted to the ground as if she were a tree and his fingers the breeze. She knew the others were watching her and she didn't dare move. She couldn't let them down. You couldn't forget the price that had been paid, or that was about to be paid if no one was to stop him.

Then, one of the gloved hands grabbed her crotch, seized the hair that guarded the entrance. It did so without permission, without pleasantries, in the full knowledge that it could do what it wanted. It went so high, she thought she might faint. But it was so insistent and so regular in its motions that she felt her body burn, and her insides moisten. Her thighs began to seek out the intruder, pushing themselves onto it, demanding they do not let her go, and the warmth became a fire.

The K was working its magic now, too. Other plague doctors appeared, emerging from out of the ruins. Her thighs trembled, her body shook, so close was she to pleasure's critical point. The Bird Man seemed to sense this and ploughed his fingers into her furrow with greater intent. She gasped, nearly fell. He held her up and her whole weight seemed to be balanced on the gloved fingers inside her. But they did not relent and the fire spread through her body, making her insides shake and causing her to grip his fingers in a vice. She groaned loudly and wondered if Tom had seen.

Let Him have his way,
Let Him have his say,
Keep Him up all night,
He will go away.

The Bird Man picked her up and lay her on a stone that had been strewn with flowers. She didn't feel the cold. She didn't feel anything. Her head was all over the place. Faintly, she smelt the herbs and spices from his beak and the aroma was sweet and sedating. She felt him spread her thighs but she didn't look down. The other plague doctors had gathered around like she was carrion, using her mouth at will and spilling themselves onto her body.

The Bird Man opened his coat. He had what looked like a thick, old rope in his hand. She felt it inside her and couldn't stop herself from moaning, a little from the cold and the roughness but mainly from desire. The she felt it in her mouth. It stank of her. Desire waned but the weirdness of the moment, and the sense of what she was doing, made her feel powerful. Finally, her mouth was filled with white seed. He wouldn't let her take it out so she had to swallow it all whole.

Who'll plant the seeds of next year's crop?

He called for the other two girls when he was done and told them to take their gowns off. She watched him catch hold of Claire with the same gloved hand. He told them to go to the two men by the annexe window. He watched them carefully, like a bird, until first the one, then the other, was done.

All the while, Tom looked on silently from the shadows.

The clock on the church tower tolled midnight and the Bird Man took his plague doctor's mask off. He sat on one of the stones in the annexe and lit a cigarette.

She watched him, swimming in the unreality of the moment. 'That was fucking amazing, you bastard.'

'I told you it would be.'

'Do you think they knew?'

'They're dumb if they didn't.'

'What about Tom?'

'What about him?'

'Do you think it hurt him?'

'Isn't that what you wanted? Besides, he should be used to it. You lot are all about free love, aren't you?'

'He's always been nice since we were little.'

The cigarette lit up like an angry firefly, then spread its ashes like a meteor shower. He put his hand on her cunt. 'You're not little any more.'

He got up. He was no longer a shadowy figure with a stick in his hand, but a large man in his fifties with a ruddy face. His prick dangled down between his legs. She couldn't help looking at it, even as he spoke. 'So, you're calling yourselves the Cult of Black Moss now?' he said.

'Tom does.'

'You're just kids playing games.'

'You don't mean that. You've seen what's going on,' she said.

'I've seen nothing,' he said.

'Well, other people have. What about the marks on our door or what Tib and Thomas said? The beacons on the hill are lit.'

'People see a lot of things when they're stoned.'

'My dad wasn't stoned.'

'It's nothing but a folk tale, Beth. The world isn't going to end because a few crackpots say it will.'

She felt cross and cold but the ketamine had her under its spell and reality had not wound its way back. 'Can you take me home now?'

'Of course,' he said. 'You want me to help you with your gown?'

She nodded or at least thought she did.

'The buttons have all been pulled off. Your boyfriend didn't make a very good job. You'll have to come the way you are,' he said.

She walked in front of him in her sandals, down the path by the river, under the branches of the trees, in the shadow of the old ruins. Once or twice, she stumbled and, seeing her on her knees, he stopped her. He was furiously stiff still.

He'd parked his silver Jag on a private road near the English Martyrs presbytery. He hadn't kissed her all evening but he did so now before they got in, long and hard on her lips so she could hardly breathe. She fell back against the car and he dug his gloved hand into her again. The breeze blew over them as they stuck there and, for a moment, they would have been mistaken for a statue, they were so closely entwined. Or maybe one of the gnarled and twisted oaks on Ridding Lane and he was the ivy that had spread over her bare boughs. They were so locked in their embrace that they didn't notice another shadow passing along the path by them down towards the abbey.

Jerking his hand free, he lay her down on the back seat of the car and took full and final advantage of the cult's membership. He did not relent till all of her had been used, and she didn't know in which order or how many times, just that she had done her bit to keep him up all night and let him have his way.

She was the sacrifice.

Hopefully, now, the Hobbledy Man would go away.

16

Johnny left the office at 8 p.m. All leave was now cancelled. Nelson was on lockdown. There were yellow-jacketed police officers all along Manchester Road. Emergency crews had dealt with the fires, but the charred, burnt out cars and smoking debris bore testimony to the violence of the previous twenty-four hours. An air of menace hung over the town. You could see it in the faces of the officers. There was none of the bonhomie of a Saturday afternoon patrol. This was something new, something unpredictable, something that had sprung up from nowhere. There were outriders on Scotland Road and patrols up and down the length of the A682. The violence had reached Colne. Resources were stretched beyond breaking point. Johnny's head spun trying to process it all: Nathan's outburst, the Cult of the Hobbledy Man, the riots in town. As mad as it sounded, he believed there was a link now – maybe not a supernatural one, but an orchestrated, mass hysteria. There were kids going round believing all this end of the world stuff. Someone, somewhere, was stirring them up.

Fires in Nelson and Colne, Ring the bells and call Him home.

As he neared Barrowford, exhaustion finally caught up with him. He sped over a pelican crossing, narrowly avoiding a pedestrian. They shook their fist and yelled at him. He didn't blame them. He would have done the same. Then he took the bridge over Pendle Water and nearly clipped its side. He shook his head to clear the fog. He felt better when the houses disappeared on either side and black copse and woodland took their place. Evening had settled on the valley.

Kat's car was in his regular spot so he had to park at the end of the road. That was the last of her belongings to appear at the house. He let himself in and there was the noise of pots and pans being thrown about in the kitchen. He looked round the door, saw her on her knees, rifling through the cupboard under the sink.

'Can I help?' he asked.

She looked flustered. 'I was trying to surprise you, make some dinner, but I can't find anything to cook with. Or eat.'

He looked at the motley collection of pans on the kitchen table, most with burn marks on the bottom and all without lids. 'I'd forgotten I had all this stuff,' he said. 'I don't think I've looked in that cupboard since I moved in.'

She put her hand on her head wearily. 'Don't you think we need to get organised?' she said.

'Organised?'

'Yes. For the baby.'

She didn't look herself today. There was an edginess about her, as if the bubble of excitement and euphoria she had lived on the last few days had finally burst, and reality had set in.

'Don't you think it's a bit…early…' he said. 'I mean, to worry.'

She shook her head. 'No. I don't.'

He was tired. She was tired. This was only going to go one way.

'Kat, I'll get it sorted. I promise.'

There was a chink of relief in her face. 'You better,' she said, and began putting the pans into a black bin bag.

He stopped her when she came to an old Pyrex dish. 'Oh, leave that, will you? My mum gave it to me when I started university.'

'You can't see through it, though, there's that much crap on it.'

'It's sentimental crap. My first cheese and onion pie. 1999.' He took it from her and put it back on the table, then took her hands. 'Come on, Kat, what's up?'

She just about stopped herself from crying. 'I don't know,' she said. 'Maybe it's baby brain. Maybe it's the hormones. Maybe it's us.'

'We've talked about this, haven't we? Things'll be okay. You're going to get a new job and so am I and I'm going to get myself sorted out.'

'You can't even get yourself to a doctor.'

A fissure of caustic responses suddenly opened up. 'I told you,' he said. 'They couldn't fit me in.' But there was a sudden twinge in his chest and it was all he could do not to show it. 'I'm going to make an emergency appointment.'

She must have sensed something was wrong because she backed off and rubbed her stomach. 'Okay,' she said. But there was a sadness in her eye he hadn't seen before and he didn't know where it had come from, if it was him or the hormones.

She went into the lounge and he heard her put the TV on. He picked the pans up off the floor and put them in the bin bag. The last to go was the Pyrex dish. It *was* dirty and needed throwing out. The fog cleared a little. Maybe this wasn't the one mum had given him.

He went outside and threw them all away. There was a strange electric calm in the air, as there was before a storm. He saw the silhouette of Pendle Hill, like an outline on a canvas, and the billowing dark grey clouds spewing from it.

He went back inside. 'Shall I order a pizza?' he said.

Kat shook her head, put her finger to her lips. She had the BBC News on.

There was a fire flickering on the screen and a red Breaking News sign at the bottom. The news ticker reeled off the same line: *Violence has spread to Colne and Blackburn. Police are dealing with disturbances in seven northern towns.*

The screen cut to different locations. Johnny recognised the centres of Burnley and Nelson, with lines of police in riot gear preparing for the worst. He'd seen their faces close up earlier on. Now, they were out on the streets again. What must they be thinking?

'Jesus. What *is* going on?' said Kat. 'It's insane.'

The female reporter who'd been on the scene yesterday appeared back on screen.

'Police are drafting in officers from neighbouring forces in what is now the largest outbreak of public disorder since the 2011 riots.'

'It's happening…' murmured Johnny, and remembered Nathan in his cell, begging him to understand. 'It's actually happening.'

Kat turned to him. 'What did you say?'

'It's what they said.'

'Who?'

'The kids. They said that something was going to happen to the town.' He was in a daze.

'Well, maybe they're involved?'

He sat on the settee next to her. 'No, you don't understand. It's not just them. It's me.'

'What are you talking about?' she said. Her voice was stretched and nervous now.

He shook his head to try and clear his mind. 'Look, this is going to sound crazy. Actually, it sounds more than crazy. It's absolutely insane, but I don't think I can deal with it any more.'

'All what, Johnny?'

'All this,' he said, indicating the world with a throw of his hands. 'I'm cracking up.'

She paused, trying to decipher what he was saying. 'You mean me, don't you?'

The fissure opened again. A searing bolt of anger came rushing kamikaze-style towards him. He did all he could to get out of its way but felt its blast in his cheeks. He wished he could just tell her: 'No, it's not about fucking you. Why is it always about you?' Then realised too late he hadn't just thought it.

Her face crumpled like it had been breached, her head sank, and tears coursed down her cheeks. 'I can't believe you just said that,' she said.

He put his head in his hands, rubbed the stubble on his cheek, tried to take the words back. 'Look, I'm sorry,' he said.

'Don't you think I know what you're bloody going through?' she said. 'It's in my face every day, too. I hear all the crap before it gets to you. It's why I want to get out and why I want everything to be perfect. We can't bring up a baby if we're not okay. You know that?'

She was right, of course. But there was a part of him that couldn't connect to her, that was still elsewhere, dialling in different numbers. Tiredness, stress, and now paranoia, the unholy trinity of child protection burnout, had today left him an empty shell.

'Have I missed something?' he said.

'What?' she said.

'Have I missed something? It's what they tell us, isn't it?'

'I don't understand what you're saying, John.'

He looked at the TV. The fires were burning brighter than ever. 'Do you believe in witchcraft?' he said.

She said nothing, just stared at him in a dead way.

'It's nonsense, isn't it? A rational person would never entertain the idea. Well, something happened today, Kat. Something that made me think otherwise.'

A look of anger, resignation, or was it sadness, appeared on her face.

'No, listen, please,' he said. 'I have to tell you. Nathan Walsh had a fit last night. He was in the riots and he saw something, a man with a stick in his hand. No one else saw him. Just Nathan. The man asked him to give me a message. *Tell John Malkin the beacon fires are lit and that he's been chosen*, he said. Those were the same lines I saw on this Twitter site yesterday.' He got out his phone, read from it. 'Listen. The end of the world is nigh. No one can stop him now. *The beacons are lit.* And look at this.' He showed her a tweet.

@plaguedoctor RIP John Malkin. No one shall forget the price you paid. #COBM

'It's all connected, Kat.'

The sadness had won out. 'John,' she said. 'You're ill.'

'No,' he said feverishly. 'You must understand. Please.' It all came tumbling out. 'There's a legend round here about someone called the Hobbledy Man. A cult grew up around him. Followers believed that the sighting of him meant the world was about to end.'

She listened carefully, a psychiatrist to his patient. 'And you think that's who Nathan saw?'

'Yes. And it's not just Nathan. There's other tweets on that site. Look.' He read from his phone again in the same frenetic manner. 'I saw him again today. In a field by Newchurch.'

She stared at him. 'Have you mentioned any of this to Daphne?'

'No. Of course not.'

'Well, maybe you should? It would be a good way of showing how stressed you are. You could also bring it up with your doctor tomorrow.'

'You don't think there's anything in it?' he asked, incredulous.

'No. I think Nathan was probably on something. And I think you need to be.'

Another searing bolt of anger came. He wasn't going to be able to hold it back. 'But what about the fucking tweets?'

Don't swear at me, John. It's just some kids reading too much into a stupid legend like you're doing. Before you went off telling your story, we were talking about *us*. You know, the important things. I think that's the thing you fucking missed.'

She got up.

'Where are you going?' he said.

'Home. I need a break from this. And I'm going to get some food.'

He got up after her. 'You can't go, Kat. It's dangerous.'

'No more dangerous than staying here with a madman.'

He smacked the wall with his fist. For fuck's sake, he should have just kept quiet.

She picked her bag up, opened the front door.

'Kat, you can't leave like this. Please stay.'

She ignored him.

He watched her click clack down the road and wanted her to turn round the way she always did after a fight. But now she wasn't for turning. He wondered if he shouldn't run after her, but her car revved up and he realised he was too late. She sped off without saying goodbye.

He slammed the front door and kicked the settee. He was angry with himself but also angry with her for not understanding. He turned the volume up on the TV. The news anchor in London was talking to some Asian woman about race relations and, as usual, was doing their best not to ask the difficult questions.

'Innocent Muslims are becoming targets for far-right groups. The actions of a tiny, tiny minority are making life very difficult for the decent, law-abiding Muslim communities in these towns.'

He flicked to Sky News. There was the same picture of the fire that he'd seen on the BBC. The caption said it was in Burnley although he didn't recognise where. There was a portly police superintendent being interviewed live from the scene.

'Can you let us know the extent of the trouble so far, sir?'

Other officers were trying to bring the booms and microphones down.

'The situation is under control,' the superintendent said gruffly.

'We have reports of wide-scale looting in other towns.'

'We're assessing those reports as we speak.'

'Are you still viewing the violence as racially motivated?'

'Our primary concern at the moment is the safety of the community. I would urge everyone to stay calm and keep indoors while we sort the situation out.'

'Have you enough resources to deal with it? Government cutbacks have hit frontline officers hardest.'

'At present, we have enough officers on the ground. Now, if you'll excuse me.'

Johnny lay on the settee. He closed his eyes, thought of the police officers out in the cold and the wild mobs running amok through the streets. He thought of brooding clouds coming up from Pendle Hill and strange bird men marching down its slopes. Then he thought of a tall hobgoblin man, with a long nose, carrying a cane in his right hand. He was looking for something. Or someone.

'You've been chosen, John Malkin.'

He opened his eyes, his heart thundering in his chest. Sleep had taken him and sleep had sent him back.

He looked at his phone. He'd been away half an hour.

He texted her.

I'm sorry. My fault. Say goodnight to baby for me. x

There was no reply.

17

The more he thought about it, the more stupid it seemed. Someone would have taken his registration; Tib would have said something; the tanker driver would. Yet he'd driven off and left the scene like a criminal, with guilt and fear as accomplices. He thought of ringing DCI Ali to explain it all, then remembered what he'd said: *It's just about us and them and about being on the right side of things.* Well, he was on the right side of things, wasn't he? He'd done what he was asked to do, followed Tib and Thomas, saved the latter's life. Surely, that would count?

He looked through the lounge curtains, half expected to see the squad car on the driveway already. He could hear mum in the kitchen making dinner, with Star Plus on in the background. She'd never got used to England; there was always that 'look over the shoulder' attitude to life back home. It made him sad to think of her that way, and made him sadder that he had to keep dodging the big question, the only question she wanted answering. How long could he keep saying he wasn't ready, he had to focus on his career, he hadn't met anyone? He knew it would make her happy to hear children in her life again. It's why she visited his sisters so often. When *was* he going to get married?

He looked at the notepaper on the table. It was the list of names DCI Ali had given him. He scribbled Tib and Thomas's names at the bottom beside John Whittle's and put the date and the time they met with a big question mark next to it. As he did, his phone vibrated in his pocket and a feeling of impending doom came over him. Was it *him*? It was a number he didn't recognise. Should he pick up or let it go to answer machine? He looked up and saw the picture of his father, riding his horse – the tough, no nonsense, manly man. What would he say if he caught him cowering?

He slid his finger across the screen. 'Hello?'

There was a pause on the other end, then a woman's voice. 'Hello, is that PC Khan?'

'Yes.'

Another pause. 'It's Beth Carver. You came to my father's farm, remember?'

Alarm bells started ringing. He'd followed Tib and Thomas; now she comes forward.

'Yes,' he said. 'I do.'

'I have some information for you.'

He put his pen on the notepaper. 'I'm listening.'

'I can't tell you over the phone. I need to see you.'

It was a trap. 'I'm busy right now. Can I ring you back later?'

'There may not be a later,' she said. 'Please. You have to come to the farm. My father and the farmhands are out for the day.'

It was laughably transparent, but like her performance at the farm, and the acts of Tib and Thomas, it was well done. 'I'm afraid I can't,' he said. 'I'm tied up with work.'

'But you have to. It's *very* important.'

Her voice was desperate now.

'If it's an emergency, you need to ring 999.'

'You're a police officer. I need to speak to you in person. I can't trust anyone else.'

Her tone was brilliant, her pitch perfect.

He stared at the names on the notepaper – Whittle, Tib, Thomas. He felt like he was walking through the coils of a python. 'I need to know what it's about,' he said. 'I need to know that or I can't come.' There it was, *his* best attempt, personal, sincere, what he got his Neighbourhood Policing Award for.

'It's about your boss.'

His heart missed a beat.

'John Whittle.'

It was *definitely* a trap.

'The superintendent?'

'That's him. I need to show you something and you need to come here quickly before my father gets back.'

She hung up.

The question mark on the notepaper suddenly got a lot bigger. He tried ringing her back but she didn't pick up.

He went into the kitchen. Mum was watching *P.I Private Investigator*. She'd got into the show because of him. He was like Raffe Roy Choudhary, she said, solving cases, looking after his mum.

'I've got to go,' he said.

'*Abhi?*'

'Yeah. Something's come up.'

'*Meh ne daal ko pakaya hai.*'

'Don't worry. I'll eat later.'

He kissed her goodbye.

A large storm cloud seemed to follow him as he headed north along the Colne Road through Brierfield towards Barrowford, sending waves and waves of Pennine rain down onto the valley. There were police cars in big convoys travelling in either direction, towards Burnley and Colne. He doubted they'd have much time looking for him, or for anyone else, given what had happened. It was hard to believe society could collapse so quickly and that madness could creep out of the very ground they'd walked on. He remembered something Tib said after the crash. It was *the start of the end*. Looking at what was happening, it was easy to believe that.

The rain came down on Pasture Lane, thick and heavy. The animals in the fields had all taken shelter and the land buckled under the weight of the sky. Sagging pools grew in hollows, the fields became waterlogged, and trees cast their branches downwards, bowing to the elements as if in supplication.

He drove as fast as he could, all the while thinking about Beth and what she was about to say and whether it was a setup, something DCI Ali had dreamed up, or maybe the superintendent himself. The rain drummed on the roof of the car, or was it his heart beating? He drove through Barley, passed the Methodist church, and took Barley Lane up to Black Moss Reservoirs. Carver's farm was on the left, down in a shallow delve. He could see the main gate. There were no cars, no tractors, and no Land Rovers outside. What did he expect? A welcoming party?

He drove down towards the outhouse, half expected the dogs to come chasing the car, then remembered there was one less. He turned the car round and parked up, ready to make a quick getaway. He took his hat and his yellow police jacket off the back seat. He wasn't in uniform today – you didn't go undercover looking all smart – but he felt he needed to. There *were* still people who trusted the uniform. And he felt safer in it.

He ran up the footpath, tried to shield himself from the rain with his arm, and approached the weathered front door. He looked for the marks on it. Only a few, faint outlines remained. Before he could knock, it opened.

She stood there in her white dress, her green eyes fixed on him like a cat. Even the squinted one seemed to be drawn to him.

'The marks on your door?' he said.

'My father sanded them off,' she said. 'Not that it will do any good.' She looked out into the rain. 'Come in. We don't have much time.'

She led him into the kitchen. The embers of a fire still flickered in the grate. There was no sign of Fang, which he was thankful for, but he couldn't help thinking of Grip and what had become of him. Maybe they'd all drowned?

She drew out a chair at the large, old oak table and invited him to sit down. His back was to the window. She sat opposite. 'I got your card from one of our farm workers. He said he'd seen you by the reservoir.'

'Yes. One of your dogs…'

'Drowned?' she said.

'Yes. I've never seen anything like it.'

Her green eyes darted across the room to the hallway. She seemed twitchy, wired, as if waiting for something. 'I'd get used to seeing strange things if I were you. It's all just starting.'

'What is?'

'The end.'

'That's a coincidence. Your farm workers said the same thing.'

'That's because they're believers, too.'

He felt tempted to ask in what, but knew time was against them. 'I came here to talk about John Whittle. You said you had information.'

'I do,' she said. 'He came round the day after you did, you know?'

'I didn't,' he lied.

'My father has known him a long time. They're old friends. I heard them arguing downstairs and came down to see what it was about. When I came in, there was a really awkward silence. I knew my father didn't want me to be there. He had that look about him. He told me we were going to have to retract the stories we'd given to you, about hearing those screams and there being an intruder. I asked him why but he wouldn't say.'

Shaf felt the coils tightening round him. Whittle had got the story changed and then promptly suspended him? 'Why did Whittle want you to do that? Did he say?'

'No,' she said. 'But I know why. He didn't want you, or anyone else, getting close to us.'

'Us?'

'The Cult of Black Moss.'

He shook his head. He'd been had. He'd come out all this way for nothing. 'A cult? This is a joke, right?'

Her eyes flashed angrily. 'No. It's not a joke. I asked you to come here to hear the truth. John Whittle has been part of the cult for years. I thought you may get it now. You've been in the woods. You saw the girls there, didn't you? You've seen the marks on our door.'

'Yeah, but no one's actually told me what it all means.'

'I thought you were a policeman?'

The comment stung.

She looked across to the hallway again, as if expecting something to come down it. 'Look, I haven't got time to explain. A lot of people round here believe it. They know the history of the area and what happens. They're prepared for it. That's all you need to know.'

'You're wrong,' he said firmly. 'I need to know *a lot* more. Believing in something is not a crime. So far, you've told me John Whittle made you change your story. That's his word against yours and not something I can do anything about.'

As if prepared for this, she put her hand in a dress pocket and produced a small plastic pouch containing a fine, white powder. She placed it carefully on the oak table in front of him. 'Okay, so how about drug dealing? Is that something you can do something about?'

He picked the pouch up. The smell was unmistakeable: ketamine. The town was full of it. 'He got you this?'

'He gets us everything. Ecstasy, dope, smack, although most of us aren't into those.'

'How do you pay him?'

'We don't.' The embers of the fire gave out a final splutter and died. Minute sparks glowed an angry red, became orange and yellow and then black. 'He gets his payment a different way.'

Shaf felt his heart sinking. There was only one way this was going.

Her eyes glazed as if remembering something, then came slowly back in to focus. 'He gets his pick of the girls. It's why he joined.'

'He's not a believer, then?'

'Only when it suits him.'

'You seem to know a lot about what he's thinking.'

'He confides in me.'

'Are you sleeping with him?'

'I wouldn't call it sleeping.'

'You have sex with him?'

'He chooses me a lot. It's part of the way we live,' she explained. 'It's written down. He gets involved in the ceremonies, takes his pick. No one complains. We've kind of got used to it. He's taken a shine to me since I first met him.'

'And when was that?'

'When I was fourteen. Maybe fifteen. Not long after my mum died. He called it having an affair. I remember he said he was having trouble with his wife. He was really cross with her, saying she didn't understand him and he wanted someone to talk to. I used to feel grown up and he used to treat me nicely.'

'Did he ever force you to have non-consensual sex? Then or now?'

She paused. 'Sometimes he goes too far but I don't stop him. He likes it that I don't. It's written down.'

Shaf knew he'd gone too far and felt guilty for it. She wasn't on trial. He was.

A sudden gust of wind brought rain lashing against the window so that it shook in its sill. A light spray came down the chimney. There was the faint fizz of water evaporating and the stirring of ashes in the grate.

'Beth, why are you telling me this now?'

She said nothing.

'Everything we have so far is circumstantial,' he said. 'Getting you to change your statement, showing me a couple of ounces of ketamine, sex with a minor though you can't be sure. We need something more. Then we can act.'

She put her hand in her dress pocket again. The material stretched over her breasts, showing the strange tumulus contours of her aureole. 'He's started taking photos of me,' she said. She took out her phone, scrolled along to a folder, and showed him the screen. She was nude, trussed up like a pig, on her knees. It wasn't the sexual acts she was committing that made him wince, but the context. She was degraded, humiliated, abused. Who the hell would do that to someone? Then the pictures began to change and the scrolling got slower so that he could pick out more details.

There were other figures in the photos with her, wearing black gowns. One wore a sinister bird mask with a large beak and red eyes. He was leading her on a chain down a narrow lane. She stopped scrolling, came to a photo of her splayed nude against a car. Her legs were spread wide, as if waiting for someone, anyone, to claim her.

'There,' she said.

'There what?' he said, trying not to look at her body.

'He's normally clever, but this time he made a mistake.'

She expanded the picture and focussed on the car. Moonlight had caught the roof. It glowed white and silver. He looked again and suddenly realised what he was looking at. The colour, the shape, the make: it was a Jaguar. She scrolled to another picture with her bent over the bonnet of the car with the chain dangling down her back. It hung like a pendulum just over the registration plate. Clever girl, her legs were far enough apart so that you could see it.

He recognised the number immediately. It was Whittle's.

'He took these and sent them to me,' she said. 'I have the texts. He told me how pleased he was with them. I didn't used to mind him taking pictures. I thought they were just for him. But these he's taking are for others.'

'You know who?'

She nodded. 'Business friends. He said they're interested in me.'

Shaf was reeling from the revelations, could hardly take it all in, but she wanted to get it all over at once, without pausing or waiting for his reactions. He guessed she didn't want to be judged. The seriousness of the accusations was beyond anything he could have imagined. To think Whittle was a part of a porno ring was mad, yet the car in the photo proved it. 'You know who these business friends are?'

'Not by name, but they're part of a grooming gang. They've been selling girls all round here. That's what they want to do to me.'

He could hardly believe what he was hearing. All the man hours DCI Ali had spent trying to nail the gang and he'd done it at the first go. It felt far too convenient. Again, he wondered if it was part of an elaborate ruse to frame him. Jenna and Alisha had accused him of sexual assault. If Beth was known to Whittle, maybe she'd do the same thing – have him arrested? And then a darker thought crossed his mind. What if DCI Ali was also in on it, springing him from suspension on a false lead, making him follow Whittle, and getting Beth to call him? He should get out of there now. But something held him back. It was not because of what she told him, horrific as it was, nor the graphic nature of the photos, but his sense of duty. He had to follow it through.

'Have you mentioned this to anyone else?' he said.

'If I mentioned it to anyone, he said he'd make sure my dad and my boyfriend saw the pictures. He would tell them what I got up to. It would kill them. And me.'

The wind blew another gust against the window and down the chimney, sending ashes scurrying down the grate.

'So,' she said. 'Can you do anything now?'

'Yes. I'm going to file a report,' he said. 'Talk to my boss.'

'Your boss?' she said, alarmed.

'Don't worry. I don't work for Whittle.' He pushed his chair back, put his hat and coat back on. 'This cult of yours, what's it really about?'

'We believe the ending of the world is upon us,' she said like she was reciting from a book. The transformation in her startled him. 'That's what we've got to stop. To remember John Malkin, to stop the Hobbledy Man. It's all written down.'

He tried to process it all. It was easy to laugh off superstitions at police headquarters, surrounded by other officers, or on the streets of Nelson, by those he was trying to lock up. But out here, in the shadow of Pendle Hill, in the old cottage kitchen, with her staring at him, those worlds ceased to exist. He'd heard of witches back home in Rawalpindi and jinn walking amongst the living. He'd heard of the Pendle Witches but, most of all, he remembered the figure in the forest pool and the drowning dog and the petrol tanker on fire and, for a moment longer than the other moments, he did believe it.

'You better go,' she said. 'My father will be back any time. And Tib and Thomas.'

He didn't tell her the latter had gone to see John Whittle, nor that they'd been involved in a crash and that Thomas was unconscious and required medical help. 'Can you get me the photos of the car?' he said. 'I need to show them to my boss.'

'As evidence?' she said.

He nodded.

'You on Snapchat?'

'What?'

'Forget it. Give me your phone.'

He let her take it.

She fiddled with some settings, then lay his phone on top of hers on the table, like they were lovers. 'Sending it by Bluetooth,' she said. She watched his face as the phones shared their guilty secret.

No sooner had she done it than they heard the sound of barking in the distance and a car door slamming.

Her face froze in panic. 'My father. He's back with the dog. He'll know something's up if he sees you.'

'Is that a problem?'

'It will be if he tells John Whittle. He'll come after you.'

'But he'll already have seen my car.'

'Plenty of people park round here before walking up to Black Moss or Aitken Wood.'

'So, which way do I go?'

She showed him out the back way. He was a criminal now, vaulting the low, stone wall round the back of the farm. He took one look at her, the wind blowing her long, brown hair and her white dress. It was hard to believe it was the same girl in the pictures, but then it was hard to believe anything that had happened the last few days.

As he ran, the sound of barking grew louder and he hoped the Pennine rain would cover his tracks.

18

The holding cells in Nelson, Burnley and Colne were full up. There was nowhere to put Nathan. There was no question that he was going to be charged this time. Arson and public disorder were a bad combination and, if previous riots had taught anybody anything, it was that the law would get you in the end. The Courts and the law-abiding public demanded justice be served.

Johnny waited by the counter for Dan the desk sergeant to reappear. Nathan was beside him, the worse for zero hours sleep, but not stoned, and not hallucinating. The waiting area still looked like a battlefield but the aftermath was uncertain, like a ring after two boxers had punched themselves out. The police officers looked drained, the rioters subdued, both wondering what would happen next.

Dan appeared round a corner to their right, his pate glistening. He made his way purposefully towards them, clutching some papers. 'Here, I'll need your signature,' he said.

Johnny filled in the blank spaces, then got Nathan to print and sign his name on top.

'You understand the conditions?' Dan said.

Johnny nodded.

The desk sergeant glanced at Nathan. 'Does he?'

'I'll make sure.'

'We'll see you in a few weeks, then…if we don't see you before.'

They went out into the grey morning. There were three Tactical Aid Unit carriers outside with police officers milling around. Some looked over as they walked down the steps. Others had taken their hats off and were wiping their faces. All of them wore the same exhausted look as the officers inside. Maybe they were also wondering how long it could go on.

Johnny shepherded Nathan to the Ford Focus. He didn't want him saying anything and fucking up the bail before it had even begun. He had his own shit to deal with.

'I'm starvin',' Nathan said as soon as he got inside.

Johnny took out a bagel from a brown paper bag. 'Here.'

'What the fuck's this?' said Nathan.

'Your breakfast.' He put the car in gear.

'Yeah, but what is it?'

'It's bread.'

'It's got a fuckin' hole in it.'

'We can't eat at McDonald's every day.'

Nathan eyed it suspiciously, then took a bite. He screwed his face up. 'It's fuckin' gross.'

'I've got a falafel wrap and a hummus sandwich, if you prefer?'

Nathan's eyes narrowed.

Johnny threw him the bag. 'You're hopeless. There's a bacon and egg McMuffin in there. The one you like.'

Nathan dived in, ate it ravenously – one mouthful, two, then gone.

Johnny wondered if he remembered anything of last night. He wanted to ask him about the Hobbledy Man – what the hell he meant by him being chosen. But he had to do right by him, and that meant getting him the help he needed.

'Where are we goin'?' Nathan asked.

'I thought you'd like to drive round.'

Nathan grinned stupidly. 'You want me to teach ya some more moves?'

'No. I want to keep my car in one piece.'

Nathan paused, the circuits in his brain slowly connecting. 'So, where are we really goin'?'

It hadn't taken him long to figure that one out.

Johnny tried to put it off. 'What do you mean?'

'You always say that when we're goin' somewhere shit,' said Nathan.

Johnny nodded. It was true. 'We're going to see a doctor.'

'I don't need a doctor.'

'I think you do.'

'I ain't goin'.'

'You have to go. It's part of your bail conditions.'

'I'd rather go to jail.'

Johnny shook his head. 'Well, you'll be going there soon enough.'

'Well, fuck you, ya cunt.'

'Thank you. The doctor's there to help you. He wants to check you out.'

'I don't need checkin' out.'

'You did last night. You had a fit.'

'I was stoned.'

'On what?'

'Fuckin' everythin'. I don't remember.'

Again, he was tempted to ask about the Hobbledy Man. 'Listen. We've got to get you sorted. It's the only way out for you.'

Nathan shook his head. 'There's another way,' he said. 'Another way you don't know about.'

'Yeah. What's that?'

He went silent. The silence was worse than the talking. It meant he couldn't keep tabs on him, didn't know what he was thinking.

The southbound lane of the A682 was blocked. The M65 and A6068 were taking the extra traffic and the queues snaked back into town from the roundabouts on Scotland Road. Police were trying to direct cars but the situation was chaotic. Johnny decided to head over to Roughlee and go over the hill. Nathan's appointment was at Calderstone Hospital. They had a special assessment unit there.

He took a detour through the back streets. This was Nathan's patch, where he'd been brought up, and where, most likely, he'd see out his days. No going to university for him, or seeking his fame and fortune elsewhere, just this empty cadaver of a town. The nearest it got to a heartbeat was the last few nights of rioting.

Johnny's eyes closed momentarily and he saw fires raging on the streets and people throwing bricks and then a tall, bent man with a stick in his hand. He was looking for something.

John Malkin

His eyes shot open and he breathed deeply. It should be him seeing the doctor, not Nathan.

They were in the countryside now. He wasn't far from home. He wasn't far from Kat's. He should call her, apologise in person. She still hadn't texted him back.

The sight of so much greenery seemed to lull Nathan into sleep. He breathed deeper and more regularly. Then, without warning, as they drove through Barley, his eyes opened and he looked at Johnny. 'I need a piss,' he said.

'Yeah?'

'Yeah. I'm desperate.'

'You want bushes or a toilet?'

'If you don't hurry, I'll use ya car.'

Johnny pulled the car over onto a grass verge beside two wooden benches and a parish noticeboard. He wondered if there was a sign that said No Pissing.

Nathan got out and Johnny followed him, just to be on the safe side.

'Well?' he said.

'Well what?' said Nathan.

'Are you going to have your piss?'

'I'm not doin' it with ya standing there, am I?'

Johnny shook his head and turned his back on him. 'You can do it behind the tree. I won't look.'

'I'm not.'

'You're not what?'

'I'm not doing it.'

Johnny turned round. 'What are you talking about? You said you wanted to piss.'

'I'm not seeing that doctor.'

Johnny cursed under his breath. He'd fallen for it. The bastard had planned it, all the while pretending to be asleep.

'For fuck's sake, Nathan,' he said, frustration and anger making him brittle. 'You have to.'

'Please don't make me go, Johnny.'

He sounded pathetic now.

Johnny shook his head. The morning air cooled his temper, tried to reason with him, find a way out, but all he could think of was getting him to the appointment. 'The doctor needs to check you out. He'll get you sorted,' he repeated. 'I promise.'

'You know that's shit, don't ya?'

He did. A sixteen-year old kid had seen through the whole system.

'They're gonna put me on some shit. Well, I'm not takin' it.'

'You don't have to. You just have to listen to him. If you don't want help, you can say so. No one's forcing you. You understand?'

'Yeah, I understand.'

There was a curious look in his eye that Johnny hadn't seen before. Normally, he could read him like a baby. When he was angry he screamed, when he was happy he laughed, when he was pissed off he'd piss on you. But now his face was blank and Johnny couldn't tell what he was going to do. 'Just get in the car, Nathan. We'll talk it through.'

Nathan twitched, shook his head, and ran right past him. He couldn't have stopped him if he'd tried. Nathan ran straight across the road, vaulted the low, stone wall, and landed on the grassy bank of White Hough Water.

Johnny ran after him. 'Nathan, where the fuck are you going?'

'I told you there was another way, didn't I, Johnny?' said Nathan and jumped into the clear, cool water. He bent down, cupped his hands, and threw it high into the air over himself, then kicked and splashed his way to the far bank like a ten-year-old.

Johnny looked into the water, wondered whether he should follow him in.

Nathan looked at him. 'See ya, Johnny.' Then he turned and ran.

Johnny swore. There was no choice. The water was icy cold and the current faster than it looked. He slipped on some loose stones, had to grab the long grass on the far bank and haul himself up. Nathan was already fifty metres ahead, racing up the hill on the other side. He watched him disappear into a copse of trees. He knew he'd never catch him running. Nathan had twenty-five fewer years on him and over twenty-five fewer pounds.

'For fuck's sake,' he swore.

The hill rose up steeply and the rain started to come down. At the top, he could see the land in every direction, the rolling, supine hills of farmland and cottongrass, the fields where sheep grazed motionless as time. Above them, to the west, stood Pendle Hill, its shadowy sides carved like an ancient barrow, its peak hidden by low forming cloud. To the north, over the brow of the adjacent hill, were Black Moss Reservoirs; and to the north-east, the black and forbidding spruces and pines of Aitken Wood. Running towards them, and far out of reach and earshot, was Nathan.

He'd lost him.

Johnny clutched his chest, breathed deeply. The palpitations were stronger this morning. He got out his phone but couldn't get a signal. He had to make a choice: follow Nathan into Aitken Wood or ring the office and let them know. Either way, the kid wasn't going to his appointment.

He shook his head, angry at himself. He went down the hill, back to his car. He picked up a signal again. Daphne was going to ask what happened, of course, see whether he could have done anything else, if he'd missed anything. If she was really pissed off, she might make him fill in her new care plan template.

Luckily, he went straight to voicemail.

'Daphne, it's Johnny Malkin. Nathan Walsh was meant to have an appointment at Calderstone this morning. Unfortunately, he's done a runner while we were on the way there and I can't find him. Can you give me a call back as soon as you get this, let me know what you want me to do?'

He hung up and felt another tremor in his chest.

Daphne looked pensively across the desk at him, confusion written all over her face. The laptop had given her no clue as to what to do. 'I just don't know how you could lose him.'

'He ran off.'

'Have you tried to ring him?'

'Yes, but he's not picking up.'

'Has he done that before?'

'Regularly.'

She looked at the laptop, took solace in the keys and the reassuring rules she had brought up on screen. 'So we don't need to get in touch with the police?'

'Is that a question?'

'I was thinking out loud, but feel free to answer.'

'Is he technically a missing person?'

'We don't know where he is, do we?'

'He's in a wood.'

'Are you being deliberately facetious, John? Considering you let him go, I think the least you could do is treat things seriously.'

Johnny pulled his chair up, put his hands on the table. 'I'm deadly serious. If we report him missing now, we'll get the police involved. He won't like that. And I don't, either. He'll panic, do something crazy as soon as he sees them, breach his bail conditions, and then he'll be back inside. More than likely, they'll keep him in. That's if they've got anyone left to guard the cells. When I came in this morning, every officer in the north of England seemed to be on patrol.'

'I'm not sure we can leave him.'

'Well, you asked for my advice.'

'I did. And I've noted it down.' Her fingers brushed the keys and she gave him a sudden, furtive look, as if she'd just remembered something. 'How's Jenna Dunham?'

'I'm putting her report together now. I'd have done it before if you hadn't got me chasing Nathan Walsh.'

'You need to manage your time better, John,' she said. 'If you kept a diary, you'd be able to see where you're up to.'

'If I filled in your diary forms every day, I'd have no time to visit anyone.'

She typed some more on the laptop, probably a note on how uncooperative he was.

'You've been to her school?'

'Yeah. They seem to think Alisha was the problem.'

'In what way?'

'Where she went, Jenna followed.'

'That's sad.'

'So's life. Hopefully, we can turn hers round.'

'How about mentally? Is she coping?'

'She's defensive and angry, and in love with the guy who pimped her. I was going to recommend some counselling, draw up a family care plan. What do you think?'

'I think that's an excellent idea. We've had some very good results with psychotherapy. Get me the report as soon as you can.'

'What about Alisha? You want me to try her again?'

'Her family won't give us access.'

'Speaking to her could be very helpful.'

'For who?'

'For all the other girls in the same boat. She might talk.'

Daphne gave him a strange look, like he'd missed something. 'I don't think that will be necessary now.'

Not necessary?

'I thought you wanted me to find out what was going on?'

'We had a memo, John.'

'A memo?'

'From the council. With all that's going on, they don't want us to alienate the community.'

'Oh, for fuck's sake,' he said.

'You've seen what's it's like out there. They think that investigating grooming cases at the moment will only make things worse.'

'So we're going to drop it?' he asked, incredulous. 'Let them get away with it? We're talking about sexual abuse here, aren't we? I mean, two girls have just been raped.'

'They know that, John. But we have to tread carefully.'

'It's the bastards who did it who should be treading carefully. Have the council said the same thing to the police? Asked them to park things to one side while they try to figure out how to get everybody back together again? It's all fucking bullshit.'

'It's an order, John.'

He got up. 'Well, it's a crap one. I'm off.'

'Where are you going?'

'I'm going to talk to Jenna Dunham, get your report finished. Let me know if you hear from Nathan.'

He heard Daphne's chair scrape across the floor, then the clacking of stilettos. 'You can't go yet, John. We haven't finished.'

'Yes, we have.'

'No, John. You were chosen, remember. You have a job to do. The town is relying on it.'

The hairs on the back of his neck stood up and he froze.

Chosen.

A shadow fell across the normally bright and cheery room. He tried to turn but fear of what lay behind made it impossible. Cosette's face in the *Les Mis* poster on the wall became suddenly misshapen. The nose lengthened and the jaw stuck out. *Tap.* Was that her stilettos on the floor? *Tap* again. No, it was too slow. Wood on wood. *Tap.* It was coming towards him. He knew what it was: the sound of a long, slender cane. *He* was coming for him.

Tap. He felt a hand on his shoulder and turned to face his adversary.

'John? Are you okay?'

He wasn't.

19

2.08. Burnley. Shaf sat nervously in the back of the TAU carrier outside the old police station. He'd been at home the nights of the previous riots but now he was in the thick of it. The streets were lined with riot police in NATO helmets all carrying their shields, and battalions of horses nervously stamping but, so far, there was no sign of trouble.

The silence outside was broken by a heavy knock on the metal door and an officer in a yellow jacket climbed in. 'Fuck, it's parky out there,' he said, rubbing his gloves together. The Darwen intonation was unmistakeable. DCI Ali closed the door with a loud clang and sat down opposite him. He took his hat off. 'Sorry about this,' he said. 'They've roped me in. Local knowledge.'

Shaf looked bemused. 'They're putting you on the front line, sir?'

'Afraid so. Last night was crazy.' He unzipped the top of his jacket. 'And dangerous. I'd have preferred your mum's. How is she?'

'Fine.'

'You told her where you were going?'

'Not exactly. But she'll be better when I'm back.' Shaf thought of her fretting by the curtains and hoped it wouldn't take long.

'Well, let's see if we can oblige. What have you got for me?'

Shaf was momentarily tongue-tied. He hadn't thought about where to begin. 'I think I've found a lead to your grooming gang.'

There was a silence, deeper than that outside. 'You have? That was quick work. Who was it? Someone on the list?'

Shaf got a notepad out of his pocket and slowly wrote on it. When he was done, he tore out the top sheet, folded it up, and handed it to the DCI.

DCI Ali smiled. 'You're learning.'

Shaf unfolded the sheet and looked down. If the name took him by surprise, he didn't show it. 'You're sure?'

'As sure as I can be, sir.'

'We've been trying to get the bastard for six months.'

'You should have got in touch with me sooner.'

DCI Ali gave him a half-smile but there was a wary look in his eyes as if he didn't quite believe him. 'We need to stick together, you and me, Shaf. We can't let this bastard get away. You understand?'

Shaf nodded but inside his heart was racing. He wondered whether he'd done the right thing. Before he could say anything, there was another bang on the van like someone had taken a hammer to it. A riot officer in blue opened the door. 'About fifty IC4's have gathered outside the Muscle Factory on Daneshouse Road, sir. More on the surrounding streets. Maybe up to a hundred.'

'Any sign of the EDL?'

'None, yet, sir. What should we do?'

DCI Ali paused. 'What did the Chief Constable say?'

'We haven't heard, sir.'

'Right. I want two units to park up on Colne Road at the junction with Hebrew Road. Then I want two others on Brougham Road by the community centre. The Jamia Masjid is next door so watch your step. Keep in your carriers till you hear otherwise.'

The officer nodded and shut the door with a clang.

'It's impossible for them, isn't it?'

'Who, sir?'

'The white lads. If they go in hard, they're accused of being racially insensitive. If they don't do anything, they're not doing their job. You imagine what's going to happen if they enter that mosque and someone gets hurt? The whole place is going to go up in flames. It'll be the start of the end.'

Shaf froze. It was the expression Tib and Beth had used. He looked at DCI Ali and tried to work out who was kidding who here. Had he been set up or was all this just coincidence?

'What if they have no choice, sir?'

'There's always a choice. That's why the Chief Constable gets paid his two hundred k. To make it for them. Come on.'

'What about the bastard you're after?'

'I want the evidence on my desk first thing in the morning. That's if there *is* a morning.' He opened the back door and got into a squad car behind it. 'Get in. I'll run you home. We don't want your mum worrying, do we?'

Shaf watched the TAU carrier fill with blue stormtroopers. Makrolon shields and riot helmets covered their tired faces. For a moment, worry about telling DCI Ali was replaced with the prospect of driving through the front line. He wasn't dressed for a fight, had never been near a riot, but he'd spoken to enough who had, and the story was always the same. You went in with the best of intentions, trying to keep the peace, and then strain and fatigue, fuelled by years of seeing injustice triumph, made a mockery of them. This was a chance to get the scum back. The law turned a blind eye to personal vendettas during a riot.

DCI Ali reversed the Ford Mondeo at speed, locked the wheels and screeched down Parker Lane towards the library. He burned rubber turning right on to Red Lion Street and then burned some more on Centenary Way. The blue light shone on top but the sirens were silent. Shaf felt sick. He guessed the DCI must have done traffic duties at some point because he drove like a madman without glancing in his mirrors.

They hurtled over the Yorkshire Street roundabout and catapulted past Poundstretcher on to Church Street. They hit sixty over the Brun and Calder and passed Thompson Park. Then, at the junction with Hebrew Street, DCI Ali hit the brakes hard. It looked like an army of ghosts were strung across the road. Ten, twenty, thirty of them in white sheets, then more on the pavements. 'Fuck,' he said, trying to reverse, but one of the TAU vans he'd ordered was blocking the way.

'What do we do?' asked Shaf.

'We stay where we are,' the DCI said. He got on the radio and ordered backup but was powerless to stop the ghost army slip by them in the night. The ghosts had white faces with red crosses painted on them and marched down Daneshouse Road in an unending line.

The car radio crackled with news. Fights had broken out by the Jamia Masjid. A police car had been overturned and set on fire.

'Do we move in?' came a desperate voice.

He could hear Gold 1, the Chief Constable, in the background, urging caution while trying to issue instructions, but no one was listening. Events had overtaken him. Local commanders strained at the leash, their dogs baying for blood, and their police horses in the side streets, blinkered and frightened, sensing the moment was near.

At first, Shaf thought it was rain coming down, or hail. It hit the windscreen hard – snip, snap, snip, snap. Then he realised it was stones, thousands of them, so that the air seemed thick with swarms of insects. Then there was a loud bang on the bonnet. Shaf held his arms in front of his face and glass shattered all around him.

'Get in the van behind!' shouted DCI Ali.

They dived out. Behind them was a Makrolon shield wall. The thin blue line had not been breached. Ghosts ran up and threw anything they could get their hands on. There were too few officers to withstand such fury.

'Fall back!' shouted DCI Ali, and the shield wall retreated down Colne Road, step by step. A roar of mocking laughter came up from the ghosts.

'Do we move in?' came the voice on the radio again. It waited forlornly for a reply, then static cut in. Sirens finally sounded in the distance. There was no need for secrecy now.

The ghosts ran down Daneshouse Road just as the convoy arrived. Officers spilled out onto the streets, batons ready. Police dogs, snarling in their handler's grasp, slavered and bayed for blood. Shaf shivered in the cold. It was like Fang had returned.

'Come on!' shouted DCI Ali, 'Get in.' He climbed into the front of the leading TAU carrier and roared at the driver. 'We need to cut them off before they reach the Muscle Factory!'

The carrier backed up, cut down Devonshire Road, the flashing blue light reflecting off the car windows and sending quicksilver shadows down the road. The driver made a sharp right on to Elm Street and hurtled towards Daneshouse Road. They were too late. A large mob had gathered on the waste ground opposite the Flooring and Furnishings warehouse. They were aiming missiles at a larger mob by Top Break snooker hall. Skirmishes had broken out. For the first time, the scale of the riots hit Shaf. This wasn't just the EDL fighting. It was everyone, Asian and white. A madness had come over them. People were fighting for their community, their property, turning on their neighbours. And the police were caught in between.

Fists, feet, sticks and stones were aimed at the TAU carriers. Shaf felt the van shake as the mob tried to turn it on its side. Officers climbed out the back and brought their batons down on anything that moved, no questions asked. He saw an Asian lad in a white shalwar kameez, maybe fourteen or fifteen, aim a brick right at the windscreen. It rebounded off the metal guard. Then, at the same moment, the boy was levelled by a blow to the head. The police officer who felled him brought the baton down again and again, crushing him.

'What the hell's going on?' Shaf whispered.

The raucous sounds of fighting shocked the night air. There was a huge roar, and a mini-army, maybe two or three hundred strong, came charging up the road from the direction of the Muscle Factory gym. They brandished snooker cues and iron bars and, fuck, yes, machetes. The police braced themselves but were totally outnumbered. Officers went down like a stack of cards, folding their hands.

DCI Ali called desperately on the radio for backup. The driver tried to get the van away but there were too many people around. Then, someone managed to jemmy his door open and he was dragged into the mob. Shaf felt sick with fear. So, this is what duty meant. He kicked the passenger door open and entered the fray the way his father would have wanted. It was his own people outside, staring up at him, like he was on a horse at the head of a phalanx of riders. They would listen to him when he told them to go home. But they didn't. They grabbed his yellow jacket and manhandled him out of the van and he was staring up into wild faces that he didn't recognise. '*Bahen'chod, ma'chod*, sister fucker, mother fucker, fuckin' traitor, bro, you fuckin' white bitch.' And someone levelled a punch at his head. Smack, it sent his head back on the pavement and nearly knocked him out. 'You're on the wrong fuckin' side, bro.'

It was the story of his life, if only anyone would have listened. It flashed by in front of him. At school, at home, there was no escape. And he had a fleeting memory of a summer day long ago – Clitheroe Grammar First XI, when he *Wasim Akramed* Burnley Grammar for 74. Dad was watching from the pavilion, Stephen Taylor behind the stumps. He jumped on top of him the moment the last wicket fell. The back of his head hit the ground with a similar thump. It nearly knocked him out, but it was the other feeling that had a more lasting effect. It was the day he realised he was batting for the other team. And, for a brief moment, the snarling Paki scally on top of him transformed into sweet Stephen Taylor, with his blond hair and selfless, blue eyes. Then cold reality wound its way back. The pain in his head brought him lurching back to the present.

A police baton knocked his assailant over. An officer knelt down, asked if he was okay, and grasped his hand in a simulacrum of friendship. Still reeling, he was led behind the police lines. He heard dogs barking nearby and what sounded like horses. He thought again of his father in the picture on the wall. Was he coming to the rescue? No. It was someone else. He heard the familiar voice at the front. DCI Ali was ordering the officers to complete a short shield advance, taking control for Queen and country. Sweat dripped off them as they approached the burning cars and masonry. DCI Ali ordered another short shield advance, trying to separate the rioters. Officers negotiated the barricades of burning vehicles and rubble. Missiles of masonry, petrol bombs, fireworks, bottles and street furniture landed at their feet. In the fiery darkness, scaffolding poles, knives and machetes glinted – anything the mob could get their hands on. For a moment, it looked like they had pushed on too far and entered hell. The pressure cooker of violence was about to explode.

Then the horses swept down the road from the direction of Brougham Street, over the canal, towards them. The rioters were scattered like chaff. Pandemonium and panic took hold. The police line on Daneshouse Road buckled under the weight of the fleeing mob but did not break. The two mobs were now separated.

Insults were thrown across the blue barricades, more incendiary than any missile. Shaf looked at the sea of red crossed faces on one side, their mouths declaiming Allah, ISIS, the Prophet, anything that would stoke the fires of bigotry and hatred. Then he looked at the sea of swarthy, brown faces on the other side, declaiming Queen and country and anyone who had died in worthless foreign fields defending them.

He began to feel faint. The cold made the blow to the back of the head ache and throb. It was then he saw him in the shadow of a streetlight, standing black and upright – a tall, slender, misshapen man. He seemed to be directing things from the side like a conductor, whipping the mob into a frenzy. And like a conductor, he was carrying something in his hand – a baton; no, not a baton – a cane. Then he disappeared and there was just a lamppost, standing tall and still.

Shaf scanned the rioters, wondered how he could have disappeared so quickly. Then, suddenly, a spark lit in the middle of the mob and a flame shot high into the air. There was a cheer and a police car was set on fire. Things were going to get worse. The horses knew it, too. They stamped nervously, feeling the heat. Then streaks of fire were flung across the sky, the luminous comet tails of Molotov cocktails. They hit the police lines and burst into flame. Horses bolted, dogs barked, and officers ran.

He heard shouts from the vans, did what he could to help. DCI Ali was nowhere to be seen. He was out on his own, as they all were: tired, frightened men at the end of their tether.

People are going to die, he thought. *No one'll get out of here.*

He tried to help the injured that came back from the front line. Some were pouring with blood where missiles had landed or machetes had hacked at them. As he bent down, he noticed that his own jacket was stained with something. It was over his arms and his collar and then he felt it trickling down his neck like ice.

'You're bleeding, mate,' an officer said. 'Sit down. Wait for an ambulance. They're on the way.'

He put his hand to the back of his head and it felt wet and cold. He sat on his haunches, looked about him as the casualties mounted and prayed they'd all live to see the day. It *was* the start of the end. The Cult of Black Moss was no longer a group of lunatics. He believed them now.

The seeds of insurrection had been sown years ago, in small, overlooked, back-to-back terraces, far from the bright lights of Burnley, or Blackburn, or Manchester. Where family had turned on family after the death of an old woman's cow, and rumour of witchcraft swept through the country, blighting the land with injustice, now street turned on street, and race turned on race, over a dead prophet's book, and the whole world was turned upside down. This was its rotten fruit, falling from the sky like pestilence. The Hobbledy Man extended his stick over the valley and the world went dark as night.

He closed his eyes, wondered what he could do to help stop it. And *Him*.

He was out there somewhere, he knew.

20

Johnny rang Mrs Dunham to let her know he'd be there. She sounded slurred and tipsy. When he got to the small, white terrace, she was waiting in the doorway, smoking a cigarette. She gave him an empty smile and looked embarrassedly at her fag. 'I only have one when I've had a drink.'

He nodded understandingly.

'I know it's a bit early,' she said. 'We had a bit of a barney.'

'With Jenna? What happened?'

'She ran off. She didn't want to go to school.'

'Any ideas where she's gone?'

She took another drag on her cigarette. 'When she's cross, she sometimes goes up to Marsden Park and sits on the swings.'

'If she comes back, can you give her my number? I need to talk to her.'

She took the card and read the name. 'I've always wanted a card.'

'You can keep it. I'll go and look for her.'

'You do that, John Malkin,' she said. 'And if you find her, bring her back with you. I want a word with her, too.'

He felt the cold, bedraggled loneliness of a woman on the verge of a nervous breakdown. He got back into his car and sped up Walton Lane. He should really have got a cappuccino from Starbucks to ward off the exhaustion, but he had to see her. It wasn't just the police that wanted answers.

She was just where her mother said she'd be, sitting on the toddler swings in a white fleece top and blue jeans. She didn't try to run off when he approached, just gave him a wary look. She threw her

143

hair back and the fine, blonde strands caught the breeze and the glare of the sun. 'Have you come to take me home?' she asked.

'No.'

'Good, because I'm not going.'

She pushed the swing with her foot, gently rocking herself. He looked round the play area. 'I went to your school and talked to your teachers.'

'Do they want me to come back, too?'

'They said they were all thinking of you and would help any way they could. Ms Houghton, particularly.'

She stopped her swinging.

'She said you'd really got into "Wuthering Heights". I remember doing it when I was your age.'

'I didn't think it was that old.'

'Nice one,' he said, then flung out a hook. 'The only reason I remember is because of this girl called Debbie. I had a massive crush on her. She always used to read the part of Cathy and I used to imagine we were out on the moors together. She didn't know it, of course. I was just the spotty kid in the corner. Anyway, one day, Mr Collins, our teacher, picked me out to read Heathcliff. It was the bit where Cathy and he first met on the moor. I just couldn't get my words out. I kept looking at Debbie and she kept waiting for me to say something. And I couldn't. Everyone in the class knew why. Everyone except Debbie.'

'You're sadder than I thought,' she said.

'Cheers.'

She looked up quickly. 'I didn't mean that. You're okay.'

'Thank you.'

She got off the swing and looked in the direction of Pendle Hill. 'Did Ms Houghton tell you anything else?'

'About what?'

'About me and Alisha.'

'No.'

'You're not a very good liar, John.'

'Who said I'm lying?'

'Miss Houghton did. She rang me yesterday.'

He did his best to keep calm. The conversation was meant to be confidential. 'I didn't realise you were that close.'

'I was going to tell you about Aitken Wood, anyway.'

'You were?'

'Yes. We heard your name mentioned there.'

The fear that had gripped him in Daphne's office came rushing back, formed a Hydra head of paranoia. Did everyone know each other? Were they all sharing secrets about him? 'What are you talking about?' he said.

She sensed his uneasiness. 'We were walking along the Sculpture Trail and there was this weird guy on a wall by an old wheel. He was just standing there looking at us and, at first, we thought he was one of the sculptures. Then he started to move and we were frightened so we ran off, but he kept following us.'

'Don't tell me,' he said, suddenly realising where it was all going. She'd spoken to Ms Houghton. They'd concocted the whole thing. 'He walked with a hobble and he carried a stick?'

'You've seen him?' she asked.

'Yeah, he's called the Hobbledy Man. Did you speak to him?'

'Alisha did. She asked him who he was and why he was following us.'

'And what did he say?' he said.

'He asked us if we'd seen you.'

The sun went in and her hair lost its lustre. She was lying. She *had* to be lying. He felt like grabbing hold of her, shaking her like a straw doll, and telling her what he thought. He knew she was up to something: her, Nathan, Ms Houghton, Daphne, everyone. They were trying to drive him mad.

'I don't believe you,' he said. 'You're making it up.'

She looked hurt. 'Why the hell would I do that?'

He took two steps towards her. 'You tell me.'

She looked frightened and backed away. 'You're acting weird, John.'

He was. Mental and physical exhaustion were eating him up. 'Can Alisha verify all this? If you rang her now?'

'She could. But I haven't spoken to her since it happened. Her mum won't let her out. She said she was going to run away the first chance she had.'

'So, ring her,' he said, and held his phone out.

She stopped, shook her head. 'I can't,' she said.

'Why not?'

'She hasn't forgiven me.'

'For what?'

'For us getting attacked in the woods that night.'

'You weren't attacked in the woods. The police report said you were attacked in the car park.'

'It's not true.'

So now the police statement was wrong. How many fucking lies was she going to tell?

'My boyfriend gave us some K. That's all he did.'

'You told me he'd given you to his mates and they'd raped you.'

'I don't know who raped us. I couldn't bloody see their faces. But we were attacked later.'

He felt a tightness in his chest, put his hand on his heart. 'I can't help you unless you tell me the truth, Jenna.'

'I've already told you and I've already told the police,' she said defensively. 'I led Alisha into the woods. I thought we could escape that way. But there were these figures in the trees that were following us. I don't remember much because the K had kicked in. Alisha was terrified and kept falling over, but I kept picking her up. We reached the Sculpture Trail and I knew the way out, but then we saw him by the wheel and he'd changed. He was wearing this big bird mask with a huge beak and he was holding a big stick. We were so frightened and tired, we could barely run. We tried to get away but only found this pool.'

At the mention of the bird mask and the huge beak, Johnny thought of the picture of the plague doctor and the nightmare of one emerging from Kat's womb.

'Alisha started to scream but one of those figures came out of the woods and struck her. She started to cry. They were all wearing masks and we couldn't see their faces. They made us kneel on the ground.'

She was crying now.

'Jenna, don't...'

'Don't you want to know now? So you can help me? They made us look at their dicks, you bastard. It was fuckin' disgusting. And then the one with bird mask made us take our clothes off and he put masks over our eyes and raped Alisha. And then he raped me. Little bits come back every day, and then little bits drop out. I don't even know what I remember most of the time. But what I did remember, I told the police.'

Johnny shook his head.

'I led her into the woods. If we hadn't gone there, Alisha wouldn't have been raped.'

'You were trying to save her, Jenna.'

'No.' She shook her head. 'It was my fault she was there in the first place. I introduced her to Tariq. I told her to come along with us.'

'You didn't know what he'd do.'

'Didn't I? We used to play Dare together at school. Everyone thought she did everything because she talked a lot. But she didn't. I shouldn't have dared her. Tariq has a bad side. He liked her and I was jealous.'

Johnny's anger was buried in an avalanche of guilt. He'd fucked up, lost sight of what he should have been doing – looking after her. 'That's some confession.'

'It's what people say when they're about to die, isn't it?'

'Who's going to die?'

'We all are.'

'The end of the world, right?'

'What's going on in the town is just the start.'

'You can't believe all that stuff?'

'It's written down. There's a group called the Cult of Black Moss, run by a guy called the Plague Doctor. He knows what's going on. It's all just starting, just as he said it would. The riots, the fires, spreading through the land.'

'But there's a way to stop it, right?'

'You know there is,' she said, and stared at him through the curtain of her long, blonde hair. She was more than pretty, in truth. In a different time, a different place, she could have been a model, or an actress, just not in this one. 'Go and see the Plague Doctor,' she said. 'He'll tell ya.' She ran off down Walton Lane.

'I'm meant to be helping *you*, not the other way round!' he shouted after her. 'Offering you counselling. I'm meant to be writing a report.'

'I don't need any help,' she called back. 'You do.'

He pulled the chain on the swing and smacked the seat in frustration. He'd lost both his clients within the space of twenty-four hours.

21

S haf sat in the passenger seat of the unmarked Golf and rubbed the back of his head. The doctor had put stitches in it last night but it hadn't numbed the pain. Nor did the painkillers. They were outside a house on Cliffe Street. Half the street had already been knocked down; the other half was waiting. To say it was condemned would have given it the appearance of life. Rather, the squat terraces were just waiting to slip their necks in the noose.

Shaf felt the same way. Last night had left him shell-shocked. It wasn't just the violence that he'd seen, but the hopelessness of it all, the feeble line in the sand that was all that separated the good from the bad, the right and the wrong. Sitting in the Golf beside DCI Ali, and with two strong-armed, white, plainclothes officers behind him, he no longer knew which side he was on. Everything was as grey as the weather. Mum hadn't wanted him to go out this morning, but he was beyond the age when a sick note could excuse him. When the Golf turned up on the drive at 8 a.m., his first thought was that he was going to be carted off to the cells, but DCI Ali was primed and ready for something else and wanted him to be part of it. The two white officers got out the back and disappeared down an alley at the end of the street. DCI Ali tapped the steering wheel and stared at the silver Skoda Rapid on the other side of the road. 'That's definitely his?'

'Yes, sir.'

'What have you got on him again?'

'There was an incident on Walton Lane a few nights ago. A resident reported a possible carjacking. The same car was seen outside Marsden Heights community college, parked on Halifax

Road. Neighbours reported the two male occupants acting suspiciously.'

'That's not much.'

'The same car was caught on CCTV outside Pendle Rise shopping precinct and the registration taken.'

'Paki on a double yellow?'

Shaf grinned, though he'd heard the joke a thousand times before. 'No, sir. Two schoolgirls got in. Descriptions matched those of Jenna Dunham and Alisha Ali.'

'Well, fuck me. What a coincidence. Anything else?'

'He's been done for ketamine possession. You'll remember Jenna and Alisha had taken ketamine the night they were attacked, sir.'

DCI Ali stopped tapping the wheel and looked at him. 'That's excellent work, Shaf. Really. Pleased to have you on board. Anything on his family?'

'Two sisters, three brothers, father deceased. They live on the other side of town. No previous convictions on any of them.'

'Well, that's going to change. He was in the thick of it last night. Some lovely shots of him lobbing blocks of concrete at our vans outside the Jamia Masjid. We'll see if we can't get the bastard to talk before we get him to the station.'

He got out the Golf and made his way to the house. Shaf followed.

The DCI knocked on the front door and Shaf's heart picked up speed. There was the sound of somebody running down stairs and then some fiddling with the latch.

A face appeared round the edge of the door. It was scruffy, white and female.

'Who are you?'

DCI Ali held a police badge out. 'Police. We're looking for Mohammed Rehman.'

'Never 'eard of 'im,' she said.

There was a crashing of doors in the back and some more thundering down the stairs. DCI Ali pushed open the front door before she had a chance to close it.

'Oi! Get the fuck out of my house!' she screamed.

There was no hallway in the property; the front door opened right into the living room. There was the usual huge plasma screen on one wall, most likely stolen, and a heap of shit everywhere else: dirty clothes, ash trays, bottles of booze and discarded takeaway cartons. An old leather settee was hanging in strips in one corner like someone had just shredded the poor cow.

There was the sound of glass being broken at the back of the house and then a short, violent struggle. A wiry Asian man, dressed in nothing but a t-shirt and trackie bottoms, was frogmarched inside by the two white officers. He had a shaved head with cuts on it and some nasty looking acne which looked as if it was about to explode. His nose had been recently bust and his eyes were swollen.

'Where were you last night, Mohammed?' said DCI Ali. 'You look like you've been in a fight.'

'I was in bed.'

The DCI looked at the scruffy white woman. 'You his alibi?'

'Where's your fucking warrant, you bastard?' she spat. 'You've no right to come into my house.'

The DCI took a piece of paper from his jacket pocket and held it in front of her.

'That's a no, then?'

She backed off. 'Yeah. He was with me.'

'Then he's got a twin knocking round Burnley lobbing blocks of concrete at us.' He nodded at the white officers who yanked Mohammed's arms behind his back and put some cuffs on him. 'I'm arresting you on suspicion of criminal damage and a breach of the peace. I'm sure you know the rest.' He pushed him towards the front door. 'Have a look round the house,' he told the white officers. 'See what you can find. Then impound his car.'

The sky was black when they got outside and it had started to rain. DCI Ali opened the back door of the Golf and shoved Mohammed inside.

'You want me in the back with him?' Shaf asked.

'Leave him. He's not going anywhere.'

He backed the Golf up Cliffe Street and reversed on to Regent Street. With a screech of wheels, he accelerated down Bankhouse Road and back into town. Shaf presumed they were going to the police station to book him but the DCI took Scotland Road out of Nelson and then on to the M65. He wondered what Mohammed was thinking, slunk in the back seat in his t-shirt and trackie bottoms. His face looked worse in the daylight.

They exited the big roundabout just outside Burnley and swung round to K Supplies, then took a narrow road with the banks of the Calder on the right and an industrial estate on the other. Shaf sensed something was wrong and Mohammed must have sensed it, too, because he asked where they were going.

DCI Ali didn't reply. He got out next to a footbridge over the river, opened the back door and grabbed Mohammed. 'Get out, *ma'chod*,' he said.

Shaf had an uneasy feeling in his gut. They were out of sight of the road now, masked by the trees and bushes. A gentle rain fell, enough to make the ground slippery underfoot. The Calder was narrow and shallow but the drop down to it was steep. A low, black, iron railing was all that divided them from it.

'Where's my solicitor?' asked Mohammed. He looked at Shaf, the whites of his eyes filled with fear. Or was it recognition?

Shaf wanted to tell DCI Ali this was not the way things were done. The law was there for a reason. Even if everyone else was breaking it, they still had to stick to it. But it seemed naïve and foolish to say anything, especially with the shit that was happening in the town.

The DCI marched Mohammed to the railing. 'You know what happens to shit like you in Pakistan, Mohammed? They get pushed over the edge. No one asks any questions and no one cares. Aren't you lucky you were born here?'

Mohammed tried to inch away from the edge.

'You get free schooling, a free health service, a nice place to live with electricity generators that don't pack up in the summer, a place to worship and a place to work. You've got shisha bars, nightclubs, that big TV in your house, all there for you to enjoy. So, why do you want to go and fuck it up?'

'I haven't done anything,' Mohammed said.

'You think picking up underage girls in your taxi and pimping them out is a good way to earn a living? You think getting them into ketamine and dope is a good way of keeping them quiet?'

'I don't know what you're talking about.'

'Your silver Skoda was seen outside Marsden Park community college.'

'I've got mates who live round there.'

The DCI pushed him up against the railing again. 'You were also seen in Nelson a few weeks ago, talking to two schoolgirls.'

'I don't remember.'

'Sure you do. It was the same two girls you raped, remember?'

Mohammed shook his head vigorously.

'I hope your car's been cleaned, Mohammed. I wouldn't like to find any long hairs in there. I mean, your hair's very short.'

'You haven't anything on me, *bahen'chod*, otherwise you wouldn't be chatting the way you are,' Mohammed grunted.

The blow came without warning, a hammer blow to the kidneys that would have sent him over the edge if he wasn't being held by his cuffs. 'We don't have to chat,' said the DCI.

Shaf saw the pain rip across Mohammed's face. Now was the time to say something, to act, but his tongue was tied and his hands weighed to his sides.

'We've already got you on CCTV,' the DCI said. 'That's going to send you down for a long time. Now, suppose you tell me who else was with you the night the girls disappeared, and maybe that video will go missing.'

Mohammed looked as though he was about to throw up. 'I didn't fuckin' touch them. Honest, it wasn't me.'

No sooner had he said it than he disappeared. One second DCI Ali had hold of him, the next he was holding on to thin air. There was a shout and a splash and then an ugly silence.

Shaf looked over the edge and saw Mohammed's body in the water, face down, arms tied behind his back, wriggling like a fish. He didn't think twice. He vaulted over the railing after him. The water was deeper than it looked, maybe a couple of feet, and it was cold. The bottom was lined with sharp stones. Mohammed had his face under the water and couldn't right himself. Shaf wondered how deep it had to be to drown a man. He grabbed his t-shirt and hauled him up.

Mohammed choked, desperate for air.

'You're okay,' Shaf said. 'I've got you.'

But Mohammed didn't seem to believe him.

Shaf looked up at the bridge for help but DCI Ali wasn't there. Where the fuck had he gone? He waded to the bank with Mohammed. The rain came down harder, making it hard to see. He blinked and looked up. At first, he thought it was the DCI reaching his hand out to him, but then realised it was no hand. It was a branch of some kind. No, not a branch, it was too even and polished for that. *A cane?* He looked into the shadows from where it came and saw a figure in silhouette. He'd seen it the night of the riots. He'd seen it in Aitken Wood when the girls got attacked. He knew who it was.

'For fuck's sake!' he shouted, and let go of Mohammed, who slipped back into the water, head first.

'Hey, this way!' came a shout.

He looked up and saw DCI Ali on the bank with his hand out. 'What the hell are you waiting for? If the bastard wants to kill himself, let him.'

He yanked Mohammed up again and succeeded in getting him up the steep slope. The ground was wet and muddy and DCI Ali had to pull whilst he pushed.

Mohammed coughed his lungs out and a stream of brackish water came out. Shaf recognised the smell. It was the same black water Alisha had coughed out in the wood.

DCI Ali stood over Mohammed. 'You're lucky the PC's got a heart.'

'You pushed me, you bastard.'

The DCI crouched down next to him. 'I want a name, that's all.'

Shaf shuffled uneasily. He wanted to say something, to right the wrong, but he knew DCI Ali's blood was up and he feared it would go worse if he said anything.

Mohammed gave another cough. 'Tariq Ibrahim,' he said. 'He's the one you want. I don't know anything about the girls.'

There was a long pause. Shaf half-thought the DCI would start again, but he just stood there and let the rain come down on them. 'Get the fucker in, Shaf.'

Shaf helped Mohammed into the Golf. As he walked round to the passenger's side, he glanced into the trees and then across the footbridge. He didn't know what he expected to see, or what the hell was happening, but there was a madness in the air, a sense of foreboding that was more than imagination.

DCI Ali had been gone an hour. Shaf waited alone in the car. Convoys of TAU carriers drove up and down Parker Lane in the rain, ferrying officers to and from the front line. He touched the back of his head where the stitches were and winced. Maybe that was why he was seeing things? He'd knocked himself out, hallucinated. The sight of the Hobbledy Man was a trick of the light, a trick of the brain. It was DCI Ali all along. He saw him coming out of the courthouse in the rain, nonchalant and at ease. He wondered how he lived with the violence, whether he was indifferent to it.

The driver's door opened and a bag of bagels landed in his lap. 'Straight from the canteen,' the DCI said. He tore into one, ate it like a wild dog. When he was done, he stared at Shaf. 'You're not hungry?'

'No, sir.'

'The violence ruined your appetite? Remember what I said. You can't fight a fire with water guns. You need to get used to it.'

'Did you have to go so hard on him?'

'He got off lightly, the dirty bastard. Anyway, it's what you wanted, wasn't it? You put his name forward. We've got to stick together, you and me. We need to trust each other.' His eyes were unrelenting. 'What do you say?'

Shaf swallowed. 'Yes, sir.'

'That's good, because I've put a lot of faith in you, Shaf, stuck my neck out. Which is why I'd like to know why you put his name forward in the first place. That piece of shit has been on my radar for six months. I know everything about him, from where he does shisha to where he has a dump. He's a low-level drug dealer with a shit job driving a private hire and a penchant for chatting to schoolgirls. You'd be surprised how many people that covers. So, when you put his name forward, I thought either I'd missed something or you were protecting someone.'

Shaf swallowed again.

'I asked you to follow John Whittle and, so far, I've heard nothing.'

Shaf thought of Beth and how she'd put her trust in him. 'I'm sorry, sir.'

'So, are you going to tell me?'

Shaf paused. There was no point keeping it in now. 'Whittle's an old friend of Carver at Blackthorn Farm. Carver's farmhands turned up not long after I'd followed him home. Whatever they were discussing, they weren't happy and left in a hurry. Whittle got the Carvers to retract the statement they gave me. He turned up the day after, told them not to mention the screams they'd heard in the wood.'

'You got that from them?'

'From his daughter, Beth.'

'Why did he do it?'

'She claimed he was a member of a cult called the Cult of Black Moss and that he didn't want me, or anyone else, getting close to it.'

For a moment, Shaf thought there was a flicker of recognition in the DCI's eyes. He thought about telling him what he'd seen, about the signs of the ending of the world and the Hobbledy Man. Then the shutters came down.

'I'm not interested in weird, fucking cults, Shaf. I'm interested in nailing the bastard. What concrete stuff have you got on him?'

Shaf got out his phone, opened the folder with Beth's photos in. He was taking a big risk.

'Whittle's been having sex with the girls in the cult. He's been sending photos of them to the grooming gang you're after.' He gave the phone to DCI Ali, saw the expression on his face change. 'The car in the background is Whittle's Jaguar. There's a shot of the registration plate between her legs.'

'Fuck me. He got her to do that willingly?'

'He's been having sex with her since she was fourteen. He threatened to show the pictures to her dad and her boyfriend.'

'Nice.'

'She said the gang are selling girls all round here. Whittle wants to sell her, too.'

'Do you think she'll give a statement if we bring her in?'

'She's terrified of Whittle and what he'll do. She thinks everything will get back to him.'

'We can protect her.'

Another convoy of vans shot by in the rain, sending spray on to the windscreen.

'Can we?'

'We can do our best. Does she trust you?'

'I don't know.'

DCI Ali's eyes lost some of their intensity. 'The girls you found in the wood, Shaf. They accused you of assaulting them. It was one of the reasons I pressed for your release. I wanted to see where you'd run to. Why did Whittle let you off after they accused you? Were you involved with him?'

'I wasn't. I saved their lives. If Carver's statement was changed, maybe theirs was, too?'

The DCI nodded. 'I wasn't in the interview with them. We'll need to get it checked out. Maybe re-interview them.'

Shaf felt slightly more at ease. 'I thought *you* were involved, sir. Setting me up with Beth. Getting me out on a false lead. Finding that stuff out about Whittle.'

'So, that's why you gave up Mohammed?'

'Until I saw how the land lay.'

'It's a good starting point if you're working undercover. Trust no one.'

But there was a darkness in his tone that filled Shaf with foreboding and he wondered if he should have kept silent.

DCI Ali looked at the photos again, then gave the phone back. 'I want those transferred as soon as you can. We're going to go after him.'

'How, sir?'

'We're going to trap him, Shaf. You and the girl are going to be bait.'

22

The television in the office broadcast the news. Even though they were all sitting on the story, it seemed more real than checking outside the window. The pictures were going round the world, with TV crews from France, Germany, America and Australia there. The Pendle Valley was the source of the biggest outbreak of rioting since 1981. The government was on standby, the army called in. Major cities were braced for copycat violence. There were familiar newsreaders on the streets of Nelson, Burnley and Colne trying to get a handle on things. People offered their tuppennyworth on who was to blame but, really, none were the wiser. The Prime Minister had called for calm and promised to take decisive action but last night's violence had rocked the country. It wasn't just Burnley. Towns as far as Lancaster and Keighley had reported rioting and protests. Casualties were mounting up. It was only a matter of time before someone was killed. Now, the Prime Minister was going to address the nation directly. Everyone stared at the screen, waiting to hear what she had to say and if it would make any difference. Everyone except Kat, who sat on the other side of the room, stroking her stomach, looking out of the window, lost in thought.

Johnny made his way across the room. He tapped her on the shoulder. 'Kat, we've got to talk.'

She shook her head slightly and kept on stroking her stomach.

'Where were you last night? I called you.'

She finally looked up as if woken from a dream. 'It's terrible what's going on, isn't it?'

'What?'

'The Prime Minister is going to make a speech.'

'Yeah, I know. It's about time.'

'Did you see the doctor?'

'Kat, I don't want to talk about the doctor. I want to talk about us.'

'You need to see one.'

Several of the office staff looked over at them. The Prime Minister was on the podium now, about to talk.

Johnny got down on his knees, held her hand, stroked it. 'I'm going to,' he said. 'But let's talk about it tonight. Please.'

He heard the PM's familiar, strident tones in the background. 'Our core values of fairness, tolerance and justice are being eroded as we speak. A minority, a dangerous minority, are trying to undermine the very fabric of our country. Unless we act now, and decisively, we risk a descent into anarchy…'

'Will you?'

Her eyes were tired and dead. 'If you like.'

'For this reason, and hopefully for a short period of time, we are sending the army in to assist the police. We cannot allow the violence to continue and we will take all appropriate measures to see it ends.'

Johnny touched her stomach. 'How's baby?'

She looked over him at the TV screen. 'He's well.'

'*He?*'

'She. I don't know.'

She wasn't right at all. He turned to follow her eyes and saw the Prime Minister fielding questions.

'Are you thinking of declaring martial law, Prime Minister? What powers will the army have? Can we blame your mishandling of Brexit for this?'

He glanced across the room and saw Daphne by her door, gesticulating that he should come over.

'I'll be right back,' he whispered to her, but she wasn't listening. She had resumed her vigil by the window.

'Well,' Daphne said when they were inside. 'I don't think things can go on like this, do you?'

'I wouldn't think so,' he said. 'But the army will put a stop to it.'

'I wasn't talking about the rioting. I was talking about you.' She handed him a crisp, white sheet, still warm from the printer. 'And your behaviour.'

He stared at the masthead and the bold letters written across the top. There was no mistaking it. 'A written warning?'

'There's a level of acceptable behaviour we've all got to adhere to, John.'

'Fiddling while Rome burns, eh?'

'What?'

'It's an expression. Occupying yourself with trivial stuff in the middle of a crisis.'

'Yes, I know what it means, thank you. I wouldn't call your behaviour trivial.'

'World War Three's going on out there and you're complaining about my attitude?' He took the piece of paper and ripped it in two. 'There,' he said. 'You can have it back. If you're following correct disciplinary procedure, you need to issue a verbal warning. If you don't want to follow correct procedure, I'll get the BASW involved.'

She stared at the shredded paper. 'We're all struggling here, John. We need everyone on board, not doing what they damn well want.'

'You asked me to help those girls.'

'You don't do that by disobeying orders and walking out when I'm in the middle of talking to you.'

'Someone's got to find out what's going on.'

'That's the police's job.'

'Well, they're not doing a very good job. I went to see Jenna Dunham yesterday. That police statement of hers is wrong.'

'What do you mean wrong?'

'She denies being raped by any grooming gang and she wasn't attacked in the car park.'

'You mean she's changed her story.'

'No.' He paused, realising how stupid it was all going to sound. 'She says they were followed into the woods and were raped by a man with a bird mask on.'

'A bird mask? Is this some kind of joke?'

'Apparently not. She called him the Hobbledy Man, something to do with a group called the Cult of Black Moss.'

For a brief second, he thought he caught a flicker of recognition in her face, before she put her own mask back on. 'We need to get her to see that psychotherapist quickly,' she said. 'Sounds like she's delirious.'

'She was quite the opposite, actually. Very calm and collected.'

'Then why would the police account be different?'

'Why don't we ask them?'

'She's stringing you along.'

'The only way to find that out is if we speak to her friend.'

She looked at him and he knew immediately something was up. 'It's too late for that,' she said.

'Why?'

'Alisha went missing last night.'

'I thought she wasn't allowed out?'

'Her mother said she was abducted.'

'That's crap.'

'There you go jumping the gun again, thinking you know what's really going on and what everyone's thinking.'

But he wasn't listening. He was thinking of what Jenna told him the day before, that Alisha was going to run away the first chance she had. 'Well, at least I'm out there and not making judgements from behind a fucking desk.'

She looked at him coldly. 'Sometimes, front line workers can get too close to things,' she said. 'We need to step back and assess things, then make decisions based on the evidence.'

'Could you, for once, drop the corporate bullshit you're talking, and put your laptop away?' He reached over the desk and shut it. 'Try engaging with me on a human level rather than treating me like a recalcitrant child?' He had her attention now but it wasn't quite what he was expecting: it was if she was encouraging him. 'Tell me, how many hours did you spend on the front line before you got your job? How many cases did you have to deal with? You spend all your time in this office crunching numbers and designing spreadsheets and talking to other managers in your knitting circle without ever getting your hands dirty and dealing in the shit the rest of us have to deal with. And that's why we're in the shit, because people like you don't listen to what people like me are telling you and, even when you're forced to, you don't act on it. You never fucking act.' His voice was raised now and a bitter, desperate anger came out of his mouth. His heart thumped wildly, trying to catch up with the speed of his thoughts. Everything was going wrong, his whole life spinning out of control. 'Those girls,' he said. 'I'm telling you they know something. We need to find out what it is rather than giving them to the doctors and psychotherapists. We're just putting them on a conveyor belt, feeding them into the system, in the hope that somewhere along the line, someone else is going to accept responsibility for them and do something with them. I'm telling you, we can get this sorted out right now. Fuck who it's going to offend, we need to find out who else is involved in this.' He was shaking with anger. The whole left side of his chest hurt. He put his right hand over his heart and willed it to slow down. 'You have to listen to me. Something's going on in this town.'

He seemed to see her through an eyeglass, down a long tunnel that had no end. He blinked and felt faint. She was receding with every second. He clutched the side of the desk to keep himself upright.

Daphne stared at him. 'I don't think you're in your right mind, are you, John?' she said.

'You're right. Me and everyone else out there. And it's going to get a whole lot worse unless we stop it. There.' He pushed the ripped up written warning across the desk. 'You can give me your verbal warning now.'

She said nothing.

He left the room and there was silence outside, too, save for the news on the television. Colleagues looked at him, some sympathetically, some judgementally, but no one said anything. They knew what the score was. They'd overheard everything, bore witness to it all.

He looked for Kat but she was gone, too. Had she overheard? Was this him sorting himself out?

He left without saying a word to anyone, with only one thing on his mind.

Alisha Ali lived half a mile away from Jenna in a small, terraced house on the other side of town. Like many houses in Nelson, it had no front garden, just a door that led onto the street. Johnny couldn't get near the street, never mind the door. There were crowds of people, young and old, milling around Leeds Road, holding banners and waving Pakistan flags and St. George's Crosses. 'Save Our Streets!' came a cry. 'United We Stand!'

He parked on Priory Street near The Zone youth centre. He had a momentary flashback of Nathan, waiting outside with his head shaved, ready to see his new landlord. He'd forgive him anything now if he'd only ring and say he was okay.

There was further chanting down the road. A large crowd had gathered on the corner of Leeds Road and Rutland Street, opposite Hanna Fashions. He saw police vans and heard the sounds of angry confrontation. Most were Asian, although there were pockets of decent-looking white people offering them their support. As he got to Rutland Street, it became harder to move. He saw a reporter in front of a TV camera interviewing some of the protestors. Every one of them wanted to tell their story.

'She was kidnapped on the street, just going to the shops. Our girls aren't safe.'

'The EDL did it. My mate saw 'em take her.'

'They're doin' it cos they think we took their girls but Islam preaches peace, ya know what I'm sayin', so no way was that happenin'. It's just an excuse. Islam preaches tolerance which is why we're 'ere protestin'.'

'Alisha was a good girl. She was never in trouble. She had no enemies.'

The reporter tried to keep her balance as the crowd ebbed and flowed around her. 'But white girls have been attacked by Asian gangs, haven't they? It's happened in Rochdale and Rotherham.'

'There's nothing like that round here. This is a decent town.'

'The violence is caused by the EDL. The media is making Muslims out to be paedophiles. Last week, we were all terrorists.'

'Our shops are being burned, our livelihoods taken away.'

'We won't stand for it.'

'Tonight's gonna be the worst night yet.'

Johnny pushed through the protestors, tried to get to Alisha's house. Their faces were tired and frightened and angry. There were too many there, forced into a bottleneck in the narrow confines of the street. People couldn't even get out of their houses. Then he heard someone on a Tannoy telling people to get back. There were yellow-jacketed police officers on horseback. Banners were unfurled like an army about to march to war. Slowly, the crowd filed out of the street behind the horses and the chants began in earnest. 'Save our streets! Racists out!' Someone had set fire to a St. George's Cross on a pole and waved it in front of the crowd. A cheer went up. England's glory made a last brave stand, then flapped uselessly in the breeze, consumed by flames. The dreadnought was sunk.

Johnny watched them depart with a feeling of terrible foreboding. There was a small knot of protestors and a couple of police officers left on the street, guarding a house. Amidst them was a pole of a woman, with long, black hair and fine china skin. He was drawn to her like he was to her daughter.

A burly Asian man barred his way. 'What do *you* want?'

'I'm Alisha's social worker. It's important I talk to her mother.'

'She doesn't want to speak to anyone.'

'It's very important,' Johnny said. 'It could help find her.'

The burly Asian looked at him dubiously.

'Mrs Ali!' Johnny shouted. The woman stared at him with a dead expression. 'I need to speak to you about Alisha.'

He tried to push past, felt iron hands holding him back.

'Who are you?' she said.

'I'm from social services. I've just spoken to Jenna Dunham. She thinks Alisha may have run away.'

Mrs Ali's eyes narrowed. 'That bitch? She's responsible for all this. She should have gone in Alisha's place.'

Johnny dug his elbow into the burly Asian's ribs and got free. 'Did she ever mention running away to you? Did she ever speak to you about the night she was attacked? It's important you tell me, Mrs Ali.'

The fist caught him flush in the midriff. He doubled up, received a clubbing blow to the back of his head, and then sank to his knees. Was he going down like the dreadnought?

Mrs Ali appeared like a ghost in front of him. 'She doesn't remember anything, you bastard. And, if she did, we wouldn't tell the likes of you.'

He saw the two police officers approaching, felt them lifting him up and dragging him away.

'Are you sure, Mrs Ali?' he shouted. 'Did she mention a group called the Cult of Black Moss? Or the Hobbledy Man?'

But she was out of earshot.

So was he. No one was listening.

23

The crown of Pendle Hill was covered in thick, dark clouds, and fine filaments of silver rain came sluicing out of them across the valley. The water in Lower Black Moss Reservoir chopped and churned under its steady pitter-patter. Shaf stood by the stone wall overlooking it and thought of Grip down at the bottom. He wrapped his coat tightly around him and looked at Beth. She had a thick fleece on and the wind blew her long, brown hair behind her.

'They won't be long,' he said.

'I hope not,' she said. 'My dad said half an hour.'

He turned to look down the path at the old, stone outhouse beside the reservoir runoff. He wondered how long DCI Ali would be. He knew he had to check everything: the masonry, the timber, the slate roof. Nothing could be left to chance.

'You sure this is the best place?' he said.

'He's brought me here before.'

'He likes the outdoors, does he?'

'He doesn't come for the view,' she said laconically.

DCI Ali came out of the outbuilding with the two white officers he'd seen the day before. 'What a shithole,' he said, then turned to Beth. 'You know what you need to do? We need to get it on tape.'

'Okay,' she said.

'The bastard will be out your life for good.'

She glanced at Shaf. 'Will you be there?'

'Yes,' he said. 'Don't worry.'

But he was worried for both of them. He felt her press close to him as they drove back in the car. He looked out of the window at the graveyard of grey, plastic cases where the young spruces were buried and had a feeling of déjà vu.

They stopped by the red telephone box next to The Barley Mow pub. No one was around. She didn't say anything when she got out and neither did he. It was as if they'd never been together.

He watched her hurry down the road towards the Village Tea Shop, a slight willowy girl caught in the rain.

'She needs to be convincing,' DCI Ali said when he got back in.

'She will be,' he said.

'We can't have any fuckups.'

'She knows that, sir. We both do.'

He closed his eyes to wipe the rainwater from his face and tried not to think the worst. It was enough time to miss the Land Rover pull out of The Barley Mow car park behind them and turn towards the Village Tea Shop.

The DCI drove like a man possessed, with multiple things on his mind. 'She's got a soft spot for you, hasn't she?'

'I'm not sure, sir.'

'Take it from me, she does. Pretty girl like that, you could do a lot worse.'

'I don't think my mum would approve.'

'She got someone else lined up?'

Shaf felt the colour come to his cheeks. 'Maybe. I don't know.' It irritated him he couldn't defend himself. He tried to steer the conversation away. 'The girl's damaged.'

'Show me one that's not.' He swerved to avoid a line of traffic cones. 'You'd be good for her after all the shit she's been through. A safe pair of hands.'

The words resonated. It was true. It was all he'd ever been and maybe all he'd ever be. It was what made him a good copper, why he'd been commended at the Neighbourhood Policing Award ceremony. John Whittle told him to his face: 'The force needs more officers like you, PC Khan.' Now, here he was, trying to bring the bastard down.

The radio was going mad with calls. There was another disturbance in Nelson. 'They've started already,' the DCI said. 'Fuck 'em.' He hit the accelerator down the Colne Road. 'I'm going to drop you back home. I need to see the superintendent, get the ball rolling.'

Shaf's stomach tightened. He wasn't in control any more.

Fifteen minutes later, the car pulled up on the drive. 'I'll pick you up later. You're to wait for me, you understand. No fuckups. When I tell Whittle I saw you at the station trying to check the girls' statements, he's going to start sweating. He may send someone round.'

'What do I do then?'

'You ring me.' He took a brown paper bag out of the glove compartment and put it in Shaf's lap. It felt heavy and cold.

'What's this?'

'A Glock 17.'

'I've never used a gun before.'

'Hopefully you'll never have to, but I'm not leaving you unprotected.'

Shaf took it out the bag.

'The internal safety lock is on. Turn this key and you're good to go. Simple.'

'What if I forget?'

'You won't. Take it with you.'

Shaf put it in his coat pocket. His dad used guns back in Pakistan, hunting wild boar and deer. It was part of the ritual of growing up. Put a gun in a boy's hands and watch him become a man. But dad was now dead and the old ways had died with him. England was not an outlaw country, at least on the surface.

He got out of the car and went inside.

Mum was in the kitchen, watching the BBC News.

'The Prime Minister was on before,' she said. 'She's going to call the army out. They're marching through town right now.'

'What for?'

'A girl's gone missing.'

'They've brought the army out for a missing girl?'

He sat down next to her on the sofa, took the remote, and turned the volume up. That feeling of déjà vu came back, like he knew what was about to happen.

'*Kia hai*?' she asked, sensing his anxiety.

'Nothing,' he said.

Her face was on screen. She looked a lot like any girl her age, into fashion and hair accessories and taking selfies. There was life in her big, brown eyes and a long future ahead of her. But he also saw what the picture didn't see – the girl in the woods with black water coming out of her mouth, her dark brown hair and olive skin caked in mud, lying on the bank of a shallow pool. It was Alisha.

'They think she was abducted,' his mum said.

He was on autopilot. 'By who?'

'The EDL.'

'It's impossible,' he said to the girl on the screen. 'I know you.'

The back of his head hurt. He put his hand on it, held it tightly.

His mum shook her head. 'You never listen, *beta*, do you? You should have stayed off work.'

24

The first thing Johnny noticed when he pulled up was that Kat's car was gone. He didn't realise what other changes had been made, but it all sank in when he went to the bathroom and realised her pots and potions were missing, too. It was the same story in the bedroom: her clothes, her shoes were all gone. She'd moved out.

Johnny rang her mobile, willed her to pick up. He was already tired and not thinking clearly. His stomach killed and the back of his head ached where he'd been punched. There was no reply. He heard the beep and was tempted to leave a message, but something stopped him. He wanted to explain everything, get her to believe what was going on, but it was a conversation he needed in person and not one left to the end of the day.

He went downstairs, took out his laptop. If he couldn't solve one crisis in his life, he'd try the other. Jenna told him to go and see the Plague Doctor; he knew what was going on. He found his Twitter page and read the latest tweets. There were more references to *Him* being seen and some lines of godawful doggerel. His followers had jumped from a few hundred to several thousand.

He made his own account, @johnmalkin, was surprised no one had taken it, then followed @plaguedoctor. He wondered what to say to him. *Hello, Plague Doctor, I need your help. Hello, Plague Doctor, how do I join your cult? #Bollocks.*

He needn't have worried.

Seconds later, he was followed back.

@johnmalkin We've been expecting you, John Malkin.

An icy chill swept suddenly through the room.

His fingers fumbled at the keys.

@plaguedoctor What do you mean?

@johnmalkin To fulfil your destiny.

His eyes were fixed on the sinister figure in the bird mask, with its downward pointing beak and red eyepieces, leading the plague victims away. He'd seen it in his dreams. Hadn't Jenna Dunham and Alisha Ali been attacked by something like this in Aitken Wood? The eyes bored out of the screen at him, looking for him.

A direct message came through. He clicked on it and a new conversation pane opened.

@johnmalkin Are you watching the news?

@plaguedoctor No.

@johnmalkin Maybe you should?

He got the remote control, turned the TV on.

The News channel hadn't been changed for days. It was all Kat watched. Where before, there were reporters in the northern towns, now there were ones in the cities: Manchester, Bradford and Birmingham. It wasn't just the old immigrant areas that faced the night with trepidation, either, but all over the country. Poles, Romanians, Latvians and Lithuanians were under attack, from Boston down to Harlow. There were pictures of police in riot gear and convoys of army trucks drawing up. Then there were shots of Nelson and Burnley and Colne, where the trouble had started, and reporters were asking how long it could go on. Surely the storm would blow itself out and people would see sense?

Johnny heard the wind outside, whipping over the house. The room seemed to get colder.

@johnmalkin We can't let it go on.

@plaguedoctor Nothing you do is going to change it.

@johnmalkin It will if we follow what's written.

@plaguedoctor You mean the sacrifice?

@johnmalkin Yes. It's the only way to appease the Hobbledy Man.

@plaguedoctor You're crazy.

@johnmalkin So why are you here?

The wind battered the windows with gust-like roars, as if something was trying to get in. In the distance, he thought he heard the sound of a dog barking and a car door slamming. The volume on the TV made it impossible to tell if it was coming from inside or out. All he knew is that the temperature was dropping.

@plaguedoctor You can prove what you're saying?

@johnmalkin If you're prepared to listen.

He heard more strong gusts. The blue twilight of evening had gone and night took its place. Shadows appeared at the lounge window, playing on the glass like puppets in a marionette show. Here was the string, here was the wood, here was the knife that spilled their blood. There was a noise, too, of something tapping. Again, he thought it had come from the TV. He turned his head, the better to hear.

@plaguedoctor I'm prepared.

@johnmalkin Then come to see me tomorrow.

@plaguedoctor Where?

@johnmalkin The Pendle Inn. I'll see you at midday.

Before he could reply, he saw something appear at the lounge window. It looked like a face, but as quickly it disappeared.

'For fuck's sake,' he whispered. 'What's wrong with me?'

The tapping returned. Only it wasn't a tapping now but a knocking. The wind had drowned it out. Was there someone at the door? Who the hell would be out there in this? The police?

Then he heard a cry. 'John!'

He looked out of the window. There was no one there. Heart pounding, he went to the door and turned the latch. He braced himself.

The wind nearly took the door out of his hands. But that wasn't what shocked him. Huddled in the entrance was Kat.

'What are you doing?' he said, stunned to see her.

'I was knocking for ages,' she said, in tears.

'I didn't hear you. The TV must have been too loud.' But it wasn't. 'Why didn't you use your key?'

'You had it on the snib.'

'I didn't. I never put it on.'

'I'm telling you it was on,' she said, cold and cross.

Another gust blew up; the rain flew in almost horizontally.

'I'm sorry,' he said.

He opened the door fully and the light from the lounge caught it. He hadn't noticed before but there was a mark on the front. Actually, it wasn't one mark but four, scratched faintly into the brown wood. There were three vertical lines going down and one that slanted to the right with a dot on it. He'd never seen them before and he was sure they weren't there when he came in.

'What were you knocking with?' he said.

'My head,' she said. 'What do you think?'

'What do you make of that?' he asked, showing her the marks.

'I don't care,' she said. 'Maybe it's always been there and you haven't noticed?'

He shook his head. Maybe kids had done it, although he couldn't remember seeing any on the street. He looked outside. The sky was black. Pendle Water would be flush with the newly fallen rain. And still Pendle Hill was spewing out masses of smoke like the chimneys did when the factories were first built. The valley would soon be covered. Another gust, more rain, and he shut the door against it.

Kat stood in the centre of the room, her back to the TV.

'You moved your stuff out,' he said.

'I had to.'

'You didn't want to talk about it first?'

'You'd have tried to stop me.'

'Naturally.'

She looked at the TV, then back at him. 'Everyone heard your rant at Daphne this morning.'

'I'm sorry.'

'She doesn't think you're in your right mind, either.'

'I agree with her.'

She paused, as if weighing up what she was going to say next. 'Doesn't that worry you, John?'

'I'm getting used to it.'

'This is not a joke.'

'I'm not laughing.'

'There's three of us to consider.'

He looked at her stomach. 'You're better here, Kat. I can look after you both.'

'You can't even look after yourself.'

It was true. He couldn't even sleep without taking something. 'I'll see the doctor tomorrow.'

'Do you know how many times you've said that?'

'I will.'

She shook her head. 'Why are you pretending?'

'I actually think it's the other way round.'

'What do you mean?'

He hesitated as another strong gust made the lounge window shudder. 'Everyone's got their head in the sand, Kat. They're not seeing what's going on round here.'

She looked at him incredulously. 'John, have you been watching *anything*?'

As if on cue, the latest pictures on the ground were broadcast. There were soldiers patrolling city streets, police behind Makrolon walls, and fleets of vans like berthed ships waiting to sail. Rain had come, and wind – now up to hurricane speed in the Pendle Valley. Weather was always the greatest deterrent to crime. Maybe that would sort them out?

'The whole thing is under control now,' she said. 'The Prime Minister said. These things can't last.'

Johnny shook his head slowly. He didn't know why he said it. It just came to him. 'It's not finished,' he said. 'I've got to finish it. I've been chosen.'

Kat's face crumbled and she started to sob.

He went to her side and sat her down on the settee. There was no escaping that he'd done this to her. If he could just tell her now that he was going to stop it, and if he could get her to believe him, the tears would dry up on her face, her skin would glow again, and the spark return to their relationship. He wouldn't be doing it just for her, either, but for the baby. That was a sacrifice worth making. He put his arm around her, drew her towards him, and kissed her forehead.

'I just want you to stop,' she implored him. 'It's not a lot to ask. The whole world's going crazy, you're going crazy, and now I feel like I am.'

She was right.

'Kat, listen to me.' He put his hand beneath her chin, lifted it up. 'Things are going to be okay.'

She placed the fingers of her left hand on her temple and tapped it gently. For a second, just a second, the middle three were resting there, while the thumb stuck out to the right. 'And do you know how many times you've said that?'

But Johnny wasn't listening. He was trying to remember where he'd seen the pattern her fingers made and then suddenly it came to him.

'Your hand,' he said.

'What about it?'

'It's the same.'

'The same as what?'

It was same as the mark on the door. There was no point explaining it to her. She wouldn't get it. Like she wouldn't believe what Nathan or Jenna had said about him being chosen and the Cult of Black Moss and seeing the Hobbledy Man. She wouldn't believe the Plague Doctor when he said he was going to prove it all to him. She wouldn't understand his dream about her giving birth to a plague doctor astride Pendle Hill and it chasing him. She was on the other side of the hill from him, where everything was black and white and there were no shades in between.

In that moment, he had a brief epiphany. This was how Nathan Walsh felt. No one could possibly understand what he saw. His perception was different. It was the same for Jenna Dunham. What possessed her to go into those woods and convince herself the man who was pimping her was not an evil bastard but someone she was going to end up living with?

'The same as nothing,' he said finally. 'Come on, you can't go back in this tonight. You'll have to stay.'

She looked at him crossly, then dubiously, then sadly and finally resignedly. 'I won't move back until you sort yourself out.'

'I know,' he said. 'But you have to think of baby.'

She looked long and hard at him and held her stomach close. She nodded. 'Yes. I've got to think of baby.'

'I'll make you a sandwich,' he said.

She went upstairs and he went into the kitchen. He made her a tuna sweetcorn and took out a large bottle of Pepsi from the fridge. The baby had funny tastes, she said.

He looked at the laptop before following her. The conversation window was still open.

He typed a reply out.

@plaguedoctor Ok. I'll be there.

The reply came back immediately.

@johnmalkin Each night is worse than the last, John Malkin. We need to act fast.

25

Shaf took the Glock out of the brown paper bag. The black polymer was cold to the touch. He looked at the clock on the mantelpiece. It was just after five and there had been no call. Part of him was relieved but part of him was fearful. He thought of Beth out on the farm, alone. If anything bad was to happen, it would be to her. He wondered if he should call her, see how she was, but orders were orders. Pensively, he aimed the Glock at the clock and imagined pulling the trigger.

There was a knock on the door and his mum came in with a tray of *chai* and biscuits. He put the gun down quickly, covered it with the brown paper bag. 'You've been in here hours, *beta*. Is everything okay?'

'Yes,' he said. 'Just waiting for a call.'

'Work?'

'Yes, mum.'

He looked at the brown paper bag. Part of the gun's frame was sticking out. If she saw it, she'd have a panic attack.

She put the tray down on the table beside him. 'Is it from your new boss?'

'Yes. Something important.'

She paused, looked round the room, as if surveying the contents of their lives. 'It's quiet, isn't it?'

'It helps me work.'

She picked up a photo from the mantelpiece. It was of him and his two sisters when they were at primary school. Funny haircuts, funny smiles and teeth missing, eyes that shone with hope and happiness. 'Ammarah rang before.'

'Did she?'

'She wants me to go over at the weekend. See the kids.'

'No problem. I'll take you.'

He never thought he'd feel it, but he just wanted her away – for her own good as well as his.

'She says she has a friend...'

His ears went deaf. Every so often she tried it and every time he said no. He knew what the quiet meant and what she really wanted. Like every mum, she wanted to rewind the clock, to be with them again when they were young and they needed her, to be surrounded by funny haircuts and funny smiles and watch the clock turn slowly through the seasons, knowing there would be more seasons to come, as long and as fruitful and precious as the last.

A tear sprang to his eye, clung to the lid like a climber to a parapet, waiting to freefall into oblivion. He saw a country churchyard in Padiham on a hot June day. A local crowd, heads bowed the ground, saying prayers, not overloud. His mum took him. It was his first confrontation with the Almighty, and the one that made the least sense. When his father died, he was already prepared. Blood looks the same when you open the veins. He stood next to the gravestone and looked at another weeping mother and father, and brothers and sisters not really understanding what it all meant, other than that the world had changed. His mother felt uncomfortable being there. Her English wasn't great and her clothes made her look more like one of the funeral bouquets than a mourner, but she was thanked for coming and he was allowed to place a wreath over the stone.

Every time his mother mentioned marriage, he'd replay the scene in his mind, still unable to come to terms with the loss.

RIP Stephen Taylor 13 years

A brain haemorrhage had done for him, whatever that was. He knew nothing at the time other than that he'd lost him and that their secret died with him. And that he missed him terribly.

Dearly beloved of **Shafiuddin Khan**.

'I can't, Mum.'

It stopped her dead in her tracks. 'You're not young any more, *beta*…'

'Mum, I can't talk.'

The phone was vibrating in his pocket. He fumbled in his jacket, took it out. It was Beth. He pressed *Accept* and put it to his ear, waited for Mum to leave. The guilt he normally felt was waylaid by fear.

'Hello?'

The line was bad. Her voice cut in and out.

'Shaf, is that you?'

'Yes. What's wrong? You're not meant to ring.'

'John Whittle's been in touch.'

He froze. That wasn't meant to happen. 'What did he want?'

'He was asking about you.'

The line crackled, broke up.

'What did you say?'

'I told him you'd been asking questions. He asked why I hadn't told him. He was really cross, said he wants me to meet somebody and I have to go with him.'

'When?'

More crackling. 'He said now but I said I couldn't because I had to help my dad, so he agreed to come at nine.'

'That's an hour earlier than we planned.'

'He said he wouldn't come later. He was cross, Shaf. He said I better be ready and do what he wants. I'm shitting myself now. You said it would be okay.'

'Beth, just stay where you are. I need to ring the DCI…'

'I can't stay. You've got to get me out of here now.' There was panic in her voice. 'One of the farmhands saw me in the car with you this morning. He must have remembered you. He knew you were police. He told my dad.'

Fuck. The whole damned thing was unravelling.

'Listen, Beth. I'm going to come and get you.'

'Please, Shaf. You have to come quickly.'

The phone went dead.

He looked at the clock: 5.20 p.m. DCI Ali had told him to wait. No fuckups. But that was before this. *Trust no one.* He said that, too. What if this was a setup? Tib could have told Whittle he'd seen him when their Land Rover crashed. He could have told him he was asking about the Cult of Black Moss. Maybe Beth had been forced to ring and it was all a trap?

He removed the brown paper bag from the gun. It was the only friend he had. He had to get Mum away now. He couldn't leave her on her own in case someone came round. Ammarah lived in Darwen, some fifteen miles away. It would delay him getting to Beth, but he had to do it.

He looked at his phone, brought up the DCI's number, and rang.

There was no reply.

Mum didn't say anything on the way. The sky was filled with black clouds and a fierce wind was blowing up the valley. It buffeted the car along the exposed parts of the M65. All the time, his right foot hovered over the accelerator impatiently, knowing that time may already have run out.

He didn't leave a message on DCI Ali's phone. He didn't want a link back to him if something went wrong. But all the time he watched his phone on the SATNAV socket, waiting for it to light up. Where was he?

He dropped Mum off outside his sister's. His nephew and niece came out to say hello and then goodbye. He wasn't staying, he couldn't stay, he had things to do.

His nephew looked up at him, smiling. 'Are you gonna arrest more bad guys, *Mamoo?*'

'You bet,' he said. 'I'm going to lock them all up.'

The little boy produced a water gun from behind his back and fired it at the car. 'Yeah!'

Mum was on the doorstep with Ammarah. He felt an awful sense of doom, like it was going to be the last time he ever saw her. He sped off down the hill, tried to figure out what his life had come to.

You can't fight a fire with water guns.

The rain came down in grey sheets on the way back. Visibility on the motorway was down to twenty, then ten feet. The faster the wipers worked, the faster the rain came down. Suddenly, like a fleet of ghost ships appearing from out of the mist, a long convoy of trucks appeared in the left-hand lane. The Prime Minister was as good as her word this time. Burnley barracks had been emptied and they weren't taking prisoners.

Shaf left the motorway, took a detour through Newchurch, hoping to save time, but got stuck behind a tractor. The roads were so narrow he couldn't pass it. The rain relented but the grey masses above Pendle Hill hadn't moved, tethered to the bald crown. He tapped the steering wheel, desperate to get past. Eventually, the tractor turned into a field and he had the open road ahead of him. The valley floor widened, revealing copses and hedgerows and miles of green, undulating fields. Where the forest had been cleared, a blanket bog lay, wild and desolate, covering the landscape as far as the eye could see. Overhead, golden plover and curlew and black-backed gulls braved the bitter wind.

He reached Barley, pulled up next to the red telephone box by The Barley Mow pub, and tried the DCI again. Still no reply. The feeling of doom got stronger. He spun the car round, drove up to Barley Lane. The chance of being spotted on it was high but, without the car, there was no chance of getting her out of there.

He stopped at the turnoff that led down to the farm and looked towards the main gate. His heart accelerated as quickly as if he'd just put his right foot on it. Whittle's silver Jaguar was there. No matter that the country was up in arms and he should be orchestrating the defence of the town, to him this was more important. What hold did Beth have on him that he would desert his post? What had DCI Ali said to make him act?

He smashed his hand down on the wheel in frustration and anger and defeat. If Whittle was there now, what was he going to do? He couldn't charge the building singlehandedly and break her out of there. He tried ringing her, then realised there was no bloody signal. He was cut off and she was cut off. He backed the car up, drove to the reservoirs. The gate to the outhouse was open. This morning, they'd left it closed. He parked the car round the back of the building, felt the Glock in his jacket pocket, and got out. Other than the wind, the only sound was the water running down the reservoir runoff. He tried her phone again but still couldn't get reception. He should have known. It was all going to happen again like it did in Aitken Wood.

He put his hand on the cold stone and went round to the front of the outhouse. He opened the grey door gently and felt a cold, wet breeze come through it. It was how they'd left it, or seemed to be. He got out his torch and flashed it around the inside of the building. Something flitted into the air in the roof space and he put one hand on the gun. He was minded to turn the key and disable the internal safety lock, but fear of setting it off accidentally stopped him. It was probably just a bat. He put his hand in his pocket, took out the listening devices they were going to use. No point having them now if no one was here.

The door creaked on its hinges, blown back by a blast of wind. He turned quickly and thought something had entered the building with him. His torch made searchlight arcs on the walls and ceiling. It was then he noticed a bale of hay on the stone floor. He didn't remember it being there earlier. Maybe Tib had been here, or Carver himself, and dropped one off? The light of the torch criss-crossed the stone floor. Shorn of daylight and at the angle he shone it, lines appeared, fainter than the cracks and crevices but surer and more cursive as if made by hand.

He touched one. It was clean cut and freshly made. He didn't need to count the lines or see which direction they lay. He'd seen the pattern before, on Carver's door and in the wood, and knew what it was. Someone had been in here after them and put it there.

As he was about to leave, he heard a car door slam. He switched the torch off and looked out. There was a Land Rover parked by the gate. He heard the sound of voices coming down the path and recognised them. One was hers. The other's was…Tib's? Thomas's?

He saw them now in the grey twilight. He wore a fleece jacket and long boots. He was holding her hand, dragging her along like a dandelion behind him, a stalk of a girl in a long, green dress, out of time.

'Please,' she said.

'I canna, Beth. You have to see it through.'

Shaf ducked back inside. There was nowhere in the outhouse to hide except the hayloft. The steps up were wooden and rackety and he didn't feel sure they'd even take his weight.

He flashed his torch along the ground, ran across the stone floor, and took them two at a time. He lay down in the shadows and peered over the edge.

Seconds later, the grey door opened wide and Beth was led in.

'You can let go now. I'm not going to run away.'

There was the sound of a match being struck and then an old-fashioned oil lamp was lit. It was lifted up and Shaf saw Tib's face in the orange glow. 'Someone's been 'ere,' he said. 'Look at the floor.'

Shaf dared not breathe in case he was overheard.

'Maybe it was that kid you saw yesterday?'

'Maybes. He won't last long on a night like this. The Hobbledy Man will find 'im. 'ere, sit down on the straw.'

'It's wet.'

'Well, there ain't no beds here.'

She sat down. Her back was to the hayloft so Shaf couldn't see her face.

'Things are gonna be bad tonight. I never seen the hill so mad.'

'If he finds you here, *he'll* be mad.'

'But he won't, will he? Or I'll tell him you were with that copper this morning. What did he want, anyways?'

'He was asking about those girls,' she said.

'Which girls?'

'You know, the ones in the wood. You helped him get them, didn't you?'

At the mention of the girls, Shaf switched on his phone's voice recorder.

Tib shook his head, agitated. 'That weren't me. Or Thomas. That was 'im on his own.'

'You could have saved them.'

'I could'na. I was'na there.'

He started to pace, swinging the lantern from side to side so that shadows see-sawed across the floor and up and down the walls.

'What if the police find out?'

He stopped suddenly and his face took on a fearful expression. 'Did ya tell 'im?'

'Who?'

'That boyfriend o' yours. The copper.'

'No,' she said adamantly. 'And he's not my boyfriend.'

'Maybes I should tell Whittle, after all?' he said slyly.

She said nothing.

Tib put the lantern down and pulled her to her feet.

Shaf tensed, sensing something bad was about to happen.

'All those times you used to make fun o' me and Thomas, watchin' us in the field all day. Teasin' us with ya looks, bathin' in sight of us. That were wicked temptation, Beth.'

'You and your brother were spying on me through the trees. A couple of Peeping Thomases. You're lucky I never told my dad.'

He grabbed hold of her arm suddenly and turned it behind her back till she cried out. 'And you were lucky I nivver told him what a whore you are.' He turned her round so that she was facing the bale of hay. 'Mr Carver brought us up like his own. We could'na hurt him. But you got found out anyway, didn't ya? John Whittle put you in your place.'

She struggled to get away. 'Get off me now, Tib.'

'He's been sending us pictures of ya, ya know.'

'What pictures?'

'Y'know,' he grinned. 'Nice ones. Thomas and I have 'em on our phones.'

'Well, that's all you're getting,' she said.

'No. Not tonight, Beth.'

'What are you talking about?'

He twisted her arm more and she stopped struggling. 'He said it's all got to stop. We've got to make a sacrifice.'

'We've already tried that.'

'Have we? You know the rhyme. *Out comes the knife to take his life.*'

'What are you saying?'

'He means to kill ya, Beth. It's the only way.'

The words seemed to sap her of all strength. 'You're crazy,' she whispered.

'You kneel on there and do as I say or I'll get him now.'

Shaf reached for the Glock. He brought it out of his pocket slowly, laid it on the wooden beam in front of him. All he needed was to turn the key.

'Take it off now or it'll get ripped,' said Tib.

The green dress came down her body like snakeskin, over her breasts and down her thighs. Shadows danced across her naked body from the lantern. The wind blew in the grey door and nearly put it out.

Shaf stared at her nude form like a boy seeing his mother's for the first time. It was alien and mysterious and dangerous.

'There,' Tib said. 'Ya not so talkative now, Beth.'

She shook her head slowly. 'What do you want?' she said.

'I want ya to let me have my way the way he has his.'

'He'll find out.'

'So, what if he does?'

'Will you let me go afterwards?'

He gave her another sly look. 'I'll consider.'

The wind blew the grey door again and the lantern flickered. A great thunder of rain came down on the grey slate roof. There were rents in the rafters and water came pouring in. Shaf rolled out of the way to escape most of the downpour but there was nowhere that was spared the deluge. The Glock got wet.

Tib was twice the size of her and strong as an ox. There was something clumsy about his overtures. He stroked her long, brown hair and tried to kiss her but she turned her mouth away. Shaf put the gun in his hand and turned the key. Could he really kill a man in cold blood? What if he missed? Could he live with Beth's blood on his hands? Fear oozed out of him. There was something else, too – a horrible, hypnotic fascination in what was happening, as if he were watching a film and only he had the power to yell CUT. He knew he'd never be able to squeeze the trigger, come what may.

Tib turned her round and started to use her like a mare. Her breasts shook and shuddered with each animal thrust. Her eyes again looked up to the hayloft and Shaf wondered if she wasn't looking for him, hoping he was there and would come to rescue her.

Tib started to grunt like a pig.

The rain continued and drowned out his grunts.

And then, suddenly, the lantern light went out and all was plunged into darkness. The wind caught hold of the door and yanked it off its hinges. Shaf looked at the rectangle of grey where the door used to be and he saw shadows moving, blacker than the night, making their way in.

He heard Tib breathing heavily down below.

There was something in the room with them.

One by one, three lights came on, spaced about a metre apart. They illuminated the ground and then the figures that were holding them.

Shaf gulped. The figures were dressed in long, black gowns which reached to the stone floor. All three wore the sinister bird masks he'd seen in the photos Beth had shown him. The Cult of Black Moss had arrived.

26

The figure in the middle held out their light and walked towards the bale of hay. Tib tried to gets his trousers on but a cane flicked out of the figure's hand and struck him hard.

'What are you doing, Tib?'

Shaf recognised the voice instantly.

'I told you to get her ready, not start without us. She's got a busy night ahead.'

Tib nodded, clutched his hand where the cane had struck.

The man called Beth over, put his torch down by his feet, and wiped her down with his gloved hands, as if checking that Tib hadn't damaged the goods. His right hand covered her fleece and tugged at it roughly.

Shaf felt sick, not just with the causal brutality of it, but her willingness to accept it. He wondered again if he'd been set up. Was this some sort of plan to get him here?

'Did you take what I gave you?' the man asked.

She nodded, quite unable to talk.

'And you understand what this is all about?'

She nodded again.

'And you're happy to go through with it?'

Silence.

He sat down on the bale of hay and put his cane on the ground beside him. He continued rummaging his hand inside her. 'Spread your legs.' He excited her right nipple with his free hand and she did as she was told. The man turned his fist this way and that till she started to groan. He dug his hand in almost to his wrist. 'Are you watching, Tib?'

Tib's eyes were on her, burning with desire and jealousy.

'Are you happy to go through with this, Beth?'

The question remained unanswered. She was shaking and groaning on his hand. Her grunts were animal, too, and louder than Tib's had been. Finally, he asked her again and she wrapped her thighs round his gloved hand and kept it there.

Tib watched her. The two plague doctors by the door watched her. Shaf watched her.

She hung her head and shook with humiliation and self-disgust.

The man withdrew his hand slowly, then looked up at the hayloft.

Shaf knew then that something had gone terribly wrong. They knew he was here. It was all part of a game. The only thing he didn't know was what part he had to play in it.

'There's really no point hiding now, is there, PC Khan?'

The words nailed him to the beam.

He watched John Whittle take off his bird mask, his face ruddy with perspiration. 'We saw your car outside. Not the best place to hide it. We should probably talk now before things go further, don't you think?'

Shaf closed his eyes. There was no choice. He stood up and looked down, the Glock in his hand.

'Nice,' said Whittle. 'Glock 17, standard issue. A gift from DCI Ali, was it?'

At the mention of the DCI's name, all Shaf's suspicions and fears were confirmed. Something *had* gone wrong. The unreturned calls, the radio silence; Whittle had found them out. He walked down the steps into the light, determined not to go down without a fight, to do the right thing. 'Why don't you let her go?'

A long, malicious smile appeared on Whittle's face. Beth was standing beside him, her head still bowed to the ground, a trinket, a flesh adornment. 'Why don't you ask her if she wants to?'

Beth didn't move, maybe couldn't move, a mannequin on a shop floor.

'She told me you wanted to save her, Shaf.'

Shaf held the gun out in front of him. 'She told me what you did, you bastard. Sex with a minor, changing witness statements, possession and supply of Class A drugs, running a prostitution racket.'

Whittle's grin broadened to a smile. 'Was that the DCI's homework or your own?'

'It's true, isn't it?'

'I've been a copper a long time. I've forgotten what truth is.'

Shaf heard a click next to his ear and felt something pressed to his head. Deaf to everything but Whittle and Beth, he'd forgotten the other two figures in the bird masks. They were now on either side of him.

'Just drop your gun, Shaf. You're not going to save her this way,' Whittle said. 'Take the brave officer's gun, Beth. And put it on the floor.'

Beth walked over to him. She still had her shoes on and her hips swayed in the torchlight. For the first time, she looked at his face. There was no hint of an apology in it. But her hands were cold and shaking, and did he imagine it, her fingers lingered on his like they were kissing them? She took the gun and put it on the floor by Whittle.

'You've put me in a rather awkward position,' Whittle went on. 'I really don't know what to do with you. No doubt you think this is all rather distasteful. Sick, almost.' He took off his glove and caressed Beth's body. 'Police work is tough. You're making tough decisions every day. I've spent thirty-five years in the force and it has cost me two marriages. The only thing that kept me together was this girl. I only ever asked one thing from her and, in exchange, I agreed to look after her, keep the farm going for her Dad, and employ the boys. Beth knows what I'm doing for her family. And she likes what I do for her.'

Beth said nothing.

Whittle nodded and the men at his side withdrew their guns. In the same instant, they took off their bird masks.

Shaf couldn't hide his shock. It was the two white officers who'd accompanied him that morning, the ones who'd arrested

Mohammed Rehman. The conspiracy was everywhere, just as DCI Ali thought. 'You knew all along?' he whispered.

'Nothing much gets by me, Shaf. The DCI came in to my office today, saying you'd been trying to get hold of those girls' statements, looking to get yourself off the hook, no doubt.'

'I didn't do anything to them,' Shaf said.

'Oh, come on. It's on record. They both said the same thing. You abused your position as a police officer and took advantage of them. You needn't pretend. Beth knows all about it. I think that's why she's attracted to you.'

'It's a lie.'

'Is it?'

'Beth told me you didn't want me getting close to the cult. She said you made them retract their stories about there being an intruder. She said Tib helped you get those girls.'

Whittle stopped stroking her. 'Well, let's see, shall we? Beth, I'd like you to tell PC Khan what you told me earlier. I want you to tell me exactly as you told me and not to leave anything out. Do you understand? He can't hurt you now.'

She nodded and looked at Shaf. There was nothing in her expression that registered anything. Whittle must have given her something: ketamine, or some other shit. He listened to her sell him down the river. She said he'd taken a shine to her when they first met, and that he'd picked her up and made her go down on him. Tib had seen them in the car. He'd confessed to attacking those girls and was frightened. He needed to blame someone quickly and thought of Whittle.

When she'd finished speaking, Whittle looked at the two white officers. 'Well, we all heard that, didn't we? Go out and tell Tariq she'll be along shortly.' He threw a set of keys at Tib. 'Tib, go to my car, get her costume ready.'

When they'd gone, Shaf felt the cold wind blowing on his face. 'What's going to happen to her?'

Whittle looked at him mockingly. 'You really have no idea?'

He shook his head.

'I'm selling her, Shaf.' He had Beth turn round so that her right buttock was directly in the torch light. 'There,' he said, pointing to four fine lines like faded burn marks on her rustic brown skin. They were the same lines he'd seen on Carver's door and the floor of the outhouse. It was the mark of the Hobbledy Man.

'You're insane,' said Shaf. 'You're bloody insane.'

'And you're a guilty man,' said Whittle, picking up the Glock from the floor. 'Now, sit down on that bale of hay and shut up or I'll put you out of your misery now.'

Tib came back in, carrying a black holdall. He was soaked.

Whittle picked up the holdall and took out a long metal chain, a metal collar, and a pair of small black boots. He had Beth come forward and let Tib put them on her.

Tib grinned stupidly. 'You think it will work, John?'

'The country's in flames, Tib. We have to try everything, do what is written.' He took out a large brown horse tail from the bag and untangled it. 'Come here,' he said to Beth. He kissed her on the mouth, long and hard.

For a moment, Shaf was tempted to run at him. He could cover the distance, knock the gun from his hand. He could save her and himself.

But Whittle broke the kiss and bent her over. Now she was looking directly at him. Her green eyes burned in the darkness. She shifted position several times, accommodating herself to Whittle's hand. Finally, he'd done what he had to and a magical tail appeared from out of her.

She looked at Shaf as if gauging his reaction. Could he still love her after all that she had done?

Tib was ecstatic and demanded he lead her round by the chain. 'Y'see,' he said to her. 'This is for all o' the times you teased us, Beth. John Whittle has put ya in ya place now. Now, you're going to get what's coming to you.'

Whittle watched them do a circuit of the outhouse. She performed like a circus horse, trotting meekly behind Tib. 'Well, what do you think of your informer, Shaf? You think she'd make a credible witness?'

'You've made her like that,' said Shaf. 'You've destroyed her.'

'You're wrong, you know. She destroyed herself. Every time we're together, she begs me.'

'I don't believe you.'

'You don't have to. You can do it later, mulling about it in Strangeways when she's gone.'

Shaf's will finally broke and he ran at him. Indignation fuelled his anger and anger fuelled his desperation. He stopped a foot short of the Glock.

'Don't think I won't pull the trigger,' said Whittle. 'I've seen better men than you go down. Bring her over here, Tib. It's time she was going.'

Tib led Beth across the outhouse.

'There's a knife in the bag. Take it out.'

Tib reached into the holdall and brought out a long, slender blade. 'Are we gonna do it ourselves, John?'

Whittle shook his head. 'No, Tib. She's going to be taken into the woods. That's why those men are here.' He took the chain from Tib and pulled Beth closer. 'Do you want to say anything to the PC before you go, Beth? He wants to save you, take you away from all this. Would you like that?'

But Beth's eyes were glazed. Whatever they'd given her had taken hold.

'Take her to the car, Tib. When you're done, tell her father it's all been sorted, then come back here and clean up. There's to be no trace of anything, you understand?'

Tib took the chain and led her out. He could have been any farmhand down the years, leading a mare to market at some bygone country fair. People may have looked up to see what strange kind of horse it was, children may have run behind her to stroke her brown tail, and men downed their pitchforks to admire her haunches. Women may have tsked under their breath and wondered what their husbands were really thinking, but the horse would have continued to its destination and earned a fat purse and given years of service to its next buyer. And that's the last the owner would have heard about it.

The rain came down hard and the wind buffeted the slates on the roof with renewed force. Whittle carried the holdall in one hand and the Glock in the other. 'Get up,' he said to Shaf.

'Where are we going?' Shaf said.

'I'm taking you in.'

'You won't get away with it, you know?'

Whittle grinned. 'Do you know how many times I've heard that crap? You should never have got involved. If you hadn't gone into Aitken Wood that night, you'd still be on the beat, doing well for yourself. I wasn't talking bullshit when I said we needed more officers like you. We could have buried that story of you attacking those girls. You could be back at home looking after your mum. But you had to listen to that fucker of a DCI.'

'He knew you were no good, that you were dealing and had sex with those girls. He knew you changed the statements.'

'And look where it's got him.'

The way he said it made Shaf turn cold and fearful. He thought again about the unreturned calls and the fact he'd never heard from him. 'Where *has* it got him?' he said. 'What's happened?'

Whittle paused, seemed on the point of saying something, then stopped himself. 'He's in the thick of it. Out on the streets. A lot can happen out there, Shaf. Come on. Get up.' He waved the Glock in front of him, got him to move.

Shaf thought of DCI Ali out on the front line. In all that confusion, anything could happen. A stray bullet could cross his path, a stick or stone levelled at his head. No one would know what he was investigating or what he'd found out. No one apart from him. He walked out to the grey door and hoped his phone was still recording. He had enough to send Whittle down for life.

The torch winked out as they made their way out of the grey door. The wind was ferocious. He screwed his eyes up and looked up the path. Tib was gone, Beth was gone, and the cars were gone – all except the silver Jaguar.

'Up there,' said Whittle, pointing to it.

Shaf looked to his left and saw the water from the reservoir runoff spilling over the side. He wondered if he could make a run for it, take the Glock from Whittle's hand, throw it into the reservoir. But Whittle was watching his every step, keeping sufficient distance behind to anticipate any move he made.

Then, after twenty yards, he stopped suddenly. There was someone by the car.

'What is it?' asked Whittle.

There was a smashing of glass in answer.

'Your car,' said Shaf. 'Someone's breaking into it.'

Whittle waved the gun and ran past him. He fired a shot over the car in warning just as the engine roared into life. Another shot was fired, this time ricocheting off the bonnet. The figure in the car ducked behind the wheel and slunk out the side.

Whittle pointed the gun. 'Stay where you are or I'll shoot, you bastard.'

There was no reply.

'Who the fuck are you?' shouted Whittle into the rain.

A figure got up slowly from behind the driver's door. It was a boy, maybe sixteen or seventeen, thin and bedraggled and soaked to the bone. Shaf thought he looked familiar, one of the kids from the Marsden Park council estate.

'Get on the ground!' Whittle ordered.

The boy sank to his knees.

'I ought to put you out your misery now, you motherfucker. Making me dent my fucking car.'

The boy shook his head. 'You need to get away,' he said.

'What are you talking about?'

The boy waved his hand vaguely towards Aitken Wood. 'He's out there.'

'Who?'

'*Him.*'

'Who's him?'

'The Hobbledy Man,' the boy said.

Whittle clubbed him with the handle of the Glock. 'Stop talking shit, you retard,' he said. 'That's superstitious bollocks.'

The boy hit the ground, a red rose of blood flaring at his temple.

It was the moment Shaf was waiting for. He dived and knocked the gun from Whittle's hand. Whittle replied with an elbow to his chest. He turned just in time and aimed a punch at Whittle's face, hoping to knock him over, but his fist met the granite jaw and the knuckles in his hand cracked. They wrestled in the rain, each of them desperate to land a blow. Shaf took a fist to his right eye socket that nearly blinded him. His head hit the ground and opened the stitches at the back. Pain erupted from two places at once. He brought his right knee up hard, felt it connect with soft flesh. He couldn't let Whittle get on top of him; he'd never get up. He wriggled away, traded wild blows before wrestling him again. He knew he was losing out. Whittle had the strength of a bear. Little by little, he was being worn down.

'Do something!' he shouted to the boy. 'Or you'll be next.'

But the boy seemed transfixed by something. He was looking past him to a point on the reservoir wall.

Shaf kicked and punched, he got kicked and punched, and then his hand struck something hard and metallic in the cold, wet grass. His fingers found a handle. It was thin and sharp. The boy must have used it to jemmy the lock. He flipped it upright, got it ready. There was really no other way. He smashed it against the side of Whittle's skull with all his strength.

At first, there was no reaction. Then Whittle roared with pain. Shaf hit him again and again, always at the same point. The metal smashed through the bone and Whittle rolled off him, clutching his head. Shaf looked down. It was some kind of poker in his hand. He felt sick but, even in his anger and desperation, he had not lost his sense of compassion. It screamed at him to stop, even though he knew Whittle would have afforded him none. His duty now was to save him, to do all he could to right the wrong.

Then, suddenly, his eyes were drawn to the reservoir wall, too. Hobbling along the narrow ledge towards him was the tall, slender man he'd seen in the riot and by the bridge. He carried a cane in his hand and seemed impervious to the wind and rain. His long nose stuck out of the shadows where his face should have been and his mouth moved stiffly like a puppet's. He pointed the cane at the body of John Whittle.

Tell John Malkin his time is nearly up and finish the job.

Shaf couldn't move his arm. It was locked with fear. The wind and the rain lashed against him and he struggled to stand. Then he felt the poker torn from his grasp and watched in horror as the boy brought it down on the head of John Whittle one last time. The skull split like a water melon.

'Fucking hell!' shouted Shaf blindly into the storm. He wrenched the poker from the boy's grasp and threw it into the air. It disappeared into the darkness over the reservoir wall, a Norman arrow loosed from a bow. Then he knelt beside the prone body. He didn't need to examine it too closely. No one was coming back from those kinds of wounds. What the hell was he going to do? He looked along the wall and the Hobbledy Man had gone. There was just him and the boy, each the witness to the other's crime. Between them, they had killed a man: a terrible man, but a man all the same.

'What we gonna do?' said the boy. He was shivering with the cold and shock.

Shaf looked at the reservoir runoff. 'We need to get rid of the body.'

He was acting on instinct now. A surge of self-preservation energised him. He had helped kill a man and now he was going to cover his tracks and destroy the evidence. He put his hands under Whittle's arms, and started to drag him up the slope to the reservoir wall. 'Help me!' he shouted.

But the boy couldn't move. 'I can't,' he said. 'I need to go.'

'Where?'

The boy gesticulated in the direction of the woods. 'I need to save her before *he* comes back.'

Shaf had no time to ask who the hell he was talking about. He pulled Whittle's body as best he could. A couple of times, he slipped on the wet grass; a couple of times the body slid down the slope before he could grab it, but finally he had it propped against the stone wall of Lower Black Moss Reservoir. The sign on the other side read: 'CAUTION Dying for a swim?' Getting the body over would have taken three or four men but there was a section of metal railings that seemed low enough to manage it. He recognised it now. It was the part of the reservoir where Grip had swum into the choppy waters and never come back. Those waters were now as rough as a small sea. The waves chopped against the sides and spray spat over the wall.

Whittle's body now felt twice the weight it did when he started pulling it. The rain had made the clothes soggy and the skin puff. He dragged it next to the railings, draped it over his shoulders and pushed with all the strength he had. Little by little, the body of John Whittle rose until it hung on the railings. He gave one last push and then gravity took the weight off his hands and the body slid onto the narrow, grassy bank and down the slope into the grey, choppy waters where it sunk like a stone. Tib said it was forty feet down to the bottom. Hopefully, the currents would take him that far, just as they had Grip.

He let the rain wash his hands and face of the terrible thing he had done.

When he was finished, he staggered back to the Jaguar. He heard the engine start up but was powerless to intervene. He watched it disappear up Barley Lane towards Upper Black Moss Reservoir. In a way, the kid had done him a favour. He'd removed a big piece of the evidence. Tib would be along later to clear up the outhouse.

Then he remembered the gun. He'd knocked it from Whittle's hand. He scoured the grass in the dark, cursed himself for not picking it up sooner. What if the kid had taken it? His boot struck something hard and he looked down at his feet. The Glock lay on its side on the ground. He picked it up, turned the key, enabling the internal safety lock. He wouldn't use it, anyway. There were other, better ways to police.

He ran down to the outhouse to where he'd left his car. He climbed in and took his phone out. The light came on. It was still working. There was enough on there to convict Whittle and himself. But, at least, he still had something. He started the engine. The wheels spun in the mud for a moment, then he was away. He sped down Barley Lane, past Blackthorn Farm, as if the Hobbledy Man were after him.

He had to find Beth.

27

As Johnny drove past the blue sign for Barley, the mood in the valley changed. Where before sunlight pierced the gloom, now it was lost behind a rampart of dark, grey clouds. The spruces and pines of Aitken Wood could still be seen on the crown of the hill but, lower down, a mist rose from the ground, petrifying the oak and ash and rowan which covered the banks of White Hough Water as it raced down to Ogden Clough. Ramblers with walking sticks and backpacks braved the inclement conditions, unaware that anything was wrong. But, even from inside the car, he could sense the valley was waiting for something, and the village had slipped back in time.

He came to the junction of Barley New Road and The Bullion, where Nathan had run away. He'd rung him every day since but his phone was dead. The valley had cut him off. He pulled in to the car park of The Pendle Inn. The sign outside showed a witch on a broomstick. It lent the building a supernatural air. The grey, leaded windows swallowed what little light there was and long shadows lent across it from the wind bent trees. He went through the arched entrance. There were two men at the bar with rotund, country faces. They nodded at him and went on drinking their ale, watching a small television screen behind the bar. Like everywhere else, there was only one channel on.

To the right of the bar was a large log fire set in an alcove. A long, wooden table and a cushioned bench ran the length of it. Sitting by the fire with some books was a man in his early twenties. He was tall and blond and thin and had a sensitive, educated face. Johnny didn't know why he expected someone older. He always expected someone older.

He sat down opposite just as the clock above the fire struck twelve.

The young man looked up. 'John Malkin?'

Johnny nodded.

'Thanks for coming. I'm Tom Whittle.' He held his hand out across the table.

'The Plague Doctor? Aren't you a little young to be a doctor?'

'I have a PhD in Witchcraft.'

It sounded like a joke, but the books on the table, and his demeanour, weren't.

Johnny picked up one of the place mats. It showed a picture of a hobgoblin. 'Okay, then,' he said. 'Let's hear it. I want you tell me everything.'

Tom opened one of the books and placed it on the wooden table in front of him. On one of the leaves was a larger version of the picture Ms Houghton had shown him. 'You recognise this?'

'Yes, I do.'

'I've been studying the legend of the Hobbledy Man since I was a kid. The first mention of him was in 1611, just before the Pendle Witch Trials.' He produced a piece of paper with some calligraphic writing on it. 'It's a bit blurry but I've put a translation on the side for you.' He pointed to some lines written in pen.

Johnny looked down it and read.

On the summer solstice, the children of the village (Barley) said they had seen a man in the shape of the devil carrying a stick. He said he had come from Padiham.

'That was written by Tomas Potts, the clerk of the Lancaster Assizes. He went on to write the most famous account of the witch trials, but in so doing, he diverted public attention away from other things that were going on in the Pendle Valley at the time. Look here.' He took out a clutch of photocopied sheets. 'It's very hard to get hold of this stuff. The books they're from are falling apart.' He laid out another sheet.

'What's this?' asked Johnny.

'It's the confession of a man called Thomas Whittle. My name, oddly. He was hanged in Lancaster in 1622, ten years after the witch trials, for robbery and murder.'

Johnny picked up the paper. As he read it, the fire began to spit and spark and flickers of light danced on the page like matchstick men. The tinderbox of doubts he had was about to go up in flames.

I, Thomas Whittle, once of Barley, in the county of Lancashire, hereby confess before God, to the murder of John Malkin, a boy of the Parish of Barley. I was chosen by the village to perform the act and, with a girl of the Parish, led the boy into the forest of Pendle and there took his life. Let God have mercy on my soul. As God is my witness, it was not my wish to kill. The boy had done nothing wrong. He was chosen as I was chosen. It was the only way to stop Him who had blighted the crops and brought plague on us.

'Jesus Christ,' whispered Johnny.

'Thomas Whittle went mad in jail before he was hanged. There are a number of accounts of him trying to escape and a curious note left in the records at Lancaster Assizes. Here.' Tom pointed to another paragraph.

The prisoner took no food this evening and spent the entire time staring out the small apex window which looked down on the courtyard. He grew fearful and restless and said he had seen Him again, he being the man he had drawn for us several times. There is no doubt he has lost his sanity. For the record of the court, the name he gave to the figure was the Hobbledy Man, a name not unknown in the Pendle Valley area.

Johnny struggled to take it in. 'What happened after he killed the little boy? Did the plague go?'

'Yes, and the furore over the witch craze died down.'

'You're suggesting they were linked?'

'They were.'

Johnny thought of the dreams he'd had and what Nathan and Jenna had said, that he was chosen. 'Can you prove it?'

Tom opened another book. 'Not definitively. But I can show you things that might convince you. As I said, the first reported sighting of the Hobbledy Man was in 1611 and confirmed by reports at the time. Now look here.' He pointed to a picture in the new book. 'This is 1662, some fifty years later, at the Bury St Edmund's Witch Trial. Rose Cullender and Amy Denny are hanged in the town for malevolent witchcraft. What do you notice?'

Johnny stared at it. It looked more like a child's scribble than an adult's, with thick, black lines and odd angles and perspectives like a Cubist painting, but one thing made him sit up. By the hangman's noose was a tall figure with a stick. His nose was long and the lower part of his jaw stuck out.

'The people of Pendle Valley had not forgotten the Hobbledy Man,' Tom said. 'There were reported sightings of him at Newchurch and Padiham and Barley in the summer of 1662. People were worried that witchcraft would again sweep the countryside. The bishop of St. Mary's in Newchurch wrote that the land 'was once again in the throes of a diabolic power' and that 'prayer alone would not suffice to turn the evil away'.'

Johnny looked at the spidery handwriting and wondered what the bishop had seen or heard. 'Okay, so how do we know it isn't just a guy in a mask? You could be confusing him for a witch finder or one of the plague doctors. They look the same.'

'It's a good question. People see what they want to see, don't they? After Roswell, everyone saw little green men. After the Patterson-Grimlin film, everyone saw Bigfoot. But, with the Hobbledy Man, there's one important distinction.'

'What's that?'

'Sightings of him are broadly regular. Every fifty years or so, there is a cluster of reports, then nothing.'

'So, we've nothing to worry about?'

Tom looked towards the bar. The television could be heard faintly in the background.

'You've been following the news?'

'Of course.'

'Then you'll know that there's plenty to worry about. Like there was in 1612, at the height of the witch craze, or in 1662, when fear of its revival and the spread of plague was gripping the countryside.'

'But that was four hundred years ago.'

Tom nodded. 'Yes, and this was fifty years ago.' He picked out a faded newspaper clipping from inside the book.

Johnny read the masthead.

The Daily Mirror June 16th, 1968

The headline was stark, the picture beneath it starker still. It showed Lower Black Moss Reservoir and Pendle Hill. They hadn't changed in fifty years.

Five-Year-Old Found in Black Moss Reservoir Search Called Off

Johnny could barely read on.

The nightmare is finally over for the family of missing five-year-old schoolboy, George House, who was pulled from the waters of Lower Black Moss Reservoir last night after a five-day search. He went missing on a family day out in the picturesque village of Barley. Police have yet to work out how the body got there and have so far not charged anyone over his disappearance.

The area around Pendle Hill has been synonymous with witchcraft since the seventeenth century and recent sightings of figures in the woods have been reported by ramblers and locals alike. Police have so far been determined to stick to facts and have not responded to speculation in the village that this is anything other than a tragic accident. Local farmers had initially claimed that a big cat was on the loose, possibly a panther escaped from a zoo, though none has been reported. Police have stepped up patrols in the area and have urged the public to remain calm and vigilant.

'I've looked at all the old newspaper reports from the time,' Tom said. 'After the death, the sightings suddenly stopped. The pattern is always the same.'

Johnny was on autopilot, trying to process everything. 'Was anyone ever charged with murder?'

'The verdict was accidental drowning. Police thought the boy just wandered off and got lost, although how he managed to get so far through thick woodland, who knows?'

Johnny looked into the fire and tried not to fear the worst, but every part of him was now alive to the possibility that it was all true. When Tom handed him another newspaper clipping from the *Northern Daily Telegraph*, he was already resigned to its content.

Satanic Cult Exposed in Lancashire Blamed for Child Kidnapping

'How much of this stuff have you got?' he said.

'Enough.'

'And you've never gone to the police with it?'

'What would I say?'

'Just what you've told me.'

'The police won't believe anything until it's staring them in the face.' He said it as if he'd already tried.

'So, what do we do?' Johnny asked.

'You mean, what do *you* do?'

'Me? I can't be responsible for all the crap that's going on out there.' He pointed to the television. 'It's all bullshit coincidence. You can't pin that on me.'

The two men at the bar looked over at him, disturbed at his raised voice.

Tom looked at him sympathetically. 'We've done all we can as a group, short of taking someone's life. We can't go that far this time. The price is too high.'

'But you're expecting me to?' Johnny said disbelievingly.

Tom collected his books and stacked them up. 'I probably wouldn't do it if I was in your shoes. But each day that this goes on, someone will die out there.'

'Listen to me,' said Johnny. The fire had warmed him, sending waves of anger through him. 'I can't go killing anybody, not for anything.'

'But you've been chosen.'

'I haven't been chosen.'

'You have. It's all over. People have seen *Him*. He's looking for you.'

'Then why doesn't he fucking come and get me?'

Tom put his bag on the table and studied him. 'Maybe he will.'

'I won't kill for him. Never.'

'We all lose somebody we love,' Tom said, and his eyes moistened in the firelight.

'I think you're a bit young coming out with stuff like that, don't you?'

'Well, perhaps there's another way this time.'

Johnny stared at him, dumbfounded. 'What's that?'

It was twenty-five past twelve and time seemed to have stood still.

'Maybe you don't need to kill someone else. You could kill yourself, make the ultimate sacrifice.'

'You're insane, do you know that? Fucking insane! You and your bloody cult!'

The men at the bar were staring at him, not with anger, but with sympathy. So was the barmaid.

Tom turned to him. 'You can't back out. The chosen one must go through with it, or something of his will be taken. Everyone round here knows what's going on. You won't hear a bad word said about you in these parts. We know what you went through and what you have to go through. No one shall forget the price you paid.'

28

The clock turned from 11.59 to 12.00 and then the horn went off. Shaf opened an eye and looked out of the car window. He was slumped at the wheel, his face sore, the back of his head sore, everywhere sore. For a moment, nothing registered. Then slowly, piece-by-piece, he put the jigsaw of the night back together. He'd been driving round, looking for Beth. Whittle had sold her to a guy called Tariq but he couldn't find a trace of them. He wondered vaguely if it was the same Tariq that Mohammed Rehman had mentioned. There was only one way to find out. Then he stopped and the rest of the night came rushing back. *Whittle*. He'd killed him, hadn't he? He was in the reservoir, lying forty feet under. There was something else there, too, something all his senses were trying to block out.

He hit the steering wheel hard. 'Snap out of it,' he told himself. It *was* superstitious bollocks. He had other things to do. He had to trim the voice recording he'd made, cut out what really happened. It wasn't an exact science, and maybe forensics could get the original back but, for the moment, it'd have to do. He'd pass it on to DCI Ali, if he was still around. He'd know what to do with it.

He started the engine and bombed down the A682. If DCI Ali wasn't answering his phone, he'd have to speak to him in person. That meant getting back into uniform and going to Nelson. It was a risk but, from now on, everything was a risk.

There was a sombre feel to the station when he arrived. Officers were sat on the steps outside with their heads bowed. There were a few squaddies in red berets, too – young lads fresh from school or college with faces not yet moulded by loss. No one raised an eyebrow. They were all waging a private war with tiredness and grief.

He saw the familiar face of Dan, the desk sergeant, behind the counter and went over to see him. Only it wasn't the Dan he remembered. His face was no longer corpulent and red, but colourless. Even his pate seemed pale and lifeless, like the skin had been taken off and only the skull left showing.

'You chose a good week to be off,' Dan said.

'Well, I'm back now,' said Shaf.

'I'll break open a bottle. Everyone here could do with a rest.'

'I'm sorry. I've been seconded to another team.'

'Any vacancies?'

Shaf studied him carefully, wondered if he was one of Whittle's men as well. 'Sorry. It's not my call. I'm looking for DCI Ali.'

The change in the desk sergeant's appearance was sudden and unscripted, like someone had let the air out of a balloon. 'I'm sorry, Shaf. You haven't heard?'

'Heard what?'

'The DCI was killed last night.'

Shaf put his hands on the counter for support. 'What? He can't have been. I saw him yesterday.'

Dan looked at him sympathetically. 'I'm sorry, Shaf.'

'What the hell happened?'

'They're going through ballistics at the moment. It was during the rioting.'

'He was shot?'

Dan shrugged.

Shaf thought about what Whittle had said. *He's in the thick of it. Out on the streets.* He knew how it had happened. Someone had taken him out with a Glock 17.

'Dan, listen to me. I need you to do me a favour.'

'What is it?'

'I need you to pull a file for me.'

'Are you saying this on the record or off the record?'

'Whichever you like. You say that no one ever tells you anything. Well, I'm telling you something now. You'll be doing DCI Ali's family a big favour if you get that file for me.' He took out his notepad and wrote down a reference number.

'I need to clear it, Shaf. I'll lose my job.'

'The file won't be gone long.'

'They all say that.'

Shaf took out another page and wrote a name down on it. 'I also want an address for this guy and a PNC check. I want to know what car he drives and if we have anything on him.'

He handed the sheets over.

Dan looked down at one and then the other.

'You know what's really funny?' he said.

'What?'

'You're the third person who's asked for this file in the last week.'

Something like panic swept through Shaf. 'Yeah? Who were the others?'

'The DCI and the superintendent.'

The names floored him. Was he going to get arrested right there and then? Had Whittle got the whole station in his grasp, even from beyond the grave?

Dan scratched his pate, smoothed down the non-existent hair. 'Whittle took me aside about a week ago, asked me to tell him if anyone requested it.'

Shaf wondered if it was some kind of test. For a desk sergeant who was meant to know nothing, he seemed very well informed. 'What did you do?'

'I kept quiet.'

'Why?'

'Whittle's a cunt. If you ask me, he should have got the bullet instead of the DCI.' He paused. 'Look, if you hold the fort for a minute, I'll see what I can do.'

Shaf was too late to stop him. He wondered if everyone felt that way about Whittle. He kept his head down, avoided looks. He didn't want anyone asking questions.

Presently, Dan returned. 'Now, isn't that the weirdest thing?' he said.

'What is?' said Shaf.

'The DCI gave me the file back yesterday and now someone's just gone and lifted it again.'

He should have known. Whittle would have taken it the first chance he had. The only way to get to the truth now was interviewing the girls and, as Alisha had just gone missing, that only left Jenna.

'But,' Dan said. 'It's not all bad news. I got you an address for Tariq Ibrahim. Drives a silver Skoda. They all do, don't they? I'll ring you later if I find anything else.'

'Thanks. I owe you one, Dan.'

'Yeah,' he said. 'You do.'

Shaf wondered how long it would take HQ to realise Whittle wasn't coming back. Or Beth. How many unanswered calls would it take before someone decided to check where they were? Police resources were at breaking point. These were exceptional times, so maybe he'd get some time, but when everything was over, they'd come after him. He was now, most decidedly, on the wrong side of things. Whittle had stepped over that mark a long time ago. DCI Ali had torn up the book and operated on both sides. Even Dan, trying to get him the file, had transgressed the law. Maybe that was inevitable. England may not be an outlaw country, but things still happened under the radar. Maintaining the law sometimes meant bending it. He'd helped kill a man and buried his body in a reservoir. Was that the actions of a police officer? He should come clean and tell them what happened, let the law take its course. But each second, minute and hour that passed, the prospect of doing so receded. He was on the run and wanted to clear his name. There would be time enough to face the consequences. He looked down at the sheet of paper and memorised the address. Silver Skodas. Yeah, they all drove them. Every last one of them.

29

As soon as Johnny left Barley, the clouds opened up and a steady stream of rain came down. It wasn't heavy but it was continual and dismal. At every twist and turn of the road, he saw Hobbledy Men and hobgoblins in the trees and on the roadside. Everyone there knew what he had to do but he was going to disappoint them: he wasn't going to sacrifice himself, or anyone else, for a bloody legend. Yet, even as he swore it, he knew that his conviction would wane as the day waned and night came calling.

But each day that this goes on, someone will die out there.

Was he prepared for that?

He drove back to the house, was surprised to see Kat's car there. She was back early from work. The mark on the door was there, too. What clearer indication could there be that he'd been chosen?

He put the key in the lock and went inside. She was in her t-shirt and leggings, curled up on the settee, watching the news.

'You okay?' he said, knowing she wasn't.

'I've rung you loads,' she said. 'But you've not picked up.'

'I didn't…' Then he remembered there was no signal in the valley. 'I'm sorry. The reception has been crap all morning.'

'I had to go to Burnley General,' she said. 'I was spotting and was really worried.'

He sat down beside her. 'Fuck, Kat. What have they said? Is the baby okay?'

She took a tissue from her pocket. 'Yes, he's okay, but they told me to lie down and relax. I'm finding it hard to do.'

'I'm sorry I wasn't there. You've got to stay off now, you hear? Your body's telling you something.'

'The nurse said it's quite normal. I just need to calm down and take things easy.' She shifted position. 'I thought you weren't talking to me.'

'How do you mean?'

'Why you weren't picking up.'

'No, there was no signal.'

'You weren't in the office?'

'No, I went looking for Nathan.'

He could tell she didn't believe him.

'Daphne called before.'

'Good. Have they found him?'

'She wasn't ringing about Nathan. She was ringing about you. She told me to tell you not to bother going in again. She'd spoken to her bosses and they were going to suspend you.'

He let it sink in. 'Great. It saves me the bother of telling her I'm resigning. This way they'll have to pay me.'

Her mouth quivered and she began to cry. Tears came pouring down her cheeks, covering the knees of her jogging pants where her head rested.

'Kat, what's wrong? I thought we wanted this, me to give up work and look after you. I'll get severance pay and I can look for something easier, less stressful.'

She wiped her eyes with the tissue. 'I know. I'm just being overemotional. Being in the hospital scared me. Seeing all those other women. That's all it is.'

He stroked her hand. 'Of course it is. It would scare anyone.'

He glanced at the latest pictures on the News. It was grim fare. Lines of police officers stood silently in ranks of grief, the way they had stood before the fury of the mobs. Shoulder to shoulder, they were the force people relied on, yet it was all too clear they were losing the battle. The army was called in. Water cannon and rubber bullets were deployed on the streets of Birmingham and Manchester, armoured vehicles were in Burnley and Blackburn – how could this be the work of any supernatural agency? Yet, he had felt in his dreams the power of the prophecy and knew a town was waiting for someone, for him, to act.

'Four dead,' Kat said, as if in a trance. 'When will it end, Johnny?'

The hairs on the back of his neck stood up. *Four?* It was as if Tom was speaking through her: *someone will die out there.* He shook his head. 'I don't know.'

She stretched her legs and lay down, her head on a cushion.

He went to get her a blanket from upstairs, but when he got back, she was asleep. He lay it on her like a shroud.

He looked out of the lounge window at the dismal rain and his eyes started to close. He heard the thump of his heart in his skull, a threadbare sound, worn out by stress and alcohol and the endless, futile stream of antidepressants.

'Have I missed something?' he whispered, and saw a grey mist in front of him. It gradually cleared to reveal a wood with dark conifer trees and a big metal wheel embedded in a stone wall. Then, the mist came down again and he was lost.

The vibration in his pocket brought him round.

He took the phone from his pocket and looked at the screen. It was Nathan.

Fucking hell. He pressed *Accept* and put the phone to his ear.

'Johnny?' Nathan's voice was faint and unclear.

'Nathan, where the hell are you?'

'I dunno, Johnny, but I need ya. I need ya to come quick.'

The signal crackled and came back. 'Are you still there, Nathan?'

'I'm here, Johnny. I need ya to come now.'

'Nathan, listen, you have to tell me where you are.'

'In that wood, Johnny. Where you left us. I'm cold and hungry and goin' mad.' He was crying now.

'Okay, just calm down.'

'I can't, Johnny. He's here, too.'

He?

'Who?'

'That guy. The one I told you about. He wants to see ya, Johnny.'

'What guy, Nathan?'

But he already knew. It was the Hobbledy Man. He couldn't run from his destiny. He was calling him.

'Nathan, listen. I want you to tell him I'm coming. Tell him to stop whatever he's doing. I'll see him. Do you hear me?'

The wind whistled down the phone and the line crackled again.

'I hear ya, Johnny.'

'Is there anywhere you can hide? Somewhere I can find you?'

'I'm on the Sculpture Trail, Johnny. I can't hide no more. Please come. Something bad's happened.'

The line cut out just as he was about to ask.

He tried ringing back but there was no answer.

He looked at Kat, sleeping on the settee, and scrawled her a note.

Kat,

Nathan called. He's in trouble and I have to go. I'll be back as soon as I can. Can you let Daphne know I've gone to find him and that I accept the suspension. Everything will be all right.

Love,

Johnny x

He lay it on the blanket next to her.

As he left, he saw the latest news headline. It spoke of the dead but only mentioned three of them. She must have been confused. It was an easy thing to do.

The rain kept falling as he made his way to the car.

Please be okay, son.

30

Shaf pulled up outside the grey terraced house and put his hat and yellow jacket on. There was no silver Skoda outside and probably no Tariq Ibrahim, but there was no harm trying; somebody knew where he was and the first person to ask was his wife.

He knocked on the door and a small, fat woman in a blue shalwar kameez opened it. Her bright red lipstick made her mouth look like a gash. 'Mrs Ibrahim?'

She tucked some stray hair into her headscarf. 'Yes.'

'I'm PC Khan. I need to speak to your husband.'

'Well, good luck with that.'

'Do you know where he is?'

'You could try the bookies. He'll be there or the taxi ranks.'

The answer caught him by surprise. 'That's where he works?'

'So he says. Has he done something wrong?'

'Maybe.'

'Well, maybe you better come in,' she said.

Inside, it was neat, tidy and rather typical. There was a sheet of plastic on the carpet to stop people treading mud in, a picture of the Kaaba on the wall, the smell of salan coming from the kitchen, and a flat screen TV nailed to the wall with Star Plus on.

She adjusted her headscarf again. 'Can I get you tea or a juice?' she said.

'No, I can't stay long. We're very stretched at the moment.'

'Yes, I understand.' She paused. 'I've been meaning to go to the police before, you know?'

'You have?'

'About my husband.'

215

'I see.'

'But you know what it's like. You don't snitch on family, do you? Everyone would prefer you suffered in silence.'

He'd heard it a thousand times. It wasn't exactly mistrust of the police as fear of what the community would say. People lived in fear of losing face, of becoming a pariah. That's why women put up with domestic abuse at home, and children with abuse at the mosques. It was part and parcel of growing up to accept what others said, and those others were usually grey-haired old men with more concern for the pronunciation of Arabic letters than the law of the land.

'Sometimes you have to,' he said. 'Otherwise it's not just you that suffers.'

She looked at him as if weighing the import of his words. He didn't feel any goodness in his heart, but he showed it, and that was enough.

She went to the sideboard, opened a blue handbag, and took a phone from it. 'My husband doesn't look after me,' she said. 'We have no children, luckily, and I can tell he's bored with me. I took his phone about a month ago because I thought he was having an affair. He'd been really distracted and kept getting texts at odd times. Anyway, normally he sleeps with it next to him, but he left it downstairs that night and I looked through it. I found some pictures of a girl, so I copied them to mine before he woke up. I was scared when I did it in case he found out, but every day since I thought I should go to the police. Especially when I heard what was going on in the town.'

'The rioting?' Shaf said.

'No, these grooming gangs. That's why you're here, isn't it?' She looked down at her phone. 'She can't be more than fifteen. There's a couple of pictures with her school uniform on. I think they're worse than the others.'

She handed the phone to him.

He really didn't want to look. He'd seen too much of Beth. But when he did, his heart sank further. The pictures were of Jenna Dunham, the girl in the wood.

Mrs Ibrahim was right. The school photos *were* the worst. They gave Jenna a personality, a life, a humanity that the nude ones didn't possess.

'Do you know who she is?' he asked.

'No,' she said. 'And I don't want to.'

'You've not said anything to your husband?'

'No. Tariq gets very cross. It's hard to talk to him when he's cross. I'm afraid he might kill me.'

She started to cry then and thick, milky tears ran down her face. He wanted to hold out his arms and stop her crying, the way he would his mum. The town he thought he knew all these years, patrolling the streets, earning his Neighbourhood Policing Award, was not the town it was now. There were secrets behind every door, skeletons in every closet, and cruelty and abuse in places people called home. Nowhere was safe and no one was safe. He thought of Beth in a car somewhere with Tariq, and of Jenna Dunham in the photos, and then what was happening on the streets, and it was hard not to think the whole world was rotten and that they were all being punished for their part in it.

'I want you to keep these photos, Mrs Ibrahim. You understand? It's very important that you keep them safe. It's evidence we can use against your husband.'

'Don't you want to take them?'

'Not yet. We need to find him first.'

'But I don't know where he is.'

'I want you to ring him.'

'He won't pick up.'

'He will if you leave him a message.'

She was panicking now. 'Well, what do I say?'

'Tell him Jenna Dunham's just called round and she's told you everything.'

'Who's she?'

He looked at her ruefully. 'The girl in the pictures.'

'You know her?' she asked, stunned.

'Yes,' he said, and handed her back the phone.

Slowly, reluctantly, she made the call. There was pain in her voice when she spoke, but that only made it more realistic. He chastised himself for using her, for putting her in harm's way, but that was the price you paid for not saying something at the time. If she'd only come forward before, Jenna and Alisha may never have been attacked, he would never have been to Carver's farm, and he would never have met Beth or Tib or Thomas or the Hobbledy Man. He would never have killed someone.

'What do I do now?' she said.

'Have you any relatives nearby?'

She nodded.

'I want you to go and stay with them. Pack what you need and go. If your husband calls, I want you to call me.' He wrote his number down for her.

'Where are you going?' she asked, bewildered.

'To see Jenna Dunham, hopefully before your husband does.'

31

Johnny drove the black Ford Focus through the rain. The windscreen wipers beat against the glass like gulls' wings in a gale. They scraped and jarred with each flap and sent a steady stream of water across the bonnet. White Hough Water had burst its banks and a light film of water had spread across the road. It was impossible to imagine the village being more cut off than this; there was no phone signal and, now, no access. Pendle Hill was spewing out more cloud, intent on covering the whole valley in darkness. He took a right turning onto Barley New Road and made towards Whitehough Education Centre. It was the quickest way into the wood.

He parked on a narrow path beyond Whitehough farm and got out, shielding his eyes from the rain. It was hard to work out if the sun had already set, so dark was the sky. He had an old, blue waterproof coat on, which he'd worn once when Kat and he had plans to hike. It smelt slightly of damp but did its job and kept him dry. He felt the bite of the wind through the polyurethane and wondered how the hell Nathan must be feeling. He'd been out here on his own all this time.

He looked across the field towards Aitken Wood. It was perhaps two hundred metres and uphill all the way. He ran for the first part, hoping to make it there quickly, but his feet got bogged down in the waterlogged grass and he wished he'd worn something more substantial than trainers. He felt the soft squelch of the insoles as his feet squeezed the water back out. He breathed deeply, checked his heart was okay. He slowed to a jog, till the first trees stretched out their wizened arms and welcomed him under their ancient canopy.

Now, the grey of evening became a dark green wall and the rain slowed to a drip as it permeated the foliage and dropped forty and fifty feet to the forest floor. He took one of the manmade paths that led into the darkness and his heart grew uneasy. He imagined a little boy being taken through here four hundred years ago, unaware he was being led to his death. Tears sprang to his eyes. Poor John Malkin. Was he about to go through the same thing? The Hobbledy Man was out here somewhere.

There was a stone wall on his right that ran roughly due east and hemmed the wood in. He used it to gauge what direction he was travelling in, but soon it disappeared and he was forced to rely on the paths. The wood wasn't so claustrophobic now. There were fewer plants and bushes on the ground. This meant he could see twenty or thirty metres in all directions. It wasn't quite as reassuring as he wanted. If he could see out, it meant others could see him, and it soon became clear that he was not alone. There were figures moving between the tree trunks and, once or twice, he caught the sound of something snapping in the woods behind him. A twig, perhaps? Whatever it was, it only moved when he did and got no closer to him.

After five minutes, he passed a wooden sign on his left that pointed straight to the Sculpture Trail. The path began to climb. He could feel the rain on his face as it found more gaps in the tree canopy. He felt like calling out to Nathan, to let him know he was here, but fear of bringing something else out into the open kept him quiet. His blood started pounding in his ears.

Thud.

Was that his heart, or something else?

Thud.

He looked behind him and saw something moving between the boughs of two Scots pine, swaying gently from side to side. It was too tall to be a man. Or was it? What if the man was hanging upside down?

His legs were rooted to the ground, yet he had to move to find Nathan. He broke into a run, felt the squelch of his feet along the path. The figures were following him on either side. Who or what the hell were they?

Soon, he came to a clearing in the wood. There were two giant wooden arches in the centre. They looked like dragons' tails coiled over each other. It wasn't the tails that stopped him, though. It was the boy underneath shivering helplessly from the wind and rain.

'Nathan?' he said.

He came out of the dragons' tails. 'Johnny?'

A tight, black cap of hair now covered his skeleton head. He was painfully thin.

'What are you doing here, son?'

'I had to hide, Johnny. I had to get away.'

'You should have come with me.'

Nathan shook his head. 'I couldn't go back.'

'Well, we'll have to now. We can't stay here.'

Nathan wavered. 'I have to do something first. '

'What is it?'

'I have to check on someone.'

'Who?'

'A girl, Johnny. I found her a few days ago. She were hidin' just like me. I been lookin' after her. The police 'copter came last night. I thought they were lookin' for me but maybes they were lookin' for her.'

'We don't have time, Nathan. We have to go now.'

'Just let me check on her, Johnny. Please.'

Johnny stared at him and thought better of it, but Nathan was insistent. He followed him down the path. The rain came down heavier through the broken tree canopy and the spruces and pines bent double, and the rowans and ashes bristled in the chill wind. He knew the figures were following at a safe distance. Every so often, there was a snap of a twig or a broken branch in the darkness. They passed the sculptures made for the kids: a bronze witchfinder with his hat and cane; something that looked like a worm coming out of the ground; and small insects hung on trees. It was meant to be a celebration of the area's history but, in this light and at this time, it was really a gallery of the macabre.

Every so often, Nathan looked behind to make sure he was there and Johnny had a vague doubt. He remembered what Tom had said that morning, about little John Malkin being led to his death by Thomas Whittle, and a terrible thought entered his head. Maybe this was no longer Nathan? Maybe it was a trap and the Hobbledy Man had killed him? Maybe *he* was the Hobbledy Man?

'How far?' he shouted, and the wind brought the answer back. 'We're nearly there.'

They had reached an old, stone wall which stretched down into the wood on their right and curled round to their left like a claw, hemming them in. It wasn't the wall which caught his attention, though, but the giant metal wheel embedded in it. It looked like it had come from one of the old mills, or a giant penny farthing. It was black and rusted and the centre of it, from where the spokes radiated out, was thick with branches like the wheel had got caught in a giant spider web. Horribly, he realised it was the one he'd seen in his dream.

Nathan approached it and Johnny drew up alongside him.

'She's in there, Johnny. I were lookin' after her.'

Johnny felt the terror in his voice. He looked at the skeleton face of his charge, the boy he was meant to save, and saw the signs of withdrawal. He'd gone cold turkey up here, starved of every 'pick me up' and 'knock me out' drug his embattled body had fought and fed on the last few years. Was this the other way he'd spoken about? To rid the toxins from his body, to purge himself, not to go to some shrink and be prescribed a whole load more? Was this not what he'd gone through with the sleeping pills and antidepressants, the slide into dependence and the long nightmare of withdrawal? No wonder he'd gone mad.

'Don't worry, son. Just show me.'

Nathan held his head in his hands. 'I tried to save her, Johnny. I really did.'

They were now only a few paces from the wheel.

Johnny looked down and realised that what he at first thought was branches knotted in the spokes of the wheel was, in fact, a body.

'Fuck, Nathan. What have you done?'

He bent down and turned the body over. It was a girl, about sixteen, with long, dark brown hair and sallow skin. She was soaked to the bone. Her jeans, her shoes, her coat were tattered and torn. But that wasn't what drew his attention. It was the black orchid bruise on her temple and the scars on her face. She'd been badly beaten. He recognised her instantly and the shock of seeing her in the flesh, and in these circumstances, froze his bones.

It was Alisha Ali.

He turned to Nathan. 'You did this, son?' His tone wasn't angry but rather resigned, like he'd finally realised there was no longer anything he could do.

Nathan shook his head. 'She fell, Johnny. Honest she did. That's what happened.'

Johnny looked at her face. She'd have needed to fall off a cliff to sustain those injuries. The ripped clothes hadn't been done by accident. Had he also tried to rape her? He turned his back on Nathan. The wounds on her face weren't fresh, she wouldn't die of them, but exposure was another thing. Why had she come out here? He felt for a pulse, and even though his hands were cold and he couldn't feel his own heartbeat, he detected the faraway sign of life in her veins. She had not given up the fight.

'Is she alive?' Nathan asked.

'Just.'

'I was gonna get help. I was gonna save her.'

'Yeah? How were you going to do that? Carry her to hospital on your back?'

His sarcasm was cruel.

'I stole a car,' Nathan said. 'I was gonna drive her. But *he* found her first.'

'And don't tell me, he wouldn't let you.'

Nathan shook his head. 'Why don't you believe me?'

'Cos I know you, son.'

Nathan's eyes flickered and flared. He could no longer take it. He leapt up at him, put his hands on his throat. His skeletal head was inches from his own, his eyes bloodshot with the pain and fury and hurt of rejection. 'Don't ever say that again. You ain't seen what I've seen. It's mad out 'ere. There's things in the wood you wouldn't believe, Johnny.'

Johnny threw him off easily. Nathan had lost his strength in the woods. 'You're right. I wouldn't.' He knelt down, tried to pick Alisha up. 'We haven't got time for this crap. And neither has she. You want to save her? That's what we're going to do.'

Nathan nodded hysterically. 'I would have saved her but *he* wouldn't let me. *He* wanted you. That's why I rang you.' He stopped. He was no longer looking at him, but behind him. 'It doesn't matter now, anyways, does it?' There was a snap in the woods. '*He's* 'ere.'

Johnny let Alisha slip to the ground.

From out of the shadows the figures began to emerge. They climbed over the wall and down the hill, coming from all directions. There were women in silver white masks carrying knives that glinted in the darkness, and men in boots with plague doctor masks carrying canes that snapped on the earth as they walked.

What the fuck was going on? He couldn't run even if he wanted to. There was nothing left in him. The figures made a broad circle around them. There were maybe fifty of them, maybe more.

'I'm trying to save the girl!' he shouted. 'She needs help!'

Save for the wind and rain, the wood was silent.

Then one of the plague doctors came forward. He was a giant of a man with a barrel of a chest and strong, thick arms. He took his mask off. He had a grey beard and a rugged face and his left eye squinted to the left. 'She doesna' nid help, John Malkin. She needs ya to do what was prophesied.'

'What are you talking about?' Johnny said.

One of the women came forward and held out a silver knife. 'We'll take care of the body.'

'Finish the job, John Malkin,' another man said. 'Or others will die.'

'You're insane,' Johnny said. 'I can't kill anyone.'

'You have no choice,' the woman said, and her voice sounded suddenly familiar. *Ms Houghton?*

She moved to the left and the man to the right. Others did the same till a path appeared between them like a church aisle and down it came, a hobbling figure in black. He looked just like the picture in the book. Either the artist had seen him close up or the figure had been made to look like the picture.

A bolt of anger coursed through Johnny. He couldn't let this charade continue. 'This is a lie!' he shouted, waving his knife in the air. 'Get back, the lot of you!'

But the Hobbledy Man waved his stick and the plague doctors and their partners moved forward as one. Johnny was helpless to stop them. The knife was taken from his hand. Others got Nathan and pinned him to the wheel. He screamed and the scream was cut short. The plague doctor with the squint made Johnny kneel on the ground, pressed the knife back into his hand and placed it over Alisha's chest.

'There is no other way, John Malkin. The boy will live and we will live and no more blood shall be shed.'

Johnny closed his eyes. He couldn't let Nathan die. The girl was already as good as dead. Even if they found her body, he could take the blame for it. He could save Nathan. Isn't that what his job was all about? Saving people and giving them chances. He looked at Nathan's terrified face and gripped the dagger handle tightly, prepared to force it through the girl's ribs.

32

'I need to speak to her!' Shaf banged on the door of the small, white terraced house and shouted through the letterbox. 'Open the door!'

'Leave us alone or I'll call the police!' a slurred voice shouted back.

'I am the friggin' police.'

'Well, I'm not opening the door.'

He stepped back into the rain and looked up at the bedroom and bathroom windows.

'Jenna! We need to talk!'

There was no answer.

He walked across the grass and rapped on the large lounge window. 'Jenna!'

Then he heard raised voices behind the front door. There was the sound of a struggle, then it opened a fraction. The chain was on and Jenna Dunham's frightened face appeared in the narrow crevice.

'Jenna?'

She recognised him immediately and tried to shut it, but he stuck his boot in the gap.

'What do you want?' she said.

'We need to talk. It's about Tariq,' he said.

Her expression changed immediately. 'What about him?'

'His wife found those photos of you.'

'What photos?'

'You know which ones. He had them on his phone. She's got your texts, too.'

She didn't move a muscle. 'He loves me.'

'He has a funny way of showing it. Have you ever heard of a girl called Beth Carver?'

She shook her head.

'There were some pictures of her on it, too.'

Her eyes were full of doubt. 'I don't believe you.'

'He's been passing the pictures round.'

She shook her head. 'He wouldn't.'

He got his phone out, scrolled to the photos, then turned the screen to her.

'It's a mistake,' she said, but her voice was trembling.

'It's not a mistake. Beth was assaulted and then bundled into a car in Aitken Wood last night. It belonged to Tariq. That ring any bells?'

'Why are you telling me this?' she said.

'Because we need to find her.'

'I don't know where she is.'

'You might know where he's taken her?'

She shook her head.

'Think,' he said. 'Think what happened to you. Where the fuck did he take you?'

The rain bounced off his jacket, ran down his hat onto his neck and splashed his face.

'The wood,' she said. 'There's a cabin nearby. He used to wait there and other cars would pull up. He was going to get us somewhere. Somewhere nice. He was going to leave his wife.'

'You may want to tell her that. Now, is there anywhere else you can think of?'

'No,' she said.

'Get your mum.'

'Are you gonna tell her?'

'I'll leave that to you.'

She looked behind her into the hall. 'She's not quite with it tonight.'

'Just open the door, Jenna.'

She took the chain off and let him in.

Mrs Dunham was lying on her side in a pool of vomit.

'She been drinking?' he said.

'What do you think?' she said. 'She won't stop drinking.'

He knelt down beside her, got a whiff of her breath. 'We've got to get her out of here. And you've got to go, too.'

'Go where?'

'Just get out. Call an ambulance, say it's an emergency.'

'Where are *you* going?'

'I need to find Tariq.'

She grabbed his arm. 'What about Alisha?'

'What about her?'

'You need to tell her, too.'

'You know where she is?'

'I got a text from her.'

'When?'

'A few nights ago.'

'Why didn't you say? Everyone's been looking for her.'

'Because she didn't want to come back.'

'So, where is she?'

'Aitken Wood, I think. She took food and a sleeping bag. She was okay till a few days ago and then the texts stopped. I thought her battery must have gone. She'll be okay, won't she?'

He looked right through her. He was thinking of a boy gesticulating in the direction of the woods. *I need to save her before he comes back.*

'Fuck the ambulance,' he said. 'We've no time. Just get in the car.'

She stared at him like she had by the pool, wary and frightened.

'What's wrong?' he said.

'Getting in…' she said.

'It's me or a taxi. And I don't think you'd want that.'

She hesitated.

'I never touched you that night,' he said. 'You know that?'

'I never said you did.'

'Your statement does.'

'Well, the statement's a fucking lie.'

Even though she had a slight frame, Mrs Dunham was heavy with drink and leaned on him like a sandbag. With Jenna's help, he managed to drape her right arm round his neck and carry her to the car. He put her in the back and Jenna got in beside her.

He drove towards Leeds Road. The town was quiet as if still paying its respects to the fallen. There were no crowds baying for blood, just yellow-jacketed police officers on street corners, watching the clocks turn towards evening with trepidation in their hearts.

He gave Jenna the money he had in his pocket and pulled up outside the Pendle Community Hospital. 'They're taking in accident and emergencies now. Just tell them she collapsed. They may give her a bed for the night. If not, get her to a hotel. Don't go home. You understand?'

She nodded.

It was the last he saw of her.

It wasn't true what they said about criminals always returning to the scene of their crimes. Of course, you always got the odd psychopath, or arsonist, who came back to admire their handiwork, but most of them kept far away. It made sense. Most criminals don't want to get caught. What that made Shaf, he wasn't quite sure, but he wasn't an arsonist and he wasn't a fool.

He was back on Barley Lane, heading towards the reservoir. There were no lights on in Blackthorn Farm. In fact, there seemed very few lights on in the village. There were no cars parked outside The Pendle Inn or The Barley Mow. It's as if everyone had suddenly left. As he drove past Lower Black Moss Reservoir, he had a strong urge to check the water in case Whittle had washed up somewhere, his body bobbing on the surface with his head exploded like he'd been harpooned. He didn't know what he'd do if he was. Fish him out and bury him? Or tie a rock to him and hope it dragged him down?

The rain came down in sheets of silver droplets, faint and unending over the wall and all down the valley. He imagined it falling on the outhouse and on Blackthorn Farm and in the village on the roofs of the abandoned houses. He imagined it on Pasture Lane and on the A682 back to Nelson, covering the land from Burnley to Colne in a film of tears. He imagined it in Darwen, in the eyes of his mother looking down the road for him, and on all the people who loved him, and all those he loved, on a gravestone in a churchyard in Padiham all those summers ago.

He set off grimly up the path to Aitken Wood and wondered what he was really doing there, if it was by volition or by some secret design. Like he had after the oil tanker explosion and the lighting of the beacon fire, he felt the cold hand of fate guiding him and he was powerless to resist.

He came to the top of the path where it forked to the right. He could see the reservoir glinting through the spruce trees in the darkness and the copses of conifers higher up, shielding the hillside from the punishing wind. Then, he came to a field of upturned broomsticks planted in the cottongrass.

He stopped. There were figures moving amongst them. At first, he thought he was imagining things. Who would be out here at this time? But then he heard voices and realised he wasn't. There were scores of them slipping through the trees. Some wore black and carried canes, others were slighter and wore silver white. He left the path and followed them, wondered where they were going. Had he stumbled across some pagan festival? What other explanation could there be?

They crossed a stream and filed down to a shallow pool in the shadow of an old rowan tree. He recognised it immediately. It was where he'd found Jenna and Alisha. A preternatural dread crept through him.

He took the Glock out of his coat pocket.

A man was addressing them now. He was a big man and spoke in a broad Lancashire accent. 'It's time!' he shouted. 'He's on his way.'

As if in answer, they all donned masks, silver white for the women and black plague doctor bird masks, like Whittle had worn, for the men.

They filed out of the hollow through the trees.

He was about to follow them when he heard a branch snap behind him.

He turned quickly.

It was a slender woman in a sheer, long, white dress.

'Are you not coming, brother?' she said through the mask.

'Not tonight,' he said.

'We're seeing the prophecy fulfilled. Haven't you been told?'

He hadn't.

He sensed her doubt even behind the mask. 'You're not…a member, are you?'

'No.'

'Then why are you here? Are you spying on us?'

'I came to save a girl.'

'Which girl?'

'She's been out here wandering round for several days. Everyone's looking for her.'

She shook her head. 'You can't save her. It's too late.'

'Why is it too late?'

'John Malkin is here.'

John Malkin? It was the name the Hobbledy Man had used.

'I can't tell you any more. I have to join the others,' she said.

He raised the Glock and pointed it directly at her head. 'Tell me.'

She took a step back. 'He's been chosen to carry out the sacrifice,' she said. 'If you try to stop him, you'll risk everything.'

'He's going to kill her?'

'It's the only way to stop the Hobbledy Man.'

'You're crazy.'

The scream got halfway out of her mouth and was then cut short. He hit her so hard, the mask came off her face. She lay on the wet ground, her straw-coloured hair spread around her. The violence he'd meted out sickened him but there was another feeling, too – a sense of righteousness and vindication. He was doing it for a reason and that made it okay.

He hurried out of the broomstick wood, over the thick cottongrass, towards the Sculpture Trail. The figures had disappeared already. He ran after them and thought of only one thing, stopping it all before it was too late.

He soon caught up with them. His yellow jacket wasn't the best camouflage in the wood, so he hung back as far as he could. The crowd had gathered by a stone wall. He heard the big man addressing them again. His voice sounded familiar now and he struggled to place it. He slunk behind the wall to try to get nearer to him, to listen to what he was saying. He crawled around, unobserved. The wall was about four feet high and made of large stones cut from the local rock. It was grey and wet and sharp. Halfway along, a wheel had been sunk into it, weighed down by logs. He peered over the top and saw plague doctors on the other side. They were holding a boy to the wheel.

Shaf recognised him instantly. It was the boy he'd seen yesterday, the one who'd finished Whittle off. A few paces away, the big man was towering over a man kneeling on the ground. He saw the glint of steel in his hand and realised time was nearly up. He had to act. He turned the key in the safety catch and felt the trigger move a hair's breadth.

'There is no other way, John Malkin. The boy will live and we will live and no more blood shall be shed.'

The knife was in the other man's hand now. It made a quick downward motion towards a girl at his feet. He fired the gun. The recoil knocked his hand upwards. The wood recoiled, too. There were screams and shouts from the crowd and another gunshot went off, this one the boom of a hunting rifle.

Shaf saw his chance. He jumped over the wall and pointed the Glock at the big man.

'Drop the knife,' he said.

The man just looked at him. His grey beard and rugged face was expressionless. Only his eyes showed any sign of life. The right one was fixed on him like a rook. Shaf recognised him now and his hand shook with fear. It was Beth's father, Mr Carver.

'What have you done?' Carver said.

'I'm saving her life,' he said, indicating the girl. 'And his.' He aimed the gun at the plague doctors by the wheel. 'Let the boy go.'

For a moment, they hung on, so he shot another round over their heads and this time they ran. The man who'd been kneeling on the ground looked over at him. 'You arrived in the nick of time.'

'You're John Malkin?' Shaf asked.

'Most people call me Johnny.'

'Is she alive?'

'Just.'

'You know what's going on round here?'

'Yeah. But I thought I was the only one.'

Shaf shook his head. 'They all know. Every fucking one of them.'

The plague doctors hadn't gone far. They'd made a wide circle round them. Some had drawn guns now and were pointing them. There was the sound of distant thunder overhead that reverberated through the valley. The rain teemed down.

'Don't make this more difficult on yourself, detective!' Carver shouted across to him. 'We've all made sacrifices. Let's hope there will be no more.'

Shaf thought of Beth. Did he know? But he had no time to ask questions because lightning lit up the sky over Pendle Hill and, for a second, he saw everything. All the plague doctors were looking behind him, their masks turned up at the sky. He turned to see what they were looking at.

The Hobbledy Man was on top of the wheel. He cracked his cane on the side of the metal and another rumble of thunder echoed across the valley.

'You have to kill her, John Malkin!' shouted Carver urgently. 'We have no more time.'

John Malkin looked at Shaf. It was his call. The gun was all that stood between them and the Hobbledy Man.

Carver came forward and the plague doctors followed him. Hands reached out to grab them. The boy climbed onto the wall and tried to get away but was quickly pulled down. The Hobbledy Man beat the wheel with his stick and his mad acolytes filled with bloodlust and frenzy the way the rioters had in Nelson and Burnley.

Shaf raised his arm and took aim. He'd already killed someone. Would it really be any worse if he took another life? He sensed Carver running at him from the corner of his eye, trying to stop him. The Hobbledy Man raised his cane above his head in victory.

The Glock exploded in his hand. He never saw whether the bullet hit its target because Carver was on top of him, knocking the gun from his hand. Then the earth shook and the stone wall collapsed and the big metal wheel came crashing down. He looked up at the sky and thought he heard the beating of thousands of wings. There was a bright light up there, beaming down on him. He guessed he'd died and this was the end. He'd be able to tell his Dad how he followed in his footsteps and that he could be proud of him now. Then he'd be able to see Stephen, maybe play cricket with him, tell him how much he missed him. That wasn't so bad.

33

Shaf woke up bound in crisp, white sheets like a funeral shroud, but he definitely didn't feel dead. There was a nurse beside him in a starched blue and white uniform. She clamped the cuff of a blood pressure machine round his arm and smiled.

'Morning,' she said. 'Or, in your case, afternoon.'

'How long have I been asleep?'

'Long enough. There. Your blood pressure's fine.'

'Where am I?'

'Burnley General Hospital.'

Shaf looked round the room. It was small but private, with a television on the wall and its own window. He was surprised to see the sun shining outside.

'Are all your rooms like this?'

She shook her head. 'Sadly not. This is only for private patients.'

He went quiet. Outside the room were two men. He recognised them immediately. They were the white officers who'd betrayed DCI Ali: Whittle's men. They'd seen everything. Were they going to arrest him?

'Excuse me,' he said to the nurse. 'Those men. What are they doing here?'

She looked up from her clipboard. 'They brought you in,' she said.

'I don't understand. They were in the wood?'

One of them knocked on the door and put his head round. 'Can he talk?' he asked the nurse.

'He can, but he's tired,' she said. 'Don't be long.'

They came in together.

She gave him a last look and shut the door behind her.

'I daresay you've got some questions,' the one on the left said.

'You could say that.'

'You'll get your chance in a minute.'

'You're going to arrest me first?'

'No. We were told to guard you. Make sure nobody spoke to you before the guvnor did.'

'The guvnor?'

He gave a wry smile. 'You'll find out.'

After a few moments, there was another knock and the officer on the right opened the door. Initially, Shaf couldn't see who it was because the officers were in the way. Then, the newcomer slipped out of their shadow and stood at the end of the bed.

He couldn't believe it. 'Fucking hell,' he said. 'I thought you were dead.'

DCI Ali smiled. 'We thought *you* were.'

'What the hell happened?'

'To me or you?'

'Both.'

'You're a hero, Shaf. You saved the girl.'

'Alisha?'

'Official commendation is on its way. Queen's Police Medal, hopefully. Exceptional bravery on duty.'

'What about the others?'

'What others?'

'There was a man with us. And a kid. They were trying to get away, too.'

'From who?'

'Those people. They were all around us. The Cult of Black Moss. They were all there. They were going to kill her.'

DCI Ali gave him a troubled look. 'There were no others, Shaf. You've had a bad night and must have imagined it. But it's going to get better. Everything's going to be okay.'

Shaf shook his head. 'Listen,' he said. 'There *were* people there with me. They wore black masks and silver masks. They were going to sacrifice the girl.'

DCI Ali looked at the other officers. They shook their heads.

'You're not listening,' said Shaf. 'The Hobbledy Man was there. I saw him.'

'There was no one there, Shaf. Just you and the girl. You went to save her. Jenna Dunham told us.'

Shaf nodded and a sliver of understanding pierced the fog. Of course, he must have imagined it all. That was the easiest way out, wasn't it? DCI Ali was offering him the chance to get out of jail. All he had to do was shut up. 'Yeah,' he said. 'I remember now.'

'All you have to do is get better, Shaf. Couldn't be easier.' He went to the window and looked out. 'I can't remember the last time I saw blue sky like this.' He nodded at the two white officers and they left the room. 'So, what do you think of it? Not bad, eh?' He picked up the lunch menu. 'Halal food, too. We got it for you, especially.'

'So I wouldn't blab. That's why you put them on the door?'

'Something like that.'

'How come you're still alive?'

'Not often you get to pretend to be dead, is it?'

'To throw Whittle off the trail?'

'He panicked when I said you were after the girls' statements. He rang Beth straight away. A bit messy but we got what we wanted.'

'How?'

'The boys were bugged. We got enough on him and Tariq Ibrahim to send them down for a long time. Our only concern was leaving you there. It would have blown their cover if they'd intervened.'

'So, you left me.'

'With a gun.'

Shaf shook his head. 'You're a bastard.'

'Sometimes you have to be.'

Shaf looked out of the window. 'Do you know what's happened to Beth?'

There was a long silence. 'That got a bit messy, too, I'm afraid.'

Shaf steeled himself. 'What do you mean?'

'We had the car Tariq was driving trailed after he left you. Dan said you were asking about it. It was involved in a high-speed chase on the M6 last night. All four occupants died at the scene. Three Asian men and one white female.'

Shaf closed his eyes. 'Her?'

'Yes.'

He couldn't stop the tears. In truth, he didn't want to. What had happened to the world in the last few days?

'I'm sorry, Shaf.'

'She trusted me.'

'There's nothing you could have done.'

'I could have not got involved.'

'She wanted you involved. That's why she came to you.'

'I should have shot Whittle when I had the chance.'

DCI Ali gave him an implacable look. 'He hasn't been seen since but we'll get hold of him, I'm sure. You leave that to us.'

Shaf knew he knew, then. It was obvious. It was also obvious it was going to get buried with everything else. A policeman had died, just not the one everyone thought. DCI Ali was one step ahead of everything.

'We need to stick together, you and me, Shaf. Look after one another. We're going to make you DCI, if you want it. Get you posted to Burnley or Manchester, make your mum proud. Here,' he said. 'I'll stick the TV on. You can hear about yourself.' He picked up the remote and turned it on. 'The boys will pick you up when you're ready to go.'

He closed the door behind him.

Shaf stared at the television screen. There was a BBC reporter outside Nelson Police HQ, speaking live to camera.

'For the first time in over a week, the streets of Nelson and the surrounding towns, Colne, Burnley, and Blackburn, have been quiet. Police and army reported no disturbances last night. I was out and about with a Tactical Aid Unit and it really was eerie. Where before there were the sounds of police sirens wailing through the Lancashire night, there was just silence. Local residents say it was just like somebody had flipped a switch and everything went back to normal. The police aren't saying that, of course. They remain vigilant but cautiously optimistic that the worst is over. We've even got blue skies for the first time since I've been up here.'

Shaf looked outside. It was over? The army on the streets had sorted it out. Things would go back to normal and the last week would be consigned to history. He wanted to believe that because it was the only rational thing to believe, but he knew something else had happened. The proof of that lay in the dark waters of Black Moss Reservoir and in Aitken Wood.

'In other news,' the reporter went on. 'I can tell you the missing teenager, Alisha Ali, presumed kidnapped by a far-right group in retaliation for the supposed grooming of young white girls in the town, was found by a policeman in a local wood last night. She remains stable in hospital. The policeman sustained minor injuries in the search but has been commended by the force for his bravery on what was really a treacherous night.'

He shook his head. No mention of the Cult of the Hobbledy Man. Nobody wanted to know. He got the remote and turned the sound down. He picked up the lunch menu DCI Ali had left, looked at the halal option. Chicken Curry. English style, no doubt. No harm in that.

The sunlight lit up the back of the paper so that he could see the other side. It looked as though someone had written on it. He flicked it over, then caught his breath. There were four lines on it. Three vertical ones and then a shorter one that veered to the right with a dot on it.

34

Johnny lay on the seats in the waiting area. Sleep had come and gone, the best he had managed in a few days, but the dreams were out of this world – police helicopters and a hill full of plague doctors. He was still running now, reliving every moment, getting Nathan out of there. The kid had nearly died of exposure; he'd nearly died of heart failure. The police could have picked them up any time, it seemed, but had let them go. Maybe they had different priorities. Maybe it was the Cult of Black Moss they were really after?

A young Pakistani doctor came out to see him.

'Mr Malkin?'

'Yes.'

'You brought Nathan in?'

'Yeah, I'm his care worker. Is he going to be okay?'

'Yes. But we're going to keep him in. His body's taken a bit of a battering. He's very weak.'

'But he's going to be okay?'

'Yes, we hope so.'

'You know, I've noticed something with you guys. You never deal in absolutes. You're always hedging your bets. You may live, you may die, you may get better. Now and again, it would be nice to know if I can relax, just for a day.'

The doctor gave him a curious look. 'Are you talking about yourself or Nathan, Mr Malkin?'

'I'm talking about the world, doctor. I'll be in touch.'

He walked out of Burnley General Hospital into bright sunlight. He tried Kat on both her mobile and the landline but there was no reply.

He rang the office and asked to speak to Daphne. There were the last rites to perform before handing in his resignation. He didn't think she'd actually pick up, but she did. She sounded, if anything, concerned.

'Johnny, are you okay?'

'I'm alive.'

'We were all very worried about you. Kat left a message saying you'd found Nathan.'

'Yeah. He's in Burnley General. I've just come out.'

'How is he?'

'Weak. But he'll live.'

'You found Alisha, too.'

'All in a night's work.'

She paused. 'The department, well, actually me, thought we may have been hasty suspending you. In light of what you've gone through the last few weeks, we're happy to grant you a paid leave of absence, so you can sort yourself out. I know Kat would appreciate that.'

'You've spoken to her?'

'Only briefly about your message.' She paused. 'She sounded quite down. She wasn't in yesterday and she isn't in today.'

'I'll go and see her now.'

'Good idea.'

'I don't want to come back,' he said. 'Ever.'

'I understand,' she said, and it sounded like she actually did. 'Before you go, I thought you'd like to know that Jenna Dunham got in touch with us.'

'She did?'

'Yes, she's going to give evidence against Tariq Ibrahim and Mohammed Rehman. We'll see if it stands up in Court.'

'It won't,' he said. 'The law's fucked up and so is the social services department. The innocent always get shafted. If you're honest, you'd tell her that now.'

She paused. 'Maybe one day, John.'

She hung up.

He drove back up to Barrowford. It was all over the radio that the night had been calm. Was he the only one who put it down to the events in Aitken Wood? There was the policeman. He knew what was going on. He said they all knew, everyone who was there. He'd saved him from killing the girl and so the prophecy hadn't come true. It was a lie. It had nothing to do with the Hobbledy Man. All that stuff he was told and believed was untrue. The Prime Minister, though completely and utterly wrong most of the time, had got it right. A dangerous minority were trying to undermine the very fabric of the country. But they had been put back in their place. The army had seen to that.

Kat's car was in his parking place. That was reassuring. Before he went in, he looked over the valley, now bathed in sunlight, and saw Pendle Hill in the distance. There were no clouds and its peak was clear.

He looked at the outside of the door and noticed that the marks no longer seemed to be there. Had Kat got them off?

He went inside and found her sitting down at the table. There was a big bunch of flowers in the middle of it and a small box. She was staring at them.

'What's all this?' he said.

She looked up at him across the table. 'I was back in hospital again last night, Johnny.'

'What do you mean?'

'The baby. I couldn't keep it, John. I didn't want to bring it into a world like this. I didn't want us to be arguing all the time.'

She passed him a card.

He took it out of the envelope, his hands shaking. It had a single flower on the front and the words Deepest Sympathy above. He opened it and read.

In loving memory of John Malkin. RIP.

'I named him after you,' she said.

The sacrifice had been made, after all.

Epilogue
One month later

Shaf walked down the steps of Burnley Magistrates Court to his new squad car. It was his first day as DCI. There were three pips on his epaulettes, the start of a new life. His mum was very proud, as his dad would have been. He drove down Parker Lane and headed for home. He took the Colne Road, the quickest way back, and passed down roads where the rioting had been worst. Things were getting back to normal. Shops were being rebuilt and people were going about their business just as they used to.

Near the old Duke of York pub, he slowed down. It was being turned into an Indian restaurant, a sign of the changing times. He saw a silver private hire taxi on the opposite side of the road. The driver was Eastern European or Syrian, one of the new wave of immigrants, and was talking to a group of white girls in short skirts. He froze when he saw Shaf approach. The dwindling evening light could not hide his face. He made his excuses and went on his way and Shaf watched him go. He looked at the girls and wondered what to say to them. He thought of Jenna and Alisha and Beth and how vulnerable they all were.

The Hobbledy Man, if he existed or not, had highlighted the fault lines in the town and country. No amount of politically correct reporting could disguise that. People were always an argument away from a fight, a fight away from a battle, a battle away from a war. It took nothing to whip up fear and loathing in a community, to turn ignorance and bigotry into an inferno of hate, to make neighbour turn on neighbour. The town would see the Hobbledy Man a thousand more times before that lesson was learned, if it ever was.

He drove on, sad and determined, into an uncertain future.

Acknowledgements

Special thanks to Betsy and all the Bloodhound team for their help bringing Pendle Fire and the Hobbledy Man to life.

Printed in Great Britain
by Amazon

58473901R00151